Vendetta Canyon

**Center Point
Large Print**

Stan Lynde titles
available from Center Point Large Print:

The Bodacious Kid
Careless Creek
Saving Miss Julie
Marshal of Medicine Lodge
Summer Snow

**This Large Print Book carries the
Seal of Approval of N.A.V.H.**

Vendetta Canyon

Stan Lynde

CENTER POINT PUBLISHING
THORNDIKE, MAINE

This Center Point Large Print edition
is published in the year 2009 by arrangement with
Kleinworks Agency.

Copyright © 2008 by Stan Lynde.

All rights reserved.

This is a work of fiction. All of the characters, names,
incidents, organizations, and dialogue in this novel
are either the products of the author's imagination
or are used fictitiously.

The text of this Large Print edition is unabridged.
In other aspects, this book may vary
from the original edition.
Printed in the United States of America.
Set in 16-point Times New Roman type.

ISBN: 978-1-60285-521-2

Library of Congress Cataloging-in-Publication Data

Lynde, Stan, 1931-
  Vendetta canyon / Stan Lynde.
     p. cm.
  ISBN 978-1-60285-521-2 (library binding : alk. paper)
  1. Fanshaw, Merlin (Fictitious character)--Fiction.
  2. United States marshals--Fiction. 3. Cowboys--Montana--Fiction.
  4. Ranchers--Montana--Fiction. 5. Vendetta--Fiction. 6. Large type books. I. Title.

PS3562.Y439V46 2009
813'.54--dc22

2009010670

*To the big hearted
cowhands
and gentle shepherds
who kindled my fire*

ONE
▼

PULLING MYSELF TOGETHER

Across a table at Ignacio's Café, Pandora raised her dark eyes and looked into mine. "I'm sorry, Merlin," she said. "You must know I never meant to hurt you."

I forced a smile. Sadness carved a hollow ache deep inside me. I choked back the hurt she never meant to give me and found it bitter as gall. As I might have done in a high-stakes game, I put on my poker face, hoping it would hide my feelings.

"I know that, darlin'," I said. "I wish you . . . and Johnny . . . every happiness."

It was a lie, of course. I wished Johnny Peters no happiness at all. And while I did wish Pandora happiness, I wished she could be happy with *me*.

Gently, she reached across the table and touched my hand. "I missed you so much," she said. "I felt so lost and lonely. The days turned into weeks, and the weeks into months, and still there was no word from you."

"I couldn't write," I said. "I was runnin' with outlaws, pretendin' to *be* one. I couldn't tell *anybody*."

Pandora looked into her coffee cup and nodded. "I know that now," she said, "but all I knew then was that you were gone."

7

She looked up. "Johnny saw my sadness, and he was kind to me. He offered me friendship. He came to the boarding house after work and took me for walks along the river. He read to me. He made me laugh."

Pandora closed her eyes, remembering. "And then, one day, we both saw that our friendship had become something else, something deeper. That's when he asked me to marry him. Two days later, the week before you came back, I told him yes."

I feared her answer, but I had to ask. "Do you love him?"

"I do," she said. "Be happy for me, Merlin."

"I am," I said. I was developing a real talent for lying.

The first thing I noticed was that I stopped being myself. Always a hearty eater, I lost my appetite. I began to show up late for work at the marshal's office. Sometimes, I didn't get there at all. I spent my nights drinking whiskey down at the Oasis Saloon, and I don't even *like* whiskey. I am sociable by nature, but I took to drinking alone. If someone tried to pass the time of day with me, I just snarled like a junkyard cur and slunk off by myself. About the only person I talked to much was the durned bartender.

I stopped taking my Saturday night bath. I allowed my hair to grow long and didn't comb it. I quit shaving; I didn't trust myself with a razor. I swaggered around, acting tough, while inside I was weepy as a Mexican love song. I sank into the slough of despond and embraced self-pity. I even took up cussing. I was a hell of a mess.

One night, maybe two weeks after Pandora's announcement, I sauntered into the Oasis and set my elbows on the hardwood. Boogles, the barkeep, took a quart of Confederate Dew off the back bar and poured me a double, out of habit.

Boogles corked the bottle but left it sitting on the bar. He made it a point to stay upwind of me.

"Good to see you, Merlin," he said. "Business has been slow this evenin', but I knew I could count on you."

I glanced around the room. Rufe Drucker, town drunk, lay passed out in a chair near the stove. His mouth was open, and so was his fly.

At a table near the front door, gambler Bones Belcourt played solitaire and sipped milk to pacify his ulcer. He met my glance and nodded. Other than Rufe and Bones, I was the saloon's only customer.

"Oh, I'm dependable, all right," I said. "Sometimes I don't make it to work, but I always seem to find my way here. You should give out attendance medals, like they do at Sunday school."

Boogles allowed himself a wry smile. "If I done that," he said, "old Rufe yonder would be decorated like a Spanish general."

9

I tossed the whiskey back. Amber fire burned a streak down my gullet. I made a face in spite of myself.

"You ought to take a little water with that," Boogles said.

It was a moment before I could answer. "Like the old Texan said, good whiskey doesn't need water," I said, "and bad whiskey doesn't *deserve* it."

I glanced around the barroom again. "Speakin' of Sunday school, have you ever noticed how much a saloon is like a church?"

Boogles frowned. "Can't say as I have," he said.

"Think about it. *You're* the pastor. You hear confessions and offer counsel. Old Rufe yonder is a pillar of your church and one of its principal elders. That skinny cardsharp over by the door helps you take up the collection. Knuckles McBride plays piano and leads the cowboy choir, and us regulars make up your congregation."

The comparison seemed to tickle Boogles's fancy. "Church-goin' folks get filled with the Spirit," he observed. "*My* customers just get full of *spirits*."

I heard the batwing doors swing open behind me. Glenn Murdoch stepped into the room and walked toward the bar. If you're wondering how I knew it was Glenn when I hadn't seen him, it was on account of his walk. Glenn had been a top cowhand until his horse fell with him during a cattle run. Now he had a stiff leg, a limp, and a deputy sheriff 's badge. I would have known the sound of Glenn's walk anywhere.

"Evenin', Glenn," I said. "Can I buy you a drink?"

Glenn was pleasant but firm. "No, thank you," he said, "and you're not havin' any more tonight, either. Let's go."

I turned to look at him. "Go where?"

"Down to the office. Now."

I felt my hackles rise. "Are you arrestin' me?"

"Do I need to?"

Glenn was an axe handle wide at the shoulders and hard-muscled both ways from his belt buckle. I pulled in my horns. "I guess not," I said. "What's this all about?"

"Some of your friends figure it's about time you took hold of yourself."

"I'd say that's none of their business, wouldn't you?"

"No, I wouldn't, for two reasons. First, you're supposed to be workin' as my deputy. Second, I'm one of those friends I mentioned, and I can't just watch you go under without throwin' you a rope. We need to talk some, Merlin."

I stepped away from the bar and followed Glenn outside. He didn't scare me, of course, but when a friend wants to talk it's only common courtesy to listen.

The moon hung high over Dry Creek and dusted

the muddy street with silver light. Dark buildings slept shoulder to shoulder in the shadows, and only the scuffle of our boots on the boardwalk broke the stillness. Glenn led the way to the office, stepped up onto the raised veranda, and opened the door. Inside, an oil lamp, turned low, lit the room.

"In case you've forgot what it looks like," Glenn said, "this is where you work."

Guilt spurred my conscience. "I guess I have missed a day or two," I said. "I've had a lot on my mind."

"You've missed the better part of a week, all told," Glenn said, "and on the few occasions you *did* show up, you were late."

I slumped into the chair beside his desk. "I don't know what to say. Most days, gettin' out of bed hardly seems worth the effort."

"A man has good days and bad days. He goes on."

I looked down at my hands. "That's the trouble. I don't much *feel* like goin' on."

"You want to talk about it?"

I said nothing for a long moment. Then I cleared my throat and said, "I reckon you heard. Pandora is fixin' to marry Johnny Peters."

Glenn took the coffee pot off the stove, poured a cup, and handed it to me. "I heard about it," he said. "So?"

I took a sip of the coffee. It was bitter from sitting too long in the pot, but it was hot and strong.

"Well, I always figured she'd be marryin' *me*."

"I guess you figured wrong," Glenn said.

I nodded. "Yeah. I guess I did."

Glenn filled his own cup and put the pot back on the stove. From the set of his jaw, I knew he had just about cut me all the slack he was going to.

"All right," he said. "Are you ready to start earnin' your pay again?"

I thought about his question for a long minute. Then I said, "I'm ready."

"That's good," Glenn said, "because I got a telegram from Chance Ridgeway this afternoon. He's comin' in on the stage tomorrow. Says he wants to see you."

All at once, Glenn had my full attention. Chance Ridgeway was U.S. marshal for the territory—and my boss. If he was coming all the way from his office in Helena just to see me, I figured he must have something special on his mind.

"Uh . . . did he say what he wanted to see me about?"

"No, and I didn't ask. He just said to tell you he was comin' in."

"I guess I'd better meet the stage tomorrow then."

Glenn's voice was heavy with sarcasm. "You think?" he asked. "Mind if I give you some advice?"

"I guess I won't know until I hear it."

"Well," Glenn said, "If I was you, I'd get a good

night's sleep. Then, come mornin', I'd treat myself to a shave, haircut, and bath. Otherwise, Ridgeway might mistake you for a vagrant. Or a coyote with the mange."

I opened the door and inhaled. The cool, clean air of early April filled my lungs. The smell was nothing like the odor of stale beer and tobacco smoke to which I had lately grown accustomed.

Just before I stepped out into the night, I turned back to Glenn. "You're a good friend," I said, "but sometimes you tend to ride roughshod over a man."

Glenn shrugged, his eyes wide. "What are friends for?" he asked.

I awoke next morning in my bed at Blair's boarding house, clear-headed for a change and feeling better than I had a right to. Birds chattered outside my window, and the eastern sky blushed red behind the mountains. Born of the dawn, a soft wind ruffled the grass and set the leaves on the trees to quivering.

Ordinarily, I would have joined the other boarders for breakfast around the big dining room table. However, Pandora worked for the widow Blair, serving meals, cooking, cleaning, and such, and the possibility of seeing her close at hand was more than I was prepared to deal with right then. I put on a clean shirt, pulled on my California pants and my boots, and slipped out to break the fast at Ignacio's Café.

• • •

The town of Dry Creek lay soggy and wet in the wake of a spring thaw. Between its facing buildings, its single main street was a soupy mix of melted snow and mud. Water pooled in the low spots and wagon ruts, reflecting the painted clouds overhead. Below the town, flanked by cottonwood and willow, the sometime creek that gave the town its name roiled brown as chocolate. By midsummer, Dry Creek would sleep in the sun like a turtle on a rock, and the creek would be dry once again.

I grew up with my folks on a hardscrabble homestead north of Dry Creek, going to school in town and working on the home place. My mother died when I wasn't but ten, and Pa and me went on without her, scratching out a living by catching and breaking mustangs. After Pa got killed in a horse wreck, the bank foreclosed on our place, and I found work in town at Walt's Livery.

Now, four years later, in the spring of 1887, I was a deputy U.S. marshal, serving at the pleasure of Chance Ridgeway, U.S. marshal for the territory. I was also acting as deputy to Undersheriff Glenn Murdoch at Dry Creek. I liked law enforcement, and Marshal Ridgeway seemed to believe I had a certain talent for the work. Still, in the wake of Pandora's announcement, it occurred to me that my job was both a blessing and a curse.

I was making two dollars a day, plus expenses, as

15

Ridgeway's deputy. Having a steady income for the first time in my life led me to believe I could maybe get married and settle down. Trouble was, the very nature of my job made marriage an unlikely proposition.

When I stopped thinking of myself, I was surprised to find I really didn't blame Pandora for taking up with Johnny Peters. I didn't even blame Johnny all that much, though he didn't exactly have my blessing. Johnny had a steady job down at the feed store. He was hardworking and reliable. Johnny would be home nights. Pandora wouldn't have to wonder where he was and if he was dead or alive, the way she had to with me.

Now I'm not saying it was easy to let Pandora go. On the contrary, I believe it was about the hardest thing I ever did in my life. I kept remembering times we'd shared—dancing at the schoolhouse, watching shooting stars and fireflies on summer nights, sitting snug beside her in an open sleigh under a winter moon, and the long ride we took together the year outlaws stole my Quicksilver horse. Like a man reading old letters, I took my memories out, looked them over, and carefully tucked them away again. Pandora would soon be married, but not to me.

When I finished my reflections, I set my pride aside and took a hard look at the facts. I saw that I was married already—to my job. Instead of a gold band on my finger, I wore a nickel-plated star on my shirtfront. And until I got me a divorce from Uncle Sam, I had no business marrying any woman.

Lawmen's wives lived lonesome lives. They made their homes in shabby cow towns and rough camps, living hand-to-mouth and raising their babies on a peace officer's meager pay. A lawman's wife soon learned that when her man came home, he was ofttimes troubled by memories and fears he couldn't, or wouldn't, share.

It was worse for her when he was gone. Then, she worried about the dangers he faced and was beset by fears of her own. In the end, she was often, too soon, a widow. If a man was a peace officer, it seemed getting married was a terrible thing to do to the woman he loved. Looking at it that way, I was glad I *wasn't* marrying Pandora. Well, almost.

Ignacio's Café didn't look like much from the outside. Weathered and forlorn, the unpainted boards of its siding were red-brown from exposure to the sun. Above the doorway hung a faded sign, which read simply: EATS. Below, in smaller letters, the word was repeated in Ignacio's native tongue: *COMIDAS*. Ignacio himself was about the only person in town who savvied Spanish, but I suppose he wanted to be ready in case a countryman showed up some day.

The bell on the front door tinkled as I stepped

inside and took a seat at the counter. Ignacio stepped out of the kitchen, wiping his hands on his apron. He grinned when he saw me.

"*Hola, amigo*," he said. "Señora Blair kick you out of her boarding house?"

"No, I just came in to see if you've learned to cook yet. I keep hoping."

Ignacio and me liked to kid each other. Usually, he teased me about Pandora, but like everyone else in Dry Creek, he had already heard the news. Ignacio was a true friend. He would not mention Pandora this day.

"Okay. What can I bring you, *hombre*?"

I studied the bill of fare, but we both knew what my order would be. Ignacio's side pork was the best I'd ever tasted, and I seldom missed a chance to have some.

"Coffee, side pork and gravy, and some fried spuds," I said. "Try not to burn the gravy this time."

Ignacio shrugged. "I should charge you extra," he said. "My cooking's too good for this damn town."

He brought my order promptly, and I wolfed it down. The banter with Ignacio continued, even as I paid my bill. The side pork was so good it was all I could do to keep from telling him so.

The O.K. Barbershop stood next to a vacant lot on Trail Street, and it was there I headed upon leaving

Ignacio's. Its proprietor, a cadaverous gent named Slim Niccum (his real name, I swear), was asleep in the barber chair when I entered the shop. He came awake in a hurry when I spoke his name.

"Mornin', Slim," I said. "Much obliged for warmin' up that chair for me. I need a shave, a haircut, and a bath."

Slim was an affable man, but he was no diplomat. He unfolded his lanky frame from the chair, wrinkled his nose, and looked me over. "You sure as hell do," he said.

An hour later, I stood before Slim's mirror and marveled at the change. My hair was short again, my scruffy beard was gone, and I was scrubbed clean and pink as a baby. The smell of bay rum and hair tonic hung about me in a fog. I looked like my old self again, only better. I paid Slim and stepped out to meet the day, and the stage.

The stage from Silver City was a standard-size Concord, full-rigged and fancy. Pulled by a six-horse team, it weighed a solid three thousand pounds and could carry a two-ton load. The coach was built to accommodate as many as twelve to fifteen passengers, but it seldom had more than three or four on board when it hit town, and usually less than that. Since the coming of the Northern Pacific in '82, fewer people rode the coach, but Montana Territory took in a heap of country. Much of it was a far piece from a railroad, and in places like Dry

Creek folks still relied on the stage for travel and the mail.

During most of the year, the Concord rolled into town right at ten o'clock every morning, but when the road was too muddy for the big coach, the company sent out a lighter rig. This coach was sometimes called a celerity wagon but was mostly known to one and all as a mud wagon. Smaller than the Concord, with canvas sides and top, the mud wagon carried only about half the load the big coach did. Pulled by four no-nonsense mules who knew their business, the mud wagon was kind of a bare-bones outfit, but it got the job done. As I stood in the doorway of the Grand Hotel and looked at the quagmire the street had become, I had no doubt which coach would be coming that morning.

At five minutes to ten, Ben Feeney, express man for the stage line, stepped up onto the hotel's long veranda and scraped mud off his boots at the edge of the boardwalk. Ben grinned at me and spat a stream of tobacco juice out onto the muddy street. "Reminds me of a sign folks in San Francisco put up during the gold rush," he said. " 'This street is impassable,' it read, 'not even jackassable.' "

I gave him back his grin. "*This* street is at that in-between stage," I said. "Too muddy for a wagon, but not quite wet enough for a steamboat."

Feeney laughed. "I ain't so sure," he said. "I've

heard some of them paddlewheel captains can run their boats on a heavy dew."

We stood together, waiting. I felt Feeney sizing me up out of the corner of his eye. "Missed you at breakfast this mornin'," he said. His tone was carefully casual. "The widow Blair made them hotcakes you like so much."

"I ate over at Ignacio's today," I said. "I'm partial to his side pork."

Dry Creek was a small town. I figured it was a safe bet everyone knew about Pandora and me breaking up, and about my wallowing in self-pity and cheap whiskey over at the Oasis. Now here I was, sporting a haircut and shave and waiting for the mud wagon. Feeney smelled the change in me, and it wasn't just the bay rum, either.

"You meetin' somebody this mornin'?" he asked.

"My boss," I said. "He's comin' here all the way from Helena just to seek my advice."

Feeney sniffed. "All right, all right," he said. "You could have just told me to mind my own business."

"And you *would* have?"

"Probably not," Feeney said, laughing. "But you could have *told* me to."

It was ten straight up when the mud wagon came bucketing onto Main Street and slid to a stop in front of the hotel. Bob Stringfellow, the driver, was alone on the box. He was spattered with mud from head to toe, but in good humor. "Dry Creek," he called out, "All ashore that's goin' ashore!"

"Mornin', Bob," Feeney said. "No shotgun guard today?"

Bob set the brake and wrapped the reins about its handle. "No need," he said. "I ain't carryin' a strongbox this trip, and one of my passengers is the U.S. marshal for the territory. This rig is safer than the Denver mint."

Feeney stepped into the street and pulled aside the canvas curtain that served as the coach's door. A tight-lipped woman in a wool Macintosh and bonnet emerged, followed by a gent I took to be her husband. "Go ahead on inside the hotel if you've a mind to, folks," Feeney said. "Coach leaves for Shenanigan in twenty minutes."

Behind the couple, Ridgeway stepped out into the sunlight. He wore the high-crowned Stetson and long, black overcoat that were his trademarks, and his faded blue eyes searched for and found me. Beneath the snowy white of his handlebar moustache, his lips framed an honest smile.

"Deputy," he said. "How is the world treating you?"

"Better than I deserve, marshal. You're lookin' fit."

"That's because I don't take life too serious. Like the feller said, we ain't getting out of it alive, anyway."

Ridgeway seemed to study me, like a jeweler examining a stone. Uneasy under the strength of his gaze, I lowered my eyes. "You puttin' up here at the hotel, marshal?" I asked.

Feeney placed the marshal's Gladstone bag on the boardwalk. Ridgeway bent over and picked it up. "I am," he said. "I'll check in, and we'll talk some."

As we approached the front desk, day clerk Burt Appleton greeted Ridgeway with a practiced smile. "Good mornin', marshal," he said. "Welcome back to the Grand."

Burt turned the register around to face Ridgeway and handed him the pen. "Your room is ready," he said. "Number one, as you requested. Best room in the house."

Ridgeway signed the book with a flourish. "Much obliged," he said. "Send up a fresh pot of coffee and two cups, will you? Deputy Fanshaw and me are fixin' to have us a *palaver*."

"Sure thing, marshal," Burt said. "Toot sweet." Burt spoke a little French, and he liked to show off.

Picking up the room key, Ridgeway turned away toward the stairway. I picked up his Gladstone and fell in behind him. Stair steps creaked beneath our feet as we climbed to the second floor. At the landing, we turned and walked toward the front of the hotel and room number one.

Ridgeway unlocked the door and swung it wide.

Somehow, I knew crossing that threshold would set my feet on a path whose end I could not foresee. I felt the old familiar excitement, took a deep breath, and stepped inside.

TWO
▼
ACROSS THE COUNTY LINE

Most of the rooms in the Grand Hotel were small and sparsely furnished, but number one—Ridgeway's favorite—was an exception. Almost twice the size of the hotel's standard room, number one was sunny and bright. A carpet of oriental design covered the floor, and curtains of Irish lace graced the two big windows that looked out onto Trail Street. In addition to the usual furnishings—bed, dresser, night stand, and commode—the room boasted a handsome oak wardrobe and a small table with two parlor chairs.

Marshal Ridgeway hung his overcoat on a peg near the door and nodded toward the table. "Sit down, deputy," he said. "Burt will bring the coffee up d'rectly."

I pulled out a chair and sat down. I have to admit, I was a mite worried. Had Ridgeway heard about my two-week slump into self-pity? Had he come to fire me for dereliction of duty? I tried to appear relaxed and confident, but I was nervous as a mealybug in a henhouse.

Ridgeway chuckled. "Rest easy, son," he said. "I'm not here to rebuke you."

I was so relieved I rebuked myself. "I'm sure glad to hear that," I said. "The truth is I've sort of been a durned fool lately."

"Last time I checked," Ridgeway said, "bein' a fool wasn't a crime. Not even a misdemeanor."

Burt Appleton appeared in the doorway, carrying a tray that held a coffee pot, two cups, a sugar bowl, and a cream pitcher. "Here's your coffee, gents," Burt said. "Anything else I can do for you, marshal?"

"Just set it on the table," Ridgeway said. "Thank you kindly, Burt."

When Burt had left the room and the door had closed behind him, Ridgeway came back to the table, sat down, and filled a cup with coffee for each of us. I expected him to get right down to business, but I guess I should have known better. The marshal was a deliberate man and never one to rush the moment.

Sitting across the table from me, Ridgeway produced a calfskin pouch and carefully filled his short-stemmed pipe. Then he spent some time tamping the bowl, cleaning the stem and what not. Finally, he produced a small silver match safe from a vest pocket and took out a sulfur match.

Just when I thought he was finally going to light the briar, Ridgeway saw where he'd spilled some tobacco on the tabletop. Well, of course, nothing would do but that he brush it off, first into his hand and then into a waste basket. After that, he lit up at last, puffing like a steam engine and looking contented as a Jersey cow.

Blue smoke drifted and eddied above Ridgeway's head as he smoked in silence. Finally, he took pity on me. "Tell me, deputy," he drawled, "are you familiar with Meriwether County?"

"Some," I said. "I went there once with my pa when I was a kid. We took some green-broke horses to a cowman name of Rainford. Good country for cattle, as I recall."

Ridgeway nodded. "It was," he said, "and I expect it will be again. But I'm afraid last year's dry summer and the Big Die-Up last winter have changed the cow business forever."

The marshal fell silent then. He drew on his pipe, staring into space as if he was seeing that country in his mind. When he spoke again, his eyes were sad. "The old ways are over," he said. "Cowmen can't just turn their herds out on the open range and leave them untended like they used to. To succeed nowadays, a man needs to buy or lease land, put a fence around it, breed better cattle, and put up hay against a hard winter. Mostly, he needs to keep a weather eye on his livestock.

"Big cowmen are facing more competition these days, and not just from other big outfits. Small ranchers and homesteaders have moved in, and they're looking for their share of the grass and water. Some of the big operators see the newcomers as a threat, and they're striking back."

Ridgeway's pipe had gone out. Again, he took a match from his match safe, struck it, and relit the briar. Sometimes it seemed to me a pipe smoker burned more matches than he did tobacco. When Ridgeway finally had his pipe going again, he looked puzzled, scratched his head, and asked, "Where was I?"

It was an old trick of Ridgeway's. The marshal knew exactly where he'd left off. He may have been pushing sixty but his mind was sharp as a razor. He just wanted to see if I was paying attention. "The big operators," I said. "They're striking back."

"Oh, yes," he said. "Well, storm clouds are gatherin' over Meriwether County. Three men—small ranchers Pete Davis and Fred Shubert, and Toby Spengler, a camp tender for a sheep outfit—have been killed there in the last two months. Big cowmen claim the dead men were rustlers."

"Maybe they *were*," I said.

Ridgeway nodded. "Maybe, but nobody's proved it. Those men weren't tried and convicted in a court of law. That troubles me."

Ridgeway took the pipe from his mouth and laid it in the saucer beside his coffee cup. Again, he stared off into the distance as though he could see all the way to Meriwether County. "What bothers me more," he said, "is *how* those men died. All three were dry-gulched—gunned down from a considerable distance by a crack shot."

That got my attention. I lowered my coffee cup. "Stock detective?"

"Could be. There's a man name of Tallon who's said to be working the range—Griff Tallon. Of course, the county sheriff claims he has no idea who might have done the shooting. *That* troubles me, too."

"Why's that?"

"County sheriff is a man named Friendly—*Ross* Friendly. I'm thinking he might be livin' up to his name, far as the big cowmen are concerned."

Ridgeway sipped his coffee. "Of course, even if the big outfits *have* hired this Tallon bird, that doesn't necessarily mean it's a bad thing. Meriwether County takes in a heap of territory, and Sheriff Friendly and his deputies can't cover it all. Landowners and livestock associations all across the West have employed stock detectives for years.

"When they work *with* the law, stock detectives can help the legal process. They can gather evidence, turn it over to the county, assist in arrests, and testify in court. But when they decide they *are* the law—that they can try, convict, and execute men all by their lonesome—the name *stock detective* takes on other meanings. Terms like *bounty killer* and *hired gun* come to mind."

I sipped my coffee, remembering. "That time I

told you about, when I was a kid—I recall my pa tellin' me the cowman named Rainford ran the biggest spread in Meriwether County. Is that still true?"

Ridgeway nodded. "It surely is," he said. "The Circle R. Zeb Rainford built up the ranch with Texas cattle back in the late sixties, just after the war. He passed away three years ago. His son Zack runs the outfit now."

"Is it still as big as it was?"

"Rainford had losses last winter, like everyone else. Last fall the Circle R ran more than fifteen thousand steers, mostly on open range. Winterkill took nearly a third of the herd, but ten thousand head is still a respectable holding."

"Yes, it is. So Zack Rainford feels his neighbors are a threat, and he's hired himself a stock detective."

"That's my guess. Him and maybe some of the other big cowmen. They've all had a bellyful of losin'."

"One thing more," he said. "A sheep man named McKenzie has moved onto the range. He's grazin' his woollies on land the Circle R claims as its own. One of those three men who were killed was McKenzie's camp tender."

Ridgeway's eyes caught mine and held them. "Not to put too fine a point on it, but I smell a range war brewin'. I want you to pack your war bag and ride over to Meriwether County. Ask around. Talk to folks. Keep your eyes open, and then get back to me. You can reach me by telegraph at my office."

I stood up and walked over to the windows that looked out on the street. Off to the east loomed the blue mass of the Brimstone Mountains. Beyond lay Meriwether County. It would be good to get away from Dry Creek for a while and see some new country. I asked, "When do you want me to head out?"

The marshal drew his watch from a vest pocket and opened the case. Smiling, he said, "Well, now. Let me see. What time is it now?"

I shoved back my chair and stood up. "I'm on my way," I said. "Anything else?"

Ridgeway's smile faded. His expression changed, the way a pleasant view does when the sun goes behind a cloud. "Just one thing," he said. "Sit back down a minute."

His tone was serious. I sat down and gave him my attention.

"I don't believe you knew Bobbie Lee Williams, my deputy over at Butte," Ridgeway said. "Bobbie Lee got himself killed last week by a man he was bringin' in. Turned his back for just a second. Prisoner had a straight razor in his boot. He cut Bobbie Lee's throat and lit out for the tall and uncut. Bobbie Lee was a good officer and a careful man, but he wasn't careful *enough*."

"There's a word folks down in Old Mexico use,"

Ridgeway said, "and I want you to take it with you. I'm just an old country marshal from Kansas. I don't speak Latin or Greek, and I don't *habla* all that much *Español*, either. But there is one Spanish word I've learned, and I aim to pass it on to you.

"That word is *Cuidado*. Down below the border, it means "be careful" or "watch out" and it can even serve as a warning to others, depending on the situation. When you ride into unfamiliar country—*¡Cuidado!*

"Be alert. Keep your eyes and ears open. Notice everything. When you enter a canyon or step inside a bar room, *Cuidado!* Are there rocks or trees in that canyon where a bushwhacker might hide? Is there a back door to that saloon? *Cuidado!*

"When you meet a stranger, man or woman— *Cuidado!* Does the gent wear a gun? On which side? Does he have a hidden weapon? Watch his eyes. Watch his hands. *Cuidado!*

"What about that good-lookin' woman? Does she smile because she fancies you, or to hide her wicked intent? A woman can be as deadly as a man— *more* so, if the truth be known. That painted saloon cat ain't your mother and she ain't your friend. *Cuidado!*"

Ridgeway lowered his eyes. For some time, he said nothing. Then he looked up and met my gaze. "I'm not sayin' all this because I lack confidence in you," he said. "You're a good officer, and I trust you. But even the best of men can slip up and lose his memory for livin'. In Bobbie Lee's case, that slip turned out to be no-more-breakfast-forever."

Ridgeway scowled. He had said more than he'd intended. He assumed a manner that was gruffer than he really was. He cleared his throat. "Now get out of here and go to work," he said. "And don't forget—*Cuidado!* You have no idea what a nuisance it is when one of my deputies gets himself killed."

I got to my feet. "I'll be careful, chief," I said, grinning. "I sure wouldn't want to *aggravate* you none."

At the livery barn, I combed and brushed Rutherford, my buckskin gelding, leaving most of his winter hair in a pile beneath him. The horse was clear-footed and steady, with no quit to him. I figured he'd be just the ticket for my trip to Meriwether County. I thought about taking along a pack horse and a camp outfit but decided I'd make better time traveling light. I had a map of the county and such provisions as I could tote; I could follow the main road or I could roam the land. I would seem to be just one more drifter riding the grub line, and I could learn from folks as I traveled.

I hadn't used the buckskin much through the winter months, so I'd left him barefooted to give him traction and to keep snow from balling up on his feet. But just the week before, I'd had him shod by a traveling farrier. Now Rutherford wore plates that would help him handle whatever terrain we happened upon.

I did have a misgiving or two. Usually, I did my own shoeing, but what with my recent busy schedule of drinking and self-pity I had hired the job done. The smithy I hired was new to Dry Creek. I didn't know much about him, but his work seemed all right, at first glance anyway.

I looked forward to the trip. As I saddled Rutherford, it seemed like he was looking forward to it, too. I slid my Winchester into the saddle boot, tied my blanket roll and slicker behind the cantle, and led the buckskin out of the corral. Minutes later, I untracked him, stepped across him, and struck out for Meriwether County.

On the map, the Brimstone Mountains were a long, reversed S, running north and south along the eastern border of Progress County. Beyond their rolling foothills, the land tumbled out onto a broad plain, covered with sage-brush and bunch grass and marked by flat-topped buttes and low hills like islands in a sagebrush sea.

Brimstone Gap, a three-mile-wide break in the mountains, divided the range nearly at its center and served as a highway between east and west. The road was a river of mud that day, meandering between aspen groves and cataracts of melting snow. I turned Rutherford up onto the sod at the side of the road where the going was easier.

Fifteen miles ahead lay Silver City, a former mining camp that now served as the region's banking and supply center. I thought about spending the night there and going on to Meriwether County the next day, but I set that notion aside almost as soon as it came to me. I was eager to get on with my assignment.

Nearing Silver City, I came to a fork in the road, the left branch leading northeast into Brimstone Basin. I turned Rutherford onto that track. An hour later, I crossed the county line.

The road before me wound uphill and down across a broad valley. In the distance, mountains reared up on their hind legs, blue and white at the edge of the world. To the north, steep bluffs overlooked a muddy creek bordered by cottonwood trees and willows. All across the plain, new grass grew thick and tender green, and wild flowers bloomed in the sunlight. A meadowlark stood tall on a yucca stalk and yodeled its bright song as I rode past. Ahead of Rutherford's thudding hooves, a cottontail made a nervous dash for cover. Smiling, I held the gelding to an easy trot and thought about the job ahead.

Ridgeway's picture of Meriwether County seemed a gloomy one. I found it hard to think about murder, hatred, and the threat of a range war on such a fine day. I didn't doubt the marshal's judgment. I had never known him to be anything but accurate in his telling of events and people.

Still, I was in no mood to ride cat-eyed and watchful. Too much *Cuidado*, I thought, could spoil a man's day.

As I crossed the valley, I began to see cattle—both alive and dead—all across the range. The rotting carcasses of steers that had perished during the winter seemed to be everywhere. I passed coulees and draws where cattle had piled up and died in great numbers. The stench was strong. Rutherford snorted and tossed his head when the death odor reached his nostrils. Carrion birds—ravens, eagles, and magpies—flocked to attend the carcasses, and in the distance, a pair of coyotes loped easily across the valley floor, looking sleek and well-fed.

I saw live cattle, too—gaunt steers, unsteady on their feet as they hungrily grazed on the new grass. Riding close enough to read their brands, I saw they mostly bore the Circle R on their right ribs. I had already entered Rainford range.

By late afternoon, my luck, my mood, and the country all began to change at the same time. The land turned rocky and dry. The creek—Whiskey Creek, according to Ridgeway's map—became sluggish and slow. Cedar breaks and sand rock buttes replaced the grassland. Clouds gathered overhead. Thunder rolled, and lightning stabbed the hilltops. I smelled rain on the gusting wind. And Rutherford fell to limping and pulled up lame.

Stepping down to search out the source of the trouble, I found the buckskin had thrown his nigh rear shoe. The frog and heel of his hoof were badly swollen and tender to the touch. I cursed myself for failing to notice the problem earlier, and I cursed the smithy back at Dry Creek for his carelessness. I shrugged into my slicker and led the little horse down toward the brush along the creek.

Rain began to fall, first in scattered drops the size of sparrows' eggs, and then settling into a steady, pattering downpour. Along the creek bank, stands of alder and willow offered scant protection from the storm. I huddled inside my slicker, my arm across Rutherford's neck, and waited for the storm to pass.

Then, in a sudden flash of lightning, I saw the cabin. It stood just up from the creek, low to the ground and nearly hidden by brush. Beyond the cabin, not forty yards distant, was a horse corral, its peeled poles silver-white in the lightning's brightness. And beyond the corral, a pair of pinto horses milled nervously inside a fenced pasture. I took hold of Rutherford's reins and stepped out to lead him to shelter.

Again, lightning flashed, and in its light I saw movement at the cabin door. A thunderclap followed close upon the lightning, loud as cannon fire. The buckskin reared, eyes rolling in fear, and I held tight to the reins and tried to calm him. Then, in the silence that followed, I heard a man's voice. "Who's there?" it asked. "Who are you?"

I held up my hands, palms out. "Man with a lame horse," I shouted. "Just lookin' for a dry place."

At the cabin door, a man stepped partway outside, into the rain. He wore a battered brown hat and a checkered shirt, and he had a Winchester carbine trained on my middle. I tend to be withy and narrow of waist, but right then I couldn't help but wish I was narrower still. The man frowned and pooched out his lower lip.

"Come ahead, then," he said, "but keep them hands where I can see 'em."

I followed his directions, my hands shoulder high and empty, except for Rutherford's reins. The man with the rifle was a pinch-faced jasper with squinty eyes and long, greasy hair. He looked like he hoped I'd try to cause him trouble. The buckskin followed me, limping.

"What'n hell's wrong with your horse?" the man asked. "His leg busted?"

"No. He threw a shoe a ways back. Hoof's all swole up and tender."

"Hell you say. How come you to be sneakin' up on my place?"

I couldn't tell if the gent was mean or just ignorant. I wanted to grab him by the neck and slap some hospitality into him, but I smiled instead. "Wasn't sneakin'," I said. "You want to point that Winchester somewhere else?"

He thought about it. Raindrops spattered against

my slicker and drummed a tattoo on my hat. I nodded at the rifle, and water spilled off my hat brim.

The man raised the carbine's barrel and took the hammer off cock. "I guess you ain't here to cause me trouble," he said. Stepping back into the cabin, he said, "There's a lean-to around back of the corral. You can put your horse up there."

"Much obliged," I said, meaning it. "I'll be back directly."

The lean-to wasn't much. Built of weathered boards thrown together in a hurry, the stable had a forlorn and temporary look. Crooked poles set in the ground supported the walls and roof, and two stalls provided space for saddle horses. Beyond the stalls lay a hay pile, a pitchfork, a saddle, and some horse gear. A halter and lead rope hung from a rusty nail. I slipped Rutherford's bridle off and replaced it with the halter.

Rain dripped in through gaps in the roof and turned the dirt floor to mud. The shed was poor shelter, not much better than being out in the weather. I wiped Rutherford down with a grain sack and forked hay into the manger. Then I bent down, leaned into him until he shifted his weight, and lifted his nigh rear hoof.

The swelling had increased, if anything. As near as I could tell, the buckskin was suffering from a corn, which on a horse is simply a bruise on the sole of the foot. Corns cause lameness and have a variety of causes, although I suspected careless work by the smithy back in Dry Creek most of all. In any case, I would not be riding Rutherford for a while. He'd need time to heal, and afterward, the attentions of a good farrier. "No hoof, no horse" goes the old saying. I was a man afoot, and no mistake.

THREE
▼

CHANGING HORSES

I stood beneath the leaky roof of the lean-to and looked out at the rain. Across the way, a pair of pinto geldings stood beside the pasture fence, their eyes closed and their heads down. Except in Indian country, pinto horses were an uncommon sight on the range. Cowpunchers tended to prefer solid-colored mounts and thought spotted horses were of low breeding. I couldn't help but wonder about a man who owned not one but two of them.

Downhill from the corral, rain drenched the sod roof of the cabin and dripped from its eaves. Wood smoke billowed from the stovepipe, drifted down, and faded in the mist. I stepped away from the lean-to and headed toward the cabin.

Passing the corral, I noticed a steer hide draped over the top rail. Stopping, I touched the rain-wet hair of the pelt. The hide was fresh, not more than a day old. The mark it bore was clear: Zack Rainford's brand, the Circle R. The man in the cabin was becoming more interesting all the time.

He opened the door as I reached it. "Come on in," he said, "See you don't track none of that mud in."

Inside, the cabin was dark as a mine shaft. I waited for my eyes to grow accustomed to the gloom and let my nose tell me about the place. I smelled coffee, hot iron, and wood smoke first of all, and the smell of meat frying in a pan. Underneath all that was the musty, sour smell of the cabin itself—like a root cellar too long shut up—and of rotten vegetables and decay.

The gent's voice was a surly pout. "Well? Who'n hell are you? What y'all doin' here?"

"Name's Merlin Fanshaw," I said. "Just passin' through. Like I said, my horse has gone lame."

I could see more clearly now. The gent stood beside a small table at a rusty kitchen range, cooking steaks in a fry pan. He poured coffee into a cup and held it out to me. "Y'all want some coffee?" he asked.

I took the cup. "Obliged," I said.

Smoke rose from the frying meat and made a fog above the stove. "Appreciate you lettin' me put my horse up at your shed," I said. "He needs time to heal up some."

The man's eyes narrowed. Beneath a wispy mustache, his lips were a tight line. "Y'all ain't leavin' him here," he said.

I took a sip from the cup and set it carefully on the table. "Let's make a new start," I said. "I've told you my name. Now you tell me yours."

The man's eyes widened then went squinty again. After a brief pause, he said, "Name's Slye. Vernal Slye."

I offered my hand and he took it. "Pleased to make your acquaintance, Vernal. You run stock hereabouts?"

His eyes shifted. He looked away, back to the meat in the fry pan. "Yeah," he said. "I got me a few cows."

"Looks like tough country to run cattle in."

"You got that right. It's rocky and it's dry, mostly. Piss-poor grazin' land."

I nodded at the fry pan. "Still," I said, "you seem to be eatin' all right."

Again, his eyes shifted. "I butchered a steer yesterday."

"Yes," I said. "I saw the hide up at your corral." I sipped my coffee, watching him. "You seem a mite nervous, Vernal. You got *troubles* around here?"

Vernal took off his hat and wiped his brow with his shirtsleeve. His eyes darted around the cabin's interior, but they wouldn't meet mine. He turned back to his cooking. "I just thought you was somebody else, is all," he said. "Set down. We'll eat some o' this beef."

I figured Vernal Slye was either a rustler or a small operator who wasn't too particular about whose steer he butchered, but I had no proof on either count. Besides, I was hungry and wet, with a lame horse stabled in the man's lean-to. I pulled up the wooden crate that served as a chair and accepted his hospitality. "Many thanks," I said. "I *could* eat a bite."

Vernal served the steaks and dished up some beans to go with them. Then he sat down across from me, and we fell to eating. I'm happy to say my suspicions did not spoil my appetite.

As we ate, I took a look around the cabin. At first it seemed the place had not been cleaned in a long time. On closer inspection, I decided it had never been cleaned at all.

Dried mud littered the floor. The cabin's lone window was filmed over with grease, and dead flies lay scattered along the sill. Cobwebs hung like filmy banners in the corners. Charred bits of food clung to the cook stove's rusted top, and wood smoke stained the upper walls and ceiling. Looking on the bright side, there was no evidence hogs had ever occupied the place. It was altogether too filthy for any self-respecting hog.

As for Vernal, he wasn't all that tidy himself. His checkered shirt was stained and ragged, and his britches were so dirty they could have stood up by themselves. His old mule-ear boots were run over at the heels, and their soles were so thin I figured

Vernal could stand on a dime and tell you heads or tails.

He scooped beans into his mouth with a spoon and ate beefsteak with his hands, letting the grease fall where it may. He was a good cook, though. The coffee was strong and hot, the beans were tender, and Vernal had fried the ill-gotten meat to perfection—probably because he'd had plenty of practice.

Neither of us said much during the meal. When we finished, Vernal put his dishes in a pan of water on the stove and walked over to the door. Looking out, I saw the storm had passed and the skies were clearing. Vernal leaned against the doorpost, staring into the distance.

"Where'd y'all come from today?" he asked.

"Silver City," I said. "I came by way of the main road."

Vernal nodded. He seemed to study the distant hills, now fresh-washed and bright with the day's last light. When he spoke, his voice sounded strained. "Did y'all see any other riders?"

"No," I said. "I had the road to myself."

Vernal turned to face me. His eyes had a haunted look. "You sure you didn't see a feller on a bay horse? A big man—wears a black hat and a canvas duster. Y'all see anybody like that?"

"No. Nobody."

Vernal shrugged. "I seen a feller like that twice

last week—way off, coyotin' the rim rocks. Probably just a drifter, passin' through."

"Talkin' about passin' through," I said. "I'm obliged for your hospitality, but I've got business in Reata. I need to move on."

"I thought you said your horse is lame."

"He is. I'll give you twenty dollars gold if you lend me one of yours."

Suddenly, Vernal was all attention. "Twenty! You'll pay twenty dollars to borrow a horse?"

"Worth it to me," I said. "I'll have him back to you in a week and pick up my buckskin. If you'll board him while I'm gone, I'll give you another twenty when I get back."

"Forty dollars for lendin' you a horse and takin' care of yours for a week? Hell, that's a deal, mister—show me the money."

I fished a double eagle from my vest and placed it on the table. Vernal couldn't take his eyes off the coin.

"You said forty," he said.

"Twenty now and twenty when I come back," I said. "And there's one other thing."

"What's that?"

I gave Vernal a cold smile. "My horse better *be* here when I come back," I said.

We ran the geldings into the corral that night. Vernal's newfound prosperity seemed to put him in a generous mood. "These ponies were a gift from a Shoshone chief," he said. "A man couldn't ask for a better pair of pintos."

The horses were passable but nothing special. I had my suspicions about where and how Vernal had acquired them. I figured they probably *hadn't* been a gift.

"They're showy, all right," I said, "but I'm told those painted ponies lack bottom. I don't need a horse that'll play out on me."

"Hell," Vernal said, "you're only goin' to Reata and back."

Both horses were colored by big, splashy patches of brown against white. There was a difference in their heights, the shorter one standing just a little over thirteen hands. The other stood fifteen hands— five feet from the ground to the top of his withers— which was more the usual height of a horse.

"Let me guess," I said. "The taller one is your personal mount, and you're lendin' me the pony."

"You called it," he said. "He's small, but he's mighty."

"I just hope my feet don't drag," I said.

I made my bed that night in the lean-to, next to Rutherford. The skies were clear after the rain, and I could look up through the gaps in the roof and see stars. I didn't much like leaving the buckskin behind, but I knew he needed time to heal. I figured he'd be safe enough with Vernal—the promised double eagle would see to that.

I thought about the morrow and the ride to Reata. Looking at my map, I guessed the town to be maybe thirty-five miles from Vernal's camp. With an early start, I could be there by full dark.

I closed my eyes and breathed in the cold night air. Only the rushing of the creek below the cabin and the sound of Rutherford scuffling in the darkness broke the stillness. I thought of Ridgeway and his warning: *Cuidado!* And, yes, I thought of Pandora, though I tried not to. I was still trying not to when I finally drifted off to sleep.

Coming daylight stained the eastern sky and brought me to cold wakefulness. The wind woke up before I did; now it stirred the sleeping grass and sighed between the warped boards of the lean-to. Shivering, I burrowed deeper into my blankets, reluctant to leave my bed.

Beside me, unseen in the darkness, I sensed Rutherford's presence. The buckskin nickered, the sound a deep rumble in his throat. I sat up and put my hat on. "Good mornin' to you, old son," I said. "How is that hoof feelin' today?"

My boots were cold and stiff, but I tugged until my feet found their place. As was my habit, I had left my spurs on my boots when I took them off, and the stamping of my feet made the rowels ring like chimes. I buckled my forty-four about my waist and slipped into my sheepskin. Reaching out, I found the gelding. I stroked his neck and rubbed his favorite spot behind the ears until he grunted his pleasure.

Down the slope, lamplight glowed orange in the cabin's greasy window, and I knew Vernal was up. I made my way downhill past the corral and knocked on his door.

"Come in," Vernal said. "Coffee's on."

I tugged the latch string and swung the door in. Vernal stood at the cook stove, stirring the bean pot. He was only partly dressed, clad in britches, boots, and hat. The dirty shirt he'd worn the day before was nowhere to be seen. Instead, he wore a ragged undershirt that was even filthier than his shirt had been. *Old Vernal sure is no slave to fashion,* I thought, *or to cleanliness, either.*

He wiped out a tin cup with a forefinger and handed it to me. I took the coffee pot off the stove and poured myself a cupful.

"Breakfast is beans and beef, same as last night," Vernal said. He opened the oven door and took out a pan of biscuits. "Y'all like biscuits, don't you?"

"Don't everyone?"

Vernal nodded. "I expect they do. Get yourself a plate there at the chuck box."

I recalled his cooking of the night before. Breathing in the good smells of beef, beans, and biscuits, I held my plate out as Vernal filled it. My folks raised me to be polite, and I surely do like to eat, so being invited to break bread with a feller tends to make me even more polite than usual.

After chuck, Vernal and me stepped outside. Sunlight painted the high places but had not yet reached the corral where the horses waited. As Vernal looked on, I opened the gate and eased inside.

I shook out a loop, walking easy and keeping the rope low. The little paint seemed fiddle-footed, dancing nervously in the mud of the corral. Still, he was well-built and chesty, though small. The pony watched my approach with a wary eye and then broke into a run as I drew near. I sailed my loop out and saw it settle about his neck.

Caught, the pony stopped, but his feet continued their jittery fandango. He was fiddle-footed for sure, but I wasn't about to complain. I figured the old saw about not looking a gift horse in the mouth was good advice, even if the horse in question was not a gift but on loan.

I set my saddle on the paint, snugged up the latigo, and swung astride of the little horse. Vernal opened the gate, and I rode out of the corral. As I passed him, Vernal held up a finger and said, "One week."

"One week," I replied. "Take care of the buckskin." I turned the pony downhill, splashed across Whiskey Creek, and rode out to meet the morning.

The road to Reata snaked through gentle hills on its way east, and I rode the paint into the rising sun at a dog-trot. Apart from his being something of a wringtail, the little horse seemed reliable and sound, and I found him a better mount than I'd expected. I pushed ahead, mostly following the road, and as the morning grew older, the land began to change once more, this time for the better.

I began to see cattle again, first in small, scattered bunches, and then in the dozens. I left the road behind and rode among them, close enough to read some of their brands. Many wore Rainford's Circle R, but other outfits were represented as well. The hard winter had laid a heavy hand on livestock, but now they were finding nourishment among the stands of old grass and grazing on the new as if the Big Die-up had never happened.

I followed a game trail to the top of a rocky butte and drew rein, letting the paint catch his breath. Below, the land stretched away to become the foothills of what my map told me was the Warbonnet range. Taking out my field glasses, I scanned the valley below, picking out the grazing cattle and studying the land.

Sudden movement caught my attention—just a flash of white below and behind me that briefly appeared and then vanished behind a low hill. Curious, I focused the glasses but saw nothing. *Pronghorn,* I told myself. *Maybe a steer or sunlight on a white rock.*

Rocks don't move, I reminded myself. There was something about the way the patch of white had disappeared, something almost *furtive.*

I swung up onto the paint and rode him along a narrow trail that angled downhill across the face of the butte. Allowing the little horse to pick his way, I twisted in the saddle, watching for movement below. The only sounds I heard were my own breathing and the clatter of the pony's hooves striking rock.

The pony hesitated and then stopped. Looking ahead, I saw that the trail ended at the edge of a big rock slide. Sixty feet of loose rock interrupted the pathway down to the valley floor, and the trail was too narrow to turn around. There was no way to go but across the rockslide. The paint was nervous, goosey. He didn't trust the scree underfoot, and I didn't blame him. "It's all right," I said, touching him easy with my spurs. "Go on, little horse."

Trembling, the paint took a shaky step ahead, and then two. Loose rock slipped, clattering down the slide. The pony snorted, his nose nearly touching his front feet. I shifted in the saddle and put my weight down hard on the uphill stirrup. I pulled the pony's head up and spurred him hard in the flanks. The little horse was out of choices. He knew he had to cross the slide rock. I believe he would have jumped the whole thing if he could have, but he couldn't. Instead, he made what he must have thought was the next best choice—he lunged hard for the other side in a desperate, all-or-nothing scramble. I took a deep seat, held on, and hoped for the best.

The best was not to be. As if struck by a giant fist, the pony seemed to strike an invisible wall. Bright blood erupted from his neck, spattering me with its wetness. The sound of a rifle shot rang out, echoing off the rocky butte. The horse fell hard on its side, trapping my leg beneath him. I heard a second shot. Pain stabbed through me like a lightning bolt and took my breath away. The earth shook at the horse's fall. Rocks flew. The pony slid, kicking, and came to rest at the bottom of the slide. I remember struggling, trying to get free of the horse. Then a red haze, bright as the pony's blood, seemed to burst behind my eyes, and the world went dark.

FOUR

▼

A GOOD SHEPHERD

I come awake to the sound of bleating. A chorus of sheep calls and answers, some sheep sounding high and nervous, some deep and somber—a jumble of noise growing louder. A dog barks. I open my eyes.

I'm lying on my back in a narrow bunk. The smells of canvas, dust, and sagebrush come to me as I breathe. I wonder: *Where* am *I? Am I in a tent? A cabin?*

Memory returns in a rush. In my mind's eye, I'm once again riding Vernal's painted pony across the face of the butte. Ahead lies the rock slide—no way down but to cross it. The pony makes a desperate lunge across the scree. A rifle shot echoes from the rocky butte. A second shot follows. The pony goes down sudden and hard, spraying me with its blood as I try to free my foot from the stirrup.

The pony falls hard on its off side, pinning my right leg. Dead or dying, the animal tumbles down the rock slide, with me beneath it. The pain takes my breath away. I think about my rifle, but it lies under the pony in its saddle boot, beneath my leg. I can't reach my forty-four. The pain grows greater; I feel sick, light-headed. And then I pass out and slide away into darkness.

Awake and hurting, I raised myself on an elbow and reached down to check on my leg. In the darkness, my fingers touched what felt like a rolled blanket, wrapped and tightly tied about my lower leg and ankle. My foot seemed to be propped up on something—another blanket, I thought, or maybe my coat. Movement caused the pain to grow. I felt light-headed again. I slumped back and lay still.

The bunk moved. I heard the sound of a latch opening, felt the cool inrush of air. Then a match flared and touched the wick of a coal-oil lamp, and light flooded the space. Raising my head, I saw a burly man smiling at me. Broad-shouldered and barrel-chested, he was dressed in dashboard overalls and a blanket-lined canvas coat, and he wore a brimless wool cap folks call a tam-o'-shanter. At a time and place in which most men packed guns, I saw that he was unarmed.

"Evenin', laddie," he said. "So ye're nae dead after all."

"I reckon not," I said. "I just don't know where I am—or how I got here."

The man laughed. "You're in ma wagon," he said. "I'm Haggis McRae. Welcome to ye."

Sheepwagons were fairly new to the range in 1887. Invented in 1884 by a Wyoming blacksmith named Candlish, sheepwagons were a big improvement over the tents and open-air camps herders used up to that time. I had never been inside a sheepwagon, and I took a few seconds to look this one over.

A little over six feet wide and nearly twelve feet long, the wagon seemed to be well designed. Hardwood bows supported a canvas top over a snug living space that held a stove, cupboards, wash basin, and water bucket, and the bed I presently occupied. Benches ran down each side, and the front held a Dutch door with a window in the upper section. Above the bed at the rear, a second window provided light and ventilation.

"And who are ye, laddie?" the man called Haggis asked. "I dinnae ken if ye're a bad man or a good man."

I managed a smile. "Mostly good, I reckon. I'm

Merlin Fanshaw, from over in Progress County. How'd I come to be here?"

"I was herdin' ma sheep over in the glen. Heard rifle shots and found ye pinned under a dead horse. I thought at first *ye* were dead, as well."

"Likewise. I'm sort of surprised I'm not."

"Do ye ken who did the shootin'?"

"No. I didn't see anyone."

Haggis nodded, then turned to his small stove and kindled a fire. "I din-nae drink coffee," he said, "but a hot cup o' tea would nae be amiss."

Once the fire was burning well, Haggis placed a battered teapot on the stove and sat back to wait. He seemed a man accustomed to silence, and waited, saying nothing more.

I used the time to size him up. Haggis McRae appeared to be in his early forties. His hair and close-cropped beard were a sort of strawberry roan. Wrinkles rioted across his ruddy face when he smiled. There was gentleness about the man, although he looked strong enough to hunt grizzlies with a switch.

"How did you get me here?" I asked.

"Ma horse Jimmy," Haggis said. "I put a rope on the dead pony, and Jimmy lifted him off ye. Ye were covered in blood, but it was the pony's blood, nae yours."

He drew the teapot off the stove and set it aside to steep. "At first, I could nae wake ye. I'm thinkin' ye struck your head."

I closed my eyes. "I've done that before," I said, "too many times."

Haggis nodded. "Then," he said, "I put ye on Jimmy and brought ye back here. It took a second trip to fetch your saddle and rifle.

"Ye have another wee problem," Haggis said. "Ye've broken your fibula. That's the smaller bone in your lower leg. I splinted and wrapped the break and put ye there in ma bed."

"That's a first for me," I said. "I never broke a bone before."

"'Tis not a thing t' make a habit of," Haggis said, "but as broken bones go, the fibula is better than most. Ye'll be good as new in three or four weeks."

Haggis poured tea into an enamelware cup and handed it to me. He said, "When the swellin' goes down, I'll fix ye up with a *stookie*—a plaster cast. Ye'll need to see the mediciner in Reata later on, but for the time bein', ye're stuck with me."

"I could be stuck in worse places," I said. "Much obliged, until you're better paid."

"Haud yer wheesht, laddie! There'll be nae talk o' payment here!"

Haggis turned back to the stove. A stewpot simmered there, filling the wagon with a rich aroma. "'Tis cock-a-leekie soup, of a sort," the big man said. "Made wi' prairie chicken and wild onions. Could ye do wi' a wee supper?"

I grinned. "Eatin' supper is what I do best," I

said, "unless maybe it's eatin' breakfast or dinner."

Haggis dished up two bowls of the rich soup and handed me one. From the stove's small oven he produced a half dozen sourdough biscuits—Haggis called them *scones*—and divided them as well. Then we ate in silence by the lamp's dim light.

When the meal was over, I swung down from the bunk, favoring my wounded leg. "Leave the dishes," I said. "I'll clean 'em up in the morning. And I'm not takin' your bunk tonight; I'll make me up a bed on the floor."

Haggis laid hands on me and lifted me back up onto his bed. "Dinnae be daft," he said. "Ye'll sleep where I've put ye! D'ye want that leg to heal proper or not?"

I protested some, but Haggis would have none of it. He was strong as an ox; I felt like a doll in his hands.

The wagon's table was a long slab of wood that slid out from beneath the herder's bunk. Haggis pulled this board all the way out and placed it crossways, each of its ends resting on a side bench. He drew extra blankets and a heavy overcoat from beneath the bunk and spread them on the board to make a bed.

Fully clothed, Haggis nestled into the blankets and covered himself with the overcoat.

"Good night to ye, laddie," said he, and he blew out the lamp.

• • •

Coming daylight faded the darkness and turned it to gray. Pain in my right leg warned me to move with care. Nearby, in the gloom, Haggis rose from his makeshift bed and built a fire in the small stove. He picked up the water bucket, opened the latch on the Dutch door, and stepped out into the morning. His voice was gentle, like a man speaking to children. "Good day to ye, Robbie," he said. "Good mornin', young Tip."

I heard him filling the bucket from the barrel. The wagon moved again, and Haggis climbed back inside, the water bucket in his hand. Setting it on the bench, he filled the teapot and put it on the stove. He looked at me and smiled. "Good mornin' to ye," he said. "And how is your poor, long-sufferin' fibula today?"

"It's feelin' sorry for itself," I said. "Complainin' about what I did to it."

Haggis chuckled. "Well, gie us a look," he said. "I'll make ye that stookie I promised."

The big man was as good as his word. As we shared a cup of strong tea, he applied a plaster of paris dressing to my wounded leg. The swelling had gone down some, but Haggis wrapped the wound loosely enough to be sure the dressing wouldn't interfere with my circulation. When I told him I was surprised he had bandages and plaster on hand, he said, "Herdin' sheep, sometimes a man is alone for weeks at a time. If he breaks a bone and there's nae one to help him— well, whit's a body to do?"

When he'd finished his doctoring, he made us a breakfast of bacon and fried potatoes, and we ate together in silence. Already, the sheep were stirring, leaving the bed ground. Mindful of his flock, Haggis scraped the remnants from his plate into a battered pan nearly filled with table scraps and opened the wagon's door. Below, watching us, were two black and white sheepdogs.

"Meet ma boys," Haggis said. "The big fella is Robbie. Knows more about sheep than most herders. Bold as a lion, but gentle as a lamb. Smaller dog there wi' the white on his tail is Tip. He's young, but he's a learner. He'll be a top dog one day."

Haggis stepped outside, set the pan on the ground, and turned away toward a hobbled piebald gelding. The dog called Robbie was already wolfing down the scraps, while Tip sat tensely three feet away, his eyes fixed on the pan.

"Peckin' order," said Haggis. "The apprentice does nae eat 'til the master has done."

The dog called Robbie raised his head from the pan and trotted over to where Haggis was saddling his horse. Seeing his turn had come, Tip lunged for the pan and quickly finished off its contents.

Haggis hauled himself into the saddle and turned the gelding toward the sheep. "Take care, laddie," he said. "I'll be back about noon." Then he rode away, following the band as it spread out on the long slope below the wagon. The flock was a moving carpet of white on the gray-green grass, and the dogs, Robbie and Tip, trotted at each side of the flock to keep the sheep from scattering. Standing in the door of the wagon as the sun's first rays touched the land, I thought it all made a fine picture indeed.

I watched Haggis guide the sheep away through the low hills, the herder and his flock growing smaller and finally vanishing in the distance. Sunlight warmed the morning. A rising breeze ruffled the grass and danced in the sagebrush. I was alone and far from the company of men. Climbing back inside the wagon. I added wood to the stove and put a pan of water on to heat.

Seated on the bench opposite the stove, I took time to look the wagon over more carefully. Up to then, my views of it had been by lamplight and the gray light of early morning. I'd never visited a sheep camp before, and I have to admit I was curious. Most of what I'd heard about sheep and sheepherders came from bunkhouse humor and the prejudice of cowpunchers and cattlemen. I had heard sheepherders called *lamb lickers, mutton punchers*, and *snoozers*, and it was said they were all a little crazy from being alone so much.

I am ashamed to admit that I laughed along with

the boys who made sport of sheepmen and sheepherders. In every saloon and cow camp, there always seemed to be some self-appointed humorist who joked about sheepmen, or homesteaders, or Indians, in a manner that scorned and slandered them. I suppose the jesters did so to elevate themselves, but for me the effect was just the opposite. They seemed to think they were wits, but in my opinion they were only *half* right.

When the water began to steam, I washed and rinsed the dishes. A flour sack on a nail beside the door served as Haggis's dish towel, and I dried and stacked the clean tableware. Hobbling about on my good leg, I tidied up the bed and swept the floor. Then I had myself a cup of tea and sat looking out the sheepwagon's open door. As the shadows changed and the morning grew older, I let my thoughts take me back to the previous day and the rifle shots that had changed my life.

I clearly recalled hearing two shots. The first killed the pinto I rode, and the second shot had missed. But who would want to shoot me? I was just a stranger, riding through. I had no enemies in the area, leastways none that I knew of.

Back in Dry Creek, Ridgeway had described the situation in Meriwether County. He said three men—suspected rustlers—had been dry-gulched over the past two months. They had been killed by a crack shot, he said, possibly a stock detective. I could understand somebody taking a shot at me if I was a cattle thief, but I wasn't. My getting ambushed didn't seem to make any sense.

Then I remembered Vernal Slye, my sometime host and the butcher of other men's beef. Vernal had been nervous as a barefoot man in a snake pit when I rode up on his cabin. He'd seemed worried when he asked if I'd seen a rider on a bay horse. I wondered: could the man he described be the stock detective Ridgeway told me about, Griff Tallon?

"The wicked flee when no man pursueth" says the Good Book, and I reckon that's a fact. Guilt sure can cause a feller to watch his back trail, all right. It struck me that Vernal Slye might have had good cause to believe he was being pursued, and that he was well aware of the reason why.

I thought: Suppose Tallon has been watching Vernal's place. And suppose he has gathered enough evidence to convince him his man is a rustler. Just when he's about to make his move, he sees me ride out on one of Vernal's ponies. Tallon figures I'm Vernal, and acts accordingly. He follows at a distance, sees me start across the rock slide, and sends a bullet my way. His shot hits the pony; the pony falls just as the rifleman fires again.

I wind up at the bottom of the slide, unconscious and pinned beneath the pony. The pony is dead, and it sure looks like I am, too. Tallon crosses another name off his list and moves on.

Of course, I couldn't be sure that's how it happened, but I figured it was a possible explanation anyway. I had gone from "no idea" to "maybe so," and I figured that was progress.

I wondered how my Rutherford horse was doing. When I left him at Vernal's place, I said I'd be back within the week. Now I was a refugee from an ambush, in a sheep camp a long way from anywhere. I had a busted fibula and a headache, and I had no idea how long I'd be there—wherever "there" was.

Holding onto the door frame of the sheepwagon with both hands, I stepped down onto the wagon tongue with my good leg and eased myself to the ground. The hills and plains were vast and treeless, but a supply of firewood had been brought in by the camp tender and lay piled nearby. Two thirty-gallon water barrels stood in the lee of the wagon, also provided for the herder's use. I tried rocking the barrels and found one empty, the other maybe half full. Judging by the amount of wood and water remaining, we weren't likely to see anyone from the home ranch for at least another week.

I found a stone in one of the outside grub boxes and put an edge on Haggis's axe. Half standing and half seated on the wagon tongue, I split some wood and stacked it inside the doorway, near the stove. Then, pulling the plug from the half-filled barrel, I filled the wagon's water bucket and set it inside as well. By the time I finished those few simple tasks, I was sweating and my leg had begun to throb. I sat back down on the wagon tongue, looked out across the plain, and allowed myself a rest.

My saddle and bridle lay underneath the wagon, where Haggis had put them. The stirrup leather on the saddle's off side was scratched and cut as a result of the pony's death slide, and so was the scabbard that protected my Winchester. Blood from the pony, now dried black and flaking, marked the saddle's front jockey and blanket. Checking my saddle bags, I found that a bottle of liniment had shattered during the horse fall, but there seemed to be no other damage.

My old cavalry field glasses were intact. I took them out and scanned the prairie in every direction. Sheep camps are located on high places so the herders can keep an eye on their flocks, and the hilltop that held Haggis's wagon made a fine observation point.

Grass and sagebrush shimmered in the distance. Cloud shadows slid smoothly over the plains. Maybe two miles away, I discovered the tan, black, and white of a lone pronghorn standing guard atop a rocky butte. Beyond and below him, at the butte's base, a herd of maybe fifty antelope—does, fawns, and bucks—grazed in the sunlight.

I saw no sign of Haggis and the sheep, but I figured they couldn't be all that far away. A long ridge to the east blocked my view, but I guessed the band would be browsing the slopes and hillsides beyond.

I lowered the glasses and closed my eyes. The sun was warm upon my face. I stretched out in the shade of the wagon and rested my head on my saddle. The next thing I knew, it was noon.

"Hoot, laddie!" the voice said. "Is it a corpse ye are, or are ye merely sleepin'?"

Haggis McRae sat his piebald gelding, looking down at me from the saddle. The sun was high in the sky behind him. I squinted against the glare. Haggis balanced a straight piece of chokecherry wood across the saddle's fork.

About five feet long, the wood was forked at one end.

"Just restin' my eyes," I said. "I must have drifted off."

Haggis dismounted. He held out the stick. "I've made ye a crutch, laddie. Wi' a bit of sheep pelt to pad it, 'twill help ye get about until ye're healed."

"Much obliged," I said. "Appears I've come to a first-class hospital."

The big man smiled. "Aye," he said. "And 'tis time I fed ye again. A wee bite o' dinner could do us nae harm."

He tied the gelding to a wagon wheel and slackened the saddle cinch. Bending, he offered me his hand. I took it, and he lifted me to my feet as if I was a child. Nodding at the wood pile, he said, "I see ye've been busy. How's your leg?"

"A little sore, but not bad. I can even walk on it some."

"Use the crutch an' gie it some time," Haggis said. "Ye may be here for quite a spell."

He stepped up onto the packing box that served as a step, and then into the wagon. I followed, helping myself up by the strength of my arms. "How long do you figure?" I asked.

"I dinnae ken, laddie. Since losin' his camp tender, the boss tends his camps himself. Could be a week, or maybe longer."

"That's too long. I'll wear out my welcome."

"Dinnae be daft," Haggis said. "I'm glad for the comp'ny. Besides, ye need time to heal."

Haggis built a fire in the stove and set the teapot on. Minutes later, seated across the slide-out table from each other, we shared a midday meal of dried beef, beans, and corn bread. We talked but little, and Haggis was soon on his way back to his sheep.

Alone again, I wondered how a man could live so totally apart from the company of men. In the days ahead, I would ask Haggis that very question.

"A man must be good comp'ny for himself," he said. "Not all men are."

FIVE

▼

A STRANGER COMES CALLING

I was restless. Each day at the sheep camp seemed much the same as the day before, and time passed slow as a turtle race.

Mornings dawned clear or cloudy. The woollies left the bed ground, with Haggis and his dogs to guide them. I stayed behind at the wagon and tried to make myself useful. I cleaned up the dishes, split wood for the stove, and helped with the cooking. The wind blew, or it didn't. One morning it rained.

The sun crept across the sky and dropped behind the mountains. Haggis and the dogs returned with the sheep and bedded them down. The sky turned red and faded to gray. Night fell. Stars came out. The moon rose. From somewhere in the distance, coyote songs disturbed the peace. We slept, rose with the dawn, and started the day all over again. Time rolled on like a river. I rode the current, but mostly I felt like I was caught in an eddy.

Haggis was affable and good-natured, fair weather or foul. I could not have asked for a better companion. A week went by, and still no one came to tend our camp. We were running low on water and groceries, but Haggis just said, "Dinnae worry. The boss will be comin' any day now."

He said the owner of the sheep was a man named Abel McKenzie, and that he was a generous man but a "wee bit stubborn and hot-headed." The way Haggis said it made those traits sound like virtues.

I was getting around pretty well on my injured leg by that time. Haggis even allowed me to ride his Jimmy horse sometimes. Early that second week, I went with him when he took the sheep out.

Herding sheep turned out to be a lot like riding day herd on cattle. Haggis worked the band slow and easy, letting the sheep spread out and graze as they wished. He said the secret to handling sheep was to make them think they were doing what *they* wanted instead of what the herder wanted.

One sheep looked pretty much like another to me, but not so to Haggis. He knew most of the ewes in his band by sight, and he had even named several of them. He would point to one and say, "There's Fiona, six years old and the best mother in the band." Or "Poor Beatrice, she's had bad luck wi' her lambs. Lost one to the weather and two to coyotes."

I loved to watch the dogs work. Robbie was steady and reliable at all times. He seemed to know what was needed before Haggis even raised an arm. When a ewe Haggis called Wanda took it on herself to stray, Robbie was there to turn her back.

Time and again the old gadabout tried to drift away from the band, but each attempt was blocked by Robbie's no-nonsense gaze and his sleek, black-furred body. Finally, the exasperated Wanda stamped her foot and bolted, but Robbie was not about to be buffaloed by a bunch quitter. With a burst of speed, he overtook the old girl and blocked her escape route. When Wanda tried to run past him, he nipped her hind leg smartly and sent her scurrying back to the band. Seconds later, Robbie was at Haggis's side, tongue lolling, watching the sheep.

Tip, the younger dog, was quick and eager but without Robbie's patience. Tip worked the band like a policeman in a tough neighborhood, ready to quell trouble if it should arise and ready to cause some if it didn't. His rough and ready ways made the sheep nervous, and they tended to shy and scatter when they saw him coming. Sometimes, when Tip got rowdy, he'd upset a ewe or tumble one of the big lambs.

"Wheesht now, Tip," Haggis would scold. "That'll *do,* damn ye!"

Chastened, the dog would slink back to Haggis and assume an innocent pose. Tip would then be on his best behavior, at least for awhile.

I didn't go out with Haggis and the sheep the next morning but stayed at the wagon instead. My leg was hurting some, and I figured I'd give it a day's rest. I didn't know it then, but our pastoral pattern was about to change forever. On that day, our camp had a visitor.

We were finishing our midday meal inside the wagon. Now that I was getting around better, Haggis mostly packed a lunch and stayed out with the sheep all day, not returning until sundown. But on that particular day, he left the band and rode Jimmy back to the wagon at noon. He had a dead lamb draped across the saddle, and he said the animal had done what sheep seem to do best—that is, it had died.

Haggis decided to celebrate the lamb's life by serving it up for our supper. The departed woollie would be both guest of honor and main ingredient, Haggis explained.

I helped him skin and butcher the lamb, and then I filled a cooking pot with water and put it on the stove to heat.

The pot was boiling away nicely, and Haggis was about to go back to the band, when I heard a dog's excited barking just outside. Looking down from the wagon's open door, I saw Robbie staring at something beyond my line of sight. His hackles were up and his teeth were bared. A growl rumbled deep in his throat.

"Wheesht, Robbie!" Haggis commanded. "What has ye so het up, dog?"

Robbie glanced quickly at his master, and then returned to staring and snarling.

I tried to see what the dog was looking at, but the narrow doorway limited my field of vision. Haggis stepped outside. I stayed inside, looking out.

Forty feet away, a man on horseback sat watching us. He rode a lathered bay gelding, and he was dressed for the trail in a flat-brimmed black hat and canvas duster. The sun was almost directly overhead, and the man's face was hidden by the shadow of his hat.

Unbuttoned, his duster hung open to reveal a belted Colt's revolver at his waist, worn on the rider's left side and reversed for a cross draw. The butt of a long-barreled rifle protruded from a scabbard on the saddle's off side. The rider rested his hands atop his saddle horn and nodded. "Howdy," he said. "You want to call your dog off?"

Haggis stepped down and took hold of Robbie's collar. "Wheesht now, Robbie. That'll do," he said quietly. The dog stopped growling, but his eyes remained fixed on the stranger.

"He'll do ye nae harm," Haggis said. "I dinnae hear ye call out."

"Didn't call out," the rider said. "I like to go quiet."

The stranger raised his head, and I saw his face. His skin was dark from the sun. A full black moustache decorated his upper lip. Cold eyes looked me over from head to toe. The man took his time about it, studying me as if I were a problem to be solved.

I had not worn my revolver since I'd come to Haggis's camp; there had seemed no need. Now, for the first time in a week, I missed its familiar weight on my hip.

The rider shifted his gaze to Haggis. "You McKenzie's mutton puncher?" he asked.

"Aye," Haggis said. "I work for Abel McKenzie."

"Your damned sheep are trespassin'," the rider said. "This is cattle range. *Cow* country."

"Nae. This is *open* range. *God's* country."

I was still wishing I had my forty-four. The gun was inside the wagon, beside the bed. I thought about going back for it but decided doing so might be asking for trouble. I scolded myself for my carelessness. Marshal Ridgeway's lecture on *Cuidado* returned to mind.

The stranger shifted his weight, preparing to dismount. The bay shuffled its feet, its eyes on Robbie.

I don't know what got into me. I guess I'd had a bellyful of the stranger's rudeness. "Nobody *asked* you to step down, mister," I said.

He stared at me, his eyes hot and his mouth a hard, thin line beneath his moustache. "I don't need no goddam invitation," he said, "especially from a pair of scab herders like . . ."

That's when Robbie made his move. Maybe the dog heard the anger in the man's voice, or maybe he somehow sensed the stranger was a threat to his master. Whatever the reason, Robbie broke free of Haggis's grasp and made a dash for horse and rider. Seeing the sheepdog streaking toward him spooked the bay; the animal shied and stepped sharply aside.

Dismounting, the man lost his grip on the saddle horn and fell, his foot caught in the stirrup. Then his foot jerked free and he toppled heavily to the ground. I turned, stepping quickly back inside the wagon. A second later, I was back in the doorway, my six-gun in my hand.

Haggis caught Robbie again. The dog strained to free himself, but the herder held him fast.

The stranger's eyes were wild. He had lost his hat and his dignity, and he was about to lose his temper. His hand jerked toward his holstered revolver.

"I wouldn't," I said, cocking my forty-four.

The stranger stared at me, calculating the odds. For a long moment he stood, considering. Then, slowly, he drew his hand back away from his gun. His face was flushed, and he was breathing hard. Slowly, he bent down, picked his hat up off the ground, and put it on. He had kept his grip on the bridle reins when he fell, and he pulled the jittery bay around and made it stand while he stepped back into the saddle. He gave the dog a last hard look. He turned his eyes to me. "Another time," he said. Then, reining the bay around, he sank spur and rode away.

Haggis stood for a time, watching the stranger fade into the distance. Then he turned, his eyes on the gun in my hand. "So," he said, "d' ye ken who the man is?"

I slid the forty-four back in the leather. This time, I strapped the gun belt about my waist. "I have a pretty good idea," I said. "I believe he's a man named Griff Tallon. Supposed to be some kind of range detective."

Haggis nodded. He said nothing but waited for me to continue.

"Ten days ago, my horse threw a shoe," I said. "I had to leave him at a cabin back in the breaks with a small-time cowman name of Vernal Slye. Slye loaned me one of his paint ponies so I could ride over to Reata. That's where I was headed when I got ambushed.

"Slye was nervous. He seemed worried—kept askin' if I'd seen a lone rider on a bay horse. Said the man wore a black hat and a canvas duster. I told him I hadn't seen such a man, and I hadn't—not until today.

"I can't say whether Slye is a rustler or not, but I figure the gent on the bay horse thinks he is. When I rode out on Slye's pinto, I believe the man mistook me for Slye. He waited until I was out in the open, crossing the rock slide, and took a shot at me."

Haggis grinned. "Aye, and killed the pony. I'm glad he missed ye, laddie."

My own grin matched his. "Not as glad as *I* am," I said.

It was nearly dark when Haggis brought the band back to the bed ground. I listened to the now familiar bleating of the sheep as ewes and lambs called out to each other, mothering up for the night. I fed Robbie and Tip while Haggis unsaddled his gelding and washed up by lantern light.

During the time I'd been with Haggis at the wagon, we had grown comfortable with each other. Now, as night settled in, we worked together on the small chores that needed attending. The big herder busied himself at the stove and in short order produced a fine boiled mutton dinner.

We talked but little as we ate. I figured Haggis was thinking about the stranger and his visit earlier in the day. I know *I* was. A range detective with a rifle was making his own decisions about who should live or die in Meriwether County, and someone was paying him to do it. My job was to investigate and build a case against the law-breakers before a full-blown range war got started. It was high time I got back to work.

I slept fitfully that night. Near me, on his makeshift bunk, Haggis seemed restless, too. Outside, the wind blustered and moaned, buffeting the wagon like a wild animal trying to break in. The moon rose, chasing the clouds and casting its light down through the wagon's rear window. I lay awake, thinking the nighttime thoughts that make mole-hills into mountains. Finally, I was able to put them aside and passed into an uneasy sleep.

I woke to the gray light of false dawn. The wind had died away to a breeze, and the wagon was cold and dark. Haggis sat up in his blankets and stretched. He dressed hurriedly and then opened the wagon's door and stepped out into the morning. Haggis believed that if coyotes struck the sheep, they were likely to do so at dawn. For that reason, he made it his habit to be up and out with the sheep before first light.

I lit the lamp and built a fire in the stove. No sooner had I put the teapot on than Haggis came back. He appeared suddenly in the doorway and climbed up into the wagon.

"Mornin', Haggis," I said. "Are the sheep all right?"

The big herder's expression was somber, worried. "Aye, the sheep are well enough," he said. "But I cannae find ma Robbie."

I tucked my crutch under my armpit and walked out with Haggis, circling the sheep. Overhead, stars faded as darkness drained from the sky. Dew clung to the bunch grass and freshened the morning. As our eyes searched the broken country above our camp, Haggis called out, "Here, Robbie! Come, boy!" We stopped after each call to listen

75

and watch, but there was no answering bark or movement.

Tip, the younger dog, followed along at Haggis's side. We stopped again. The big man looked down at Tip and said, "Where's yer partner, Tip? Go, now, and look for him—find Robbie."

Tip must have wondered what he was being asked to do. There were no sheep to gather where we walked, no lost lamb or cantankerous ewe to deal with. He looked up at Haggis and then dashed out in front of us. Back and forth, in and out of the sagebrush, Tip roamed. We followed, watching the dog as he appeared and disappeared from view, only his white-tipped tail waving behind him like a flag.

Suddenly, Tip froze in his tracks and barked. Fifty yards away, an old cottonwood tree clung to the edge of a dry wash. Magpies scolded in its branches, fluttering from branch to branch. Again, Tip barked, and raced toward the tree. Haggis followed, as did I, but my passage was slowed some because of my leg. Looking ahead, I saw that Tip was staring upward toward the forks of the tree. Haggis quickly reached his side, and I saw that he, too, had his eyes fixed on something I could not yet see.

A moment later, I was with them, and I saw what they saw. Hanging from a tree branch was the lifeless body of the faithful Robbie!

The dog hung head down, secured to the branch

by a cord tied about its hind legs. The flies had already found him, and his sleek black fur was matted with blood. A ragged, gaping hole behind the shoulder marked the place where the bullet had passed through the dog's body. Tip continued to stare at his lifeless comrade, whining piteously. Haggis trembled as he lifted Robbie's body and cut the cord that suspended it from the tree.

The big herder gathered the dog in his arms. I looked at his face and was surprised by what I saw. His mouth was a thin, tight line, pulled down at the corners, but his overall expression was not one of anger or even of grief. Instead, he looked bewildered, as if to ask how anyone could do such a senseless and terrible thing.

Then Haggis breathed a great sigh, and it was as if all his strength left his body. He sank to his knees in the dirt of the dry wash, still holding the lifeless dog. When he spoke, his voice sounded sad beyond the bearing. "Och, Robbie," he said. "My brave and faithful Robbie."

The story was written in the dirt. Some time during the night, the man on the bay horse roped a ewe and dragged her away from the others. Robbie followed, as the stranger knew he would. As soon as the man lured the dog far enough to suit him, he killed it with a single shot.

We found tracks where the killer dismounted and

released the sheep. Then he rode away into the night. We hadn't heard the shot because of the wind.

Haggis buried Robbie on a gentle slope above the bed ground, and we made our way back to the wagon. The big herder said nothing, but I believe I saw tears brimming in that big man's eyes. I can't be sure of that, though. Somehow, my *own* vision had gone a bit blurry.

Six
▼

Life Among the Sheepmen

We heard the wagon coming long before we saw it. Two days after we buried Robbie, we were grazing the sheep on good grass maybe two miles from camp. The rumble of iron-shod wheels on rocky ground came clearly, the sound growing louder with the wagon's approach.

Haggis sat cross-legged on a knoll, watching the sheep. Tip lay at his side. I squatted nearby in the shade of Haggis's Jimmy horse. Since our encounter with the stranger and the killing of Robbie, sadness seemed to hang over the valley like a cloud. The silence between Haggis and me had grown, too. I reckon we both just sort of felt the need to be alone with our thoughts.

The wagon, pulled by a team of gray horses, rattled into view atop a nearby hill.

Two men occupied the wagon seat, and the driver drew rein when he saw us. I watched him set the brake and step down. A moment later, he was walking down the hill toward us.

Haggis got to his feet. "It's ma boss," he said quietly. "Abel McKenzie."

I watched the sheepman approach. McKenzie appeared to be a man in his late forties, solid and stocky. I saw him glance my way and then turn his attention to the grazing band. He strode up to Haggis and gave him his hand. "Haggis," he said. "The sheep are looking well."

"Aye," Haggis replied. "The new grass is like a tonic."

McKenzie looked at me, taking my measure. He was shorter than me, maybe five foot seven or eight, and his skin was freckled from the sun. He may have been a sheepman, but he had all the earmarks of a cowpuncher.

His walk was the rolling gait of a horseman on foot. He wore a narrow-brimmed hat of beaver felt, which must have set him back ten dollars at least, and he wore it pulled low above deep-set eyes of faded blue. His shirt was of gray flannel, and his pants were Levi's, the color of his eyes. His boots were hand-made and fancy stitched.

"I'm Abel McKenzie," he said. "Who might you be?"

Asking a man's name was still considered bad manners on most parts of the range, but somehow

I didn't take offense. Abel McKenzie was facing pressure from the cattlemen of Meriwether County and from range detectives like Griff Tallon. Seeing a gun-toting drifter with his woollies gave him more than the right to ask.

"My name's Merlin Fanshaw," I said. "Haggis pulled me out from under a dead horse a week ago and brought me back to his wagon. I'm grateful to him, and to you."

"Sounds like there's a story there somewhere. Let's go up to Haggis's wagon. You can tell it to me over a cup of tea."

McKenzie's offered his hand, and I took it. "It's a deal," I said.

At the sheep wagon, Abel McKenzie introduced me to his companion. "This is my son, Ian," he said. "Since Toby, my camp tender, got killed, Ian's taken to riding with me most places."

Ian was taller than his dad, but he bore little resemblance to him. He was dark-skinned and slender, and his hair was black as midnight. Abel was short and barrel-chested, fair of skin, with ginger-colored hair. Only the eyes were the same—deep-set and faded blue. I guessed Ian to be about twenty, maybe a little younger.

The wagon the McKenzies came in was loaded with supplies for the camp. The wagon box held freshly filled water barrels to replace Haggis's nearly empty ones, groceries in wooden boxes, oats for Haggis's saddle horse, a five-gallon can of coal oil, and a generous supply of firewood.

Haggis built a small fire in the cook stove and set the teapot on to boil. While we waited, he told Abel all that had happened since he found me trapped beneath Vernon Slye's pony. When Haggis spoke of the stranger on the bay and the death of the faithful Robbie, his voice grew soft, and there was pain in it.

"He killed ma Robbie," he said, "for spite."

Abel's face flushed beet red. "Sounds like that damned hired killer the cowmen brought in. Zack Rainford and the rest of those high-and-mighty beef barons won't be happy until they run everyone off the range but themselves."

Abel turned to me. "Tell me the straight of it, Fanshaw. Seems plain to me that bushwhackin' bastard took you for a rustler. Any reason he should?"

I met his eyes and held them. "I won't take offense at that, Mr. McKenzie, because you don't know me yet. The answer is no. I was just ridin' through."

The sheepman looked away. "Sorry," he muttered. "No offense meant. I guess I've just been pushed and prodded to where I've forgot my manners."

Haggis poured the tea. Abel raised his cup and looked at me. "I'm glad Haggis found you," he said. "How can I help?"

"I need to get to Reata. I could use a ride."

He nodded. "You've got one. Reata is only twelve miles from our home ranch. Ian has to go to town this week. You can ride in with him."

"I'd be obliged."

Abel and Haggis walked off by themselves, talking about the condition of the range and the sheep. I helped Ian lift the empty water barrels into the supply wagon and added my saddle, rifle, and bridle to the load.

I still used my crutch some, but most of the time I was getting along without it. The plaster cast Haggis had made me was looking more disreputable every day. I was looking forward to taking it off for good.

Ian nodded at my cast. "Does your leg still hurt?" he asked.

"Some," I said. "Mostly, it itches. Can't scratch it because of the durned cast."

"Like Dad said, I'll be goin' into Reata this week. Doc Reynolds can take it off."

"Reynolds, huh? Is he a good doctor?"

Ian laughed. "Best doctor in town. Only one, too."

"Glad to hear he's the best," I said, grinning. "Nothin's too good for me."

Abel and Haggis came back to the wagon, still talking. "Start the sheep for the home ranch a week from tomorrow," Abel said. "The other herders will be movin' their bands about the same time. We'll shear week after next and trail the sheep up the mountain to summer pasture."

"Aye," Haggis said. "D'ye ken what part of the mountain?"

"Where the grass is up to their bellies. Vendetta Canyon."

I said my good-byes to Haggis and thanked him for his kindness. He blushed like a schoolgirl and gruffly denied he'd done anything special. "Dinnae mention it, laddie," he said. "I was glad t' have ye."

I took the seat beside Abel in the supply wagon. With Ian in the box behind us, Abel shook the reins, and we rattled away, headed down to the valley floor.

Minutes later, we picked up a little-used wagon road at the base of the slope, and Abel turned the team onto it. The road rose and fell through hills and valleys studded with sage and scrub cedar, winding steadily east with the sun at our backs. "My home place is twenty miles from here," Abel said. "We'll be there before sundown."

He turned toward me. "Haggis told me how you stood up to that stranger the day he rode into camp. Said you pulled a gun on him."

"The man was rude. Said your sheep were trespassin' on cattle range. When he went to dismount,

I told him not to. I said nobody asked him to get down."

"That took guts," Abel said. "If the man is Griff Tallon, he's a hard case and a killer."

"Like I said, he was rude."

Abel was silent for awhile. Then he said, "Look here, Fanshaw. How would you like to work for me? I'm short a camp tender."

"I heard. A man named Toby. He got killed, you said."

The sheepman's face went hard. He nodded. "Zack Rainford claimed Toby was a rustler. Said Tallon caught him changin' brands on a Circle R calf. It's a damned lie! Toby never stole a thing in his life."

"But you can't prove it."

"Hell no, I can't prove it! But I knew Toby."

I had brought it on myself. When I threw down on the stranger back at Haggis's camp, I drew cards in another man's game. I couldn't blame Abel for looking for help, but I hadn't been sent to Meriwether County to take sides.

"I appreciate you askin' me," I said, "but I've got business of my own. If I was lookin' for a war, I'd join the army."

Abel looked disappointed. "You're plain-spoken, by God, but I like that in a man. I sometimes call a spade a shovel myself."

"I mean no offense. Like I said, I have business of my own."

"None taken. And I still appreciate you standin' up for Haggis."

Abel said nothing further for some time, seeming to pull back into himself and his thoughts. Ian sat in the wagon box behind me, a rifle cradled in his arms and his eyes alert as he scanned the hilltops. The way ahead appeared peaceful and serene, but it was clear that father and son were taking no chances on being bushwhacked.

The road led into a lush, green valley bounded by low hills. A rambling creek, marked by stands of willow and alder, twisted across the valley floor and caught sunlight in its ripples. Shadows lengthened as the day grew older, and the light lost its hard edge. Then, just at sundown, Abel turned the team away from the creek and up a long grassy slope.

As the wagon crested the hilltop, Abel pointed down the other side into a shadowed valley. There, at the bottom of the grade, stood a ranch house, corrals, and a scatter of outbuildings. Lamplight glowed in a window of the house, and a stream flowed past the barn lot, reflecting the sunset.

"There it is," Abel said proudly. "Headquarters for the McKenzie Sheep Company. Also home to our branch of the McKenzie clan."

"You have other children?"

"Aye. Ian's the oldest. Then there's Ginger, my

daughter. Fifteen years old, and caregiver to all creation. Her brother, Keith, is ten and a bold explorer. He gives his sister constant opportunities to practice her nursing skills."

As we reached the bottom of the grade and drove up to the ranch house, an aging sheep dog ambled out to bark at us, but his challenge was short on enthusiasm. "Hush now, Rascal," Abel said. "It's only us."

Abel stepped down from the wagon and handed the reins to his son. "Ian will show you the bunkhouse and help you get settled," he said. "I'll tell my wife to set an extra place."

"I don't want to put her to any trouble," I said.

"No trouble," Abel said. "She'll be glad for the company. She doesn't get away from the home place much these days."

With the dog walking beside him, Abel turned toward the house's front door.

At a weathered barn near the creek, two men watched as Ian drove up and parked the wagon. They were hard-looking gents, cat-eyed and watchful, and the way they wore their belted six-guns told me they were more than ranch hands. They said nothing but unhitched the team and led the horses inside the barn.

I looked at Ian. "Sheepherders?" I asked.

"No, I guess not," he said. "That's Bill Packer and Al Wilson. They're more like—bodyguards. If

Rainford's men bring trouble, Dad aims to show fight."

"Hired gunhands take careful handling. If trouble doesn't come soon enough to suit them, they're liable to go out and *start* some."

"Sounds like you know something about gunhands."

"I've known a few."

Ian glanced at the ivory-handled forty-four at my waist and then met my gaze. He said nothing, but the question was in his eyes.

He looked away, toward the fading light in the west. "Just between us," he said, "I wish *both* Dad and Zack Rainford would pull in their horns. If they'd just try to get along, there's plenty of grass in this county for both cattle *and* sheep."

Ian smiled. "But enough second-guessing," he said. "Let's find you a bed at the bunkhouse and wash up for supper."

"Suits me," I said.

The McKenzie bunkhouse held six iron bedsteads, two of them empty. I tossed the blanket roll from my saddle onto one of the vacant bunks, rolled up my sleeves, and scrubbed the trail dust from my face and hands at the wash stand. Then, with Ian leading the way, I limped across the rutted barn lot to the cook shack.

Stepping up onto the porch, I waited while Ian opened the door. Following him inside, I removed my hat and my gun belt and hung them on a peg near the door. The aroma of fresh-baked biscuits, roast beef, and gravy reminded me how hungry I was. Lamplight cast a soft glow over the room.

Abel was sitting at the head of a long table, drinking coffee. Behind him, at the stove, a handsome woman tended the pots and pans. She turned, looking at me, and smiled. Abel stood, speaking to the woman.

"Teresa, this is Merlin Fanshaw, the man I told you about. Merlin, meet my wife, Teresa."

"Ma'am," I said.

Teresa McKenzie's laugh was a throaty chuckle. She seemed neither demure nor forward, but met my eyes with honest interest, the way a man might. "Our cook has gone to Reata for a few days, so you'll have to put up with my cooking," she said. "You're very welcome here. My husband told me how you stood up for Haggis."

Teresa McKenzie's eyes were deep and dusky brown, and her skin was the color of coffee with cream. Her hair was long and black, with streaks of gray appearing, and she wore it loose about her shoulders. I judged her to be about forty years of age, but it's hard to tell with women.

"It was Haggis who took care of *me,* ma'am," I said, "He found me and brought me back to his wagon after my horse wreck."

She smiled again. I don't believe I ever saw teeth so white.

I realized I was staring. With some effort, I turned my eyes away and looked at Abel.

"Sit here, next to me," the sheepman said. "We'll get acquainted some."

I eased myself onto the bench at Abel's right hand. Ian took a seat at his father's left, directly across from me. Now that I'd met Mrs. McKenzie, it was plain where Ian got his coloring. Except for his blue, deep-set eyes, he was made in his mother's image.

Packer and Wilson came in and sat down at the table. They didn't take their guns off, and Abel didn't ask them to. Then an older man I figured was the ranch's chore boy came in and sat down. We traded nods, but we didn't howdy.

The supper was a good one, consisting of roast beef and gravy, carrots and spuds from the root cellar, sourdough biscuits, and hot, black coffee. I ate my fill and then some, going back for seconds of the beef and the biscuits. It sure was good to drink coffee again. I have been a coffee drinker since my youth, and I found during my stay with Haggis that I missed having my daily supply. Tea is fine, and many prefer it, but to me, coffee is the water of life.

Abel kept up a running talk all through the meal, bragging about how much better the sheep business was than the cow business and doing his best to convince me that Zack Rainford was the worst villain since Nero rode herd on the Romans.

"Cattle raising, the way Rainford does it, is wasteful and inefficient," he said. "Why, it takes a cowman three or four years to see a profit from his herd's increase, but a sheepman can expect a 20-percent profit the first year and similar increases the second, third, and fourth years!

"Cowmen would have you believe sheep ruin the land by overgrazing, that they eat the grass down to the roots and leave nothing but bare dirt behind. Well, so do cows if you hold 'em too long in one place and over-crowd the range! Cowmen say cattle won't graze where sheep have been or drink from the same water hole. 'Tain't so!

"There's plenty of room on the range for *both* sheep and cows! Cattle and sheep like different plants—sheep prefer tender grasses and forbs; cows can make out fine on coarser stuff. Cattle like to hold to the creek bottoms and graze the low land; sheep prefer the hilltops and ridges.

"The truth is the big cow outfits have had it all their own way for too long, and they don't like havin' to share the range. Dog in the manger is what I call it; the big cowmen don't make efficient use of the grass, but they resent it like billy hell if somebody else does!"

I found myself only half hearing Abel's tirade. I'd heard the same old argument many times before. Now and then, I'd nod or mumble "Uh huh" just to be polite and let him know I was listening, but my mind was occupied else-wise. Mostly, I was watching his missus.

Teresa McKenzie busied herself at the stove, tending to her cooking. When the meat ran low, she added more to the platter. She brought out biscuits fresh from the oven and kept the coffee pot filled. She moved with a quiet grace that put me in mind of deer grazing in a mountain meadow.

There was nothing put-on or flirtatious about the lady, and I swear I entertained no improper thoughts about her. She was simply a 100 percent, full-blooded woman, and mighty easy on the eyes. I watched and admired her same as I would a good-looking quarter horse. Well . . . maybe not *quite* the same.

"In a few weeks I'll be bringin' my sheep here to the home place," Abel was saying. "We'll shear 'em and trail 'em up into the mountains to summer range. Only this time they'll be on land Zack Rainford claims as his own: Vendetta Canyon.

"There's a world of grass up there, and good water, too. That's open range, and I have a right to it. If Rainford crowds my sheep, I'll crowd his cows. If he pushes me, I'll push back. And if he tries to run me off, he'll think a ton of brick has fell on him. That's no brag; that's just the way it is."

The supper ended. The two hard cases stacked their plates on the counter top by the door and went outside. The chore boy did the same, and I was left alone with the McKenzies.

Abel pushed himself back from the table and nodded at his son. "Ian will be takin' the wagon into Reata in the mornin'," he said. "You can ride along with him."

I got to my feet. "I'm obliged," I said. As the other men had done, I added my dishes to the stack by the door. I picked up my hat and buckled my gun belt on.

Teresa McKenzie was heating water at the stove. "It's been a pleasure to meet you, ma'am," I said. "Your dinner was mighty fine."

She nodded, her eyes merry. "Thank you," she said. "Welcome to our home."

The woman's smile could have lit up a coal mine.

SEVEN

▼

THE STREETS OF REATA

Breakfast came early at McKenzie's. The wash-up bell jangled at four thirty, and I was out of my blankets and into my boot before the echoes faded. With any luck, I'd be out of my cast and into *both* boots by evening. I was ready to see the town of Reata and meet Doc Reynolds. Truth is I was *more* than ready.

I thumbnailed a match and lit the coal-oil lamp. Soft light flooded the bunkhouse, and shadows leaped against the walls and ceiling. Bill Packer stirred beneath his bed tarp and grumbled, "It sure don't take long to stay all night at this outfit." I combed my hair by the broken mirror above the washstand, washed up in cold water, and hobbled outside to greet the day.

Above the dark mass of the mountains, the morning sky was sprinkled with stars. To the south, Orion's belt glittered like frozen fire, and over north, the Dipper sat brimful just above the horizon. A fresh breeze sighed up from the creek, stirring the dew-wet grass beside the bunkhouse. Across the barn lot, lamplight shone yellow in the cook shack window, and I set a course for the light like a sailor bound for port.

When I walked in, Abel himself was at the stove, cooking hotcakes and ham. He greeted me with a nod. "Ian is taking the wagon to Reata this mornin'," he said. "He'll be along directly. He's already had his breakfast, over at the house."

I sat down. Abel filled my cup from the coffee boiler. "You can ride in with him," he said. "I'd appreciate it if you'd keep an eye out."

"You expectin' trouble?"

Abel shrugged. "It could come any time."

"Well," I said, "if you're worried, why don't you send those two gunnies along?"

"Ian's just goin' in to pick up supplies and bring the cook back. Sendin' Packer and Wilson might *provoke* trouble."

"Yeah," I said. "All right, I'll ride shotgun, one

way. But I'll be stayin' in town for a few days. Ian will be on his own comin' home."

"I'll send somebody out to meet him this evenin'," Abel said. "I'm obliged to you, Fanshaw."

"That's all right," I said, grinning. "I just took my pay in hotcakes and ham."

Bill Packer and Al Wilson came in and sat down at the table. The chore boy followed them. We ate in silence. Even Abel seemed to have nothing to say. As they did the night before, the hard cases and the chore boy finished their meal, scraped and stacked their plates, and left the cook shack. I sat, drank a third cup of coffee, and followed suit.

I was waiting at the bunkhouse with my blanket roll and war bag when Ian drove up from the barn. He reined the team to a stop and smiled down from the wagon's spring seat. "Good morning," he said.

I squinted up at him against the sun's brightness. "Good mornin'," I said. "Nice day for a wagon ride."

Ian was clean-shaven and dressed in what appeared to be his Sunday best. Beneath a business suit of black wool, he wore a white flannel shirt and a blue silk neck scarf. A low-crowned stockman's hat sat squarely on his head, and he had polished his boots to a high gloss.

I grinned. "You dress up mighty doggy just to

pick up the ranch cook," I said. "She must really be somethin'."

Ian blushed. "I don't . . . she's not . . . that is, our cook is an old lady! She's old enough to be my grandma, and she weighs nearly three hundred pounds!"

I shrugged. "Not *my* type," I said, "but tastes have a right to differ, I guess."

Seeing that Ian had already loaded my saddle, bridle, and Winchester, I tossed my right-hand boot, my blanket roll, and my war bag into the wagon box and climbed up beside him.

Ian was smiling now, but my joke had clearly caught him off stride. He was still red-faced as he turned the team down toward the creek. Minutes later, the wagon rumbled across the bridge and out onto the road to Reata. I wondered about his reaction to my foolery; then I turned to watching the scenery and forgot all about it.

The road stretched out before us along a clear, fast-moving stream. Low hills sloped away, dotted with wildflowers. Chokecherry and wild currant bushes grew thick along the stream, and willows and cottonwoods caught the early morning light on their upper branches. I slid my Winchester from its scabbard, checked its loads, and placed it within easy reach.

As Abel asked me to, I kept watch on the wooded bottoms and hilltops as we traveled. Ian noticed my precautions but said nothing. If he had asked what I was looking for, I couldn't have told him exactly. I was practicing what my boss Chance Ridgeway had urged me to, this time for someone else. My brush with death back at the rock slide had convinced me: *Cuidado* was indeed the name of the game.

Making conversation, I asked Ian what the town of Reata was like. "Well," he said, "it's a cow town, as you might guess from its name. Early day cowmen built some big ranches hereabouts on free government grass and gumption. The town sprang up to serve them."

"Now it serves homesteaders and sheepmen, too," I said. "How did your dad come to be in the sheep business?"

"He wasn't always. He started out as a cowboy with the Circle R."

"Your dad worked for Zack Rainford?" I must have shown my surprise, for Ian looked at me and smiled.

"He rode for the brand. Zeb Rainford, Zack's father, owned the Circle R then. Doc Reynolds told me Dad and Zack were the best of friends in those days. According to Doc, they cowboyed together, hunted together, chased wild horses, and raised hell in town."

"You wouldn't know it now," I said. "What happened?"

Ian shrugged. "I guess they had some kind of falling out. Dad quit the Circle R. Married my mom. Went into the sheep business. Now Dad and Zack are sworn enemies. It doesn't make sense to me."

"Did you ever ask your dad what happened?"

"I tried to once. He said he didn't want to talk about it, then or ever."

That pretty much ended our conversation. We fell silent, each thinking our own thoughts. I recalled a line by Robert Burton that my pa used to quote sometimes. It didn't answer the question but only deepened the mystery: "Old friends become bitter enemies on a sudden for toys and small offenses."

I went back to watching the country. As we drew closer to town, the land leveled off into hayfields, crop land, and homesteads. Fences marked the boundaries, and cabins and outbuildings came into view along the creek.

Sunlight warmed the land, and only the sound of the horses' hooves on the rutted road and the creaking of the wagon broke the stillness. Twenty minutes later, we rounded a bend in the road, crossed the railroad tracks, and turned onto the main street of Reata.

The town was laid out roughly in the shape of a cross, with wide, tree-lined streets and a bustling business district. At the town's center, where Main and Trail Streets met, stood Reata's tallest buildings: the Cattleman's Bank and Trust, the Sanchez Mercantile, the Meriwether County Courthouse, and the Rainford Hotel. These pillars of law and commerce faced each other across a broad town square and stood a full story—in the case of the hotel and courthouse, *two* stories—above their neighbors. All four were built of brick or stone, which further set them apart from most of the other buildings.

Ian pulled up in front of the hotel and pointed. "Doc Reynolds lives just south of here—a white house with a picket fence. He should be at home if he hasn't been called out of town. If you miss him, you can usually find him evenings at the Longhorn Saloon. He likes his brandy, and he sometimes sits in on a poker game.

"I'll be around until one o'clock. That's when I'm supposed to pick up the cook. What do you want me to do with your saddle and bridle?"

Picking up my blanket roll, war bag, and Winchester, I climbed down from the wagon and tucked my right boot under my arm. "This town have a good livery stable?"

"Sure. Peabody's, at the end of Main Street."

"Leave 'em there. Say I'll be along directly."

I gave Ian my hand. "Much obliged for the ride," I said. "Thank your dad for me, too."

"I will. Luck to you, Merlin."

"And to you."

Ian touched his hat brim with the fingers of his right hand, swung the team around, and drove the wagon clattering up the street. I watched him drive away and then stepped up onto the hotel's covered veranda.

The sign above the double doors read "Hotel Rainford," and I remember wondering how many other things in town bore the name of the county's biggest cowman.

Inside, the lobby was spacious and well appointed. Oriental rugs decorated the floor, and upholstered chairs and divans provided seating for guests and visitors. Potted ferns and palms decorated the sitting areas, and polished brass spittoons reflected the sunlight that slanted in through the big front windows.

Beneath the high ceiling, mounted heads of pronghorn, deer, and elk gazed down on a world they had not seen in life, while below them framed paintings of cowboys working cattle and breaking broncs graced the walls. I crossed to the front desk and tapped the bell.

A balding man in a fancy silk shirt stepped out of a side room and quickly took his place behind the desk. "You caught me eating lunch," he said, smiling. He wiped his mouth and fingers on a napkin. "What can I do for you?"

"I need a room for a while," I said. "How much by the week?"

"Single rate is a dollar and half a day. Nine dollars for the week."

He glanced at my blanket roll, war bag, boot, and rifle. Raising an eyebrow, he leaned over the counter and said, "No luggage? I'm afraid I'll have to . . ."

"Yeah, I know. You'll have to ask me to pay in advance."

He gave me a rueful smile, as if to say he didn't agree with the hotel's unfriendly rules but there was nothing he could do. "That's right," he said. He raised his eyebrows. "Hotel policy. You understand."

"Sure, pardner." I dug two gold half eagles out of my pocket and laid them on the desk. The clerk took the coins and gave me back a silver dollar in change. He swung the register around so that it faced me. I signed "Merlin Fanshaw" and listed my address as "General Delivery, Dry Creek, Montana Territory."

The clerk handed me a room key. "Number five," he said. "Top of the stairs, on your right. Welcome to the Rainford, Mr. Fanshaw. I hope you enjoy your stay."

"That makes two of us," I said.

Across the lobby, I stood at the foot of the stairway and looked up to the landing at the top. A sharp pang of pain in my gimp leg reminded me that climbing those stairs wouldn't be easy. I was not looking forward to the trip, to put it mildly. Shifting my plunder to my left hand, I grasped the railing and took the stairs one step at a time up to the top. Minutes later, I found room number five and let myself in.

The room was clean and tidy and furnished with the bare essentials: a bed, a chair, a small dresser, and a washstand. I laid my Winchester and blanket roll on the bed and sat down until the hurting eased a bit. Then I picked up my boot and limped out to pay Doc Reynolds a visit.

I found the doctor a block north of the hotel, seated on the front porch of his house. He looked to be a man of about fifty or so, with snow white hair and friendly eyes. He raised his coffee cup as I stopped at his gate and answered my question before I could ask it. "Yes," he said, "I'm Doctor Reynolds. What can I do for you?"

I opened the gate and limped inside. "Busted my fibula a few weeks back in a horse fall. I need you to cut the cast off and see how she's healin'."

Doc Reynolds got to his feet. "I'll be happy to remove your cast," he said. "As for how she's healin', I'd say you're a better judge of that than I am. You seem to be getting around pretty well."

Inside, the doc led me through his parlor and into an office and examination room. Pointing to a raised table at the room's center, he said, "Climb on up there, cowboy. Let's have a look at that leg."

I have to admit the stookie that Haggis applied had seen better days. It was scuffed and dirty beyond belief but still doing its job. Doc Reynolds put on a pair of wire-rimmed spectacles and examined the cast.

"Who applied this cast?" he asked.

"Sheepherder name of Haggis McRae. Works for Abel McKenzie."

"The man should have been a doctor. I couldn't have done better myself."

Moments later, the doc had cut away the cast and cleaned my foot and lower leg. Free of the cast's protection, the pain returned with a vengeance. I gritted my teeth and tried to look unconcerned.

"Yes," he said. "The injury is healing nicely. You are lucky. Fractures of the fibula are among the least serious fractures. You'll have to be careful for a few weeks, maybe use a cane for a day or two, but you should be good as new after that."

He removed his spectacles and carefully placed them in a vest pocket. Then he leaned back, looking me over. He glanced at my belted six-gun. "Your clothing and manner say you're a cowhand," he said casually, "but there's something of the gunhand about you, as well. Are you riding for McKenzie?"

"No," I said. "Not for McKenzie, or Rainford, either. I have business of my own here."

"Forgive me, young man, but trouble is on the rise in Meriwether County, and it's only fair to warn you. If you stay around here, I expect you'll be called on to take sides."

I made no answer. "What do I owe you, doc?"

He smiled. "Fifty cents for the examination. The advice is free."

I fished a half dollar out of my pocket and handed it to him. "And worth every penny," I said.

Doc Reynolds loaned me a cane, and with my boots on both feet at last, I hobbled back to the hotel. My injured leg was still plenty tender, but it felt good to be free of the cast. I was impatient; I could hardly wait until I could get myself horseback again.

When I reached the hotel, I turned left and walked west on Main Street. I was eager to become acquainted with the town, but I also wanted to exercise my leg a bit. I passed three saloons, a hardware store, and a second bank. People on the street were going in and out of the various business places. Wagons and buckboards were parked along the street, and men on horseback rode up and down. Reata gave every sign of being prosperous and busy.

The desk clerk's comment about eating his lunch reminded me it had been a long time since breakfast, so I stopped at a hash house for a bowl of chili and a piece of apple pie. Thus fortified, I set out to continue my explorations.

Passing a barber shop, I promised myself a

haircut and bath later in the day. The front of the shop was shaded by a big cottonwood tree, and there was a bench out front for loafers and waiting customers. I decided to sit there in the shade, let my food settle, and watch the world pass by.

Across the street, saddle horses stood loose-tied in front of a saloon called the Longhorn. Piano music drifted out the open door, and cowpunchers sauntered outside and stopped to talk before turning to their mounts. I smiled. The Longhorn was a cowboy bar if ever I saw one. I knew that come evening there'd be more horses at the hitch rack and more waddies inside. *These boys have just stopped by for a beer*, I thought.

Suddenly, the palaver between the punchers stopped. Every head turned to the street, and each man seemed to give his full attention and respect to what he saw there. It was as if a parade was coming, and men were carrying the flag. Curious, I turned to see what they saw. When I did, I understood the attention, and the respect.

She came riding up the street on a hot-blooded Arab filly that was shiny black under the midday sun. The woman—or girl, for she looked to be no more than seventeen or eighteen—sat her saddle with style, her shoulders back, her elbows close to her body, and her back straight as a picket pin.

She was dressed in a white blouse, red silk neck scarf, and a high-crowned Stetson hat pulled low above her eyes. She wore high-topped boots with silver spurs and a divided riding skirt that fell just below her knees. She rode astride, as a man does, self-confidence and pride in every line of her.

Across the street, the cowboys watched her pass. I only glanced at them; I couldn't take my eyes off the girl. I got to my feet, my fingers touching my hat brim. The girl turned to me, our eyes met, and she rode on at a trot.

In that moment, I noticed most her sense of purpose. Wherever she was headed, she was determined to go there directly and without distraction.

I realized I'd been holding my breath. Beginning to breathe again, I took a quick inventory of what I saw. The girl's face was a rich tan, her cheekbones high and smooth. Her eyes were large, her nose and chin small and well-formed. Her hair was black as the filly she rode, long and done up in a single braid at the back of her head.

"She's really somethin', ain't she, cowboy?"

I turned. The barber had come out of his shop and stood beside me, watching the girl ride away. "There ain't near enough beauty in this tired old world," he said, "so when she passes by, I make it a point to come out of my shop and watch."

"Who is she?" I asked.

"You must be new in town," the barber said. "That's Morgan Rainford, Zack Rainford's only daughter. Her daddy's pride and joy."

"You're right," I said. "She really is somethin'."

The barber turned to go back inside his shop. He stopped at the door and laughed. "She's good for business, too. When Morgan's in town, I sell *twice* as many haircuts."

I was about to tell him to put me down for his next available spot when I changed my mind. Far up, at the end of the street, Miss Rainford drew rein at the livery stable, dismounted, and went inside. Ian had agreed to leave my saddle, bridle, and Winchester with the proprietor before leaving town; I had business of my own at the stable.

I thought, *If I just happen to be there when Miss Rainford is, it will only be good manners to introduce myself.* I stepped into the street and set my course for Peabody's stable.

I had nearly reached the barn when I saw a man coming toward me. He was a gent in his late forties, bandy-legged and burly. He stopped as I drew near and looked me in the eye. "You comin' to see me?" he asked.

"That depends," I said. "Who are you?"

"Calvin Peabody. I own the livery stable back yonder."

"Why, yes. I was just on my way to—"

"Sorry, friend. Stable's closed. I'm goin' uptown and have me some lunch. Be back in an hour."

"A friend of mine, Ian McKenzie, said he'd leave my saddle and bridle with you. I just wanted to—"

"Nobody's at the barn right now. Come back in an hour."

I looked down the street at the stable. The black filly was no longer in sight. I was about to argue that I'd just seen Miss Rainford go inside when I realized that Peabody already knew that. Why would the man lie to me?

"All right," I said. "I'll see you in an hour."

I turned around and made my way back toward the barbershop. On the other side of the street, Peabody continued his walk uptown.

As soon as he was out of sight, I headed for the barn. Nobody's there, Peabody said. Well, I'd just go see if maybe I could *meet* Miss Nobody.

When I reached the stable, I found the big front doors open to the street. Stepping inside, out of the sun's bright glare, I stood, waiting until my eyes grew accustomed to the darkness. Stalls receded away toward the rear. Pigeons cooed and fluttered somewhere in the loft. The familiar odors of hay and horse wafted my way. Except for the pigeons, the barn was silent. I scratched my head. *Calvin Peabody was right*, I thought. In spite of what I'd seen, there seemed to be no one in the stable.

Inside and to the left of the big doors was the stable's office, where a liveryman would keep his records and receipts and attend to his paperwork. A painted sign on the door read "Private." A small window beside the office door allowed light into the room. I passed the office and walked back along the stalls. They were empty and dark. I turned and was about to return to the front when I heard a horse nicker. I peered into the gloom. There, in the last stall, stood Morgan Rainford's black filly!

Where was Morgan? I went back to the office area, checking the stalls as I passed, and stopped. The glass in the window beside the office door was dimmed by dust and grime, but I shaded my eyes against the brightness of the street and peered inside.

I caught my breath. There, on an old divan across from Peabody's cluttered desk, sat Morgan Rainford. She was not alone.

Beside her on the divan, a dark-haired young man held her in his arms. Above his shoulder, facing me, Morgan's pretty face nestled close beside his. Her eyes were closed. Then, just for a moment, they opened, and she seemed to look directly at me!

I felt my face flush. Confused, I held my breath. Would Morgan think I was some kind of Peeping Tom? I wanted her to know I was only there by chance. I wanted to tell her I was not the sneaky yahoo I appeared to be. Mostly, I wanted to crawl into a hole and pull the dirt in over me. However, Morgan gave no sign she'd seen me and seemed lost in her lover's embrace.

I turned away from the window and stepped back. *Had* Morgan seen me? I decided she had not. I told myself that she and her young man had eyes only for each other.

Breaking in on a lovers' tryst had not been my intention, but that surely was what I'd done. Now I had seen what I had seen. I *recognized* the man in Morgan Rainford's arms. He was Ian McKenzie—the son of her father's enemy!

EIGHT

▼

GETTING ACQUAINTED

Back at the barbershop, I picked up a dog-eared copy of *The Police Gazette* and took a seat on the bench outside. Inside the shop, the barber had one customer in the chair and three waiting. I knew it would be some time before he got around to me. I leafed through the salmon-colored pages of the *Gazette* and pretended to read, but my attention was fixed on the livery stable up the street.

Twenty minutes later, Ian McKenzie left the barn by way of the corrals in back. He disappeared behind the building and a moment later reappeared on the seat of the wagon on which we'd come to town. He turned the team up a tree-lined street and drove away toward the residential part of town.

At the front of the barn, Morgan Rainford came out of the shadows, leading her black filly. Swinging into the saddle, she rode up the street past the bench where I sat. I stood up, tipping my hat. She glanced my way briefly and rode on.

My thoughts returned to the scene I stumbled

onto at the barn. Finding Ian in the arms of a pretty girl was not really all that surprising. Ian was a good-looking boy; I'd have been surprised if he *didn't* have a sweetheart. What was surprising—and a whole wagonload of complications, to my mind—was that his sweetheart was Zack Rainford's daughter.

I recalled Ian's words back at the ranch: *I wish both Dad and Zack Rainford would pull in their horns. If they'd try to get along, there's enough grass in this country for both cattle and sheep.* Ian was a loyal son, but he wanted no part of a feud between his dad and the Circle R.

I shared Ian's sentiments. When he expressed them that night, I gave him credit for clear thinking and sound judgment. I had by no means changed my mind about that, but now I knew he had a *personal* reason for wanting peace between the families.

The Meriwether County Courthouse stood foursquare and solid at the corner of Main and Trail Streets. Three stories tall and built of quarried granite, the building seemed a very monument to dignity and justice. I climbed the wide front steps and went inside. A vestibule with a marble floor led into a long hall, with doorways opening onto various county offices. Following the signs above the doors, I made my way up the hall until I reached the last office. A heavy oak door stood closed before me. The sign above the doorway read "Sheriff." I turned the knob and walked in.

The room was spacious and well-lit, with large windows and a rear door on the opposite wall. A lanky deputy stood at the room's potbelly stove, pouring himself a cup of coffee. Behind him, at a large desk, a beefy man I took to be the sheriff chewed on a dead cigar as he shuffled through a stack of wanted posters. The deputy looked up as I entered. "He'p you?" he drawled.

"I'm here to see the sheriff," I said. "I'm Merlin Fanshaw, deputy U.S. marshal out of Progress County."

"Hell you say," offered the deputy. He turned to the big man. "Hey, Ross," he said. "We got us a fed'ral lawman lookin' for y'all."

The big man laid the posters down and took the cigar from his mouth. His eyes widened in mock surprise. "Lookin' for me?" he said, "Hell, I'm *innocent,* deputy—I ain't broke no fed'ral laws all day!" Laughing, he waved me to a chair beside his desk. "Set a spell. Take a load off."

My leg was hurting again. I was glad to accept his offer. We shook hands, and I sat down.

"I'm Friendly," the man said. "That's my disposition and my name. Ross Friendly, sheriff of Meriwether County. What can I do for you, son?"

The sheriff was big-bellied and bullnecked, with a drinker's nose and close-set eyes. I met his gaze. "I had a little trouble a week or so back," I said.

"My horse threw a shoe in the cedar breaks country above Whiskey Creek. I left him there with a man named Slye and borrowed a pony from him.

"I didn't get far. Crossing a rock slide that day, somebody shot my borrowed pony and killed it stone dead. Pony fell, trapped me under him. Broke the small bone in my leg and knocked me colder than a wolf's nose. I'd likely be at the foot of that slide yet if a sheepherder hadn't found me."

The sheriff's expression was sympathetic and, like his name, friendly, but he had suspicious eyes. He laced his fingers across his belly and leaned back in his chair. "Somebody shot your pony. Didn't happen to *see* the shooter, did you?"

"No."

Sheriff Friendly stroked his jaw thoughtfully. "You say you left your horse with a man named Slye. That wouldn't be Vernal Slye, would it?"

"That's his name," I said.

"That *was* his name," Friendly said. "He's dead."

I kept my poker face. "Too bad. Natural death?"

"Natural for a rustler, I guess. Range detective caught him stealin' Circle R cattle. Slye decided to make a fight of it. Bad decision."

"Any witnesses?"

"Range detectives work alone."

I slid my chair back and stood up. "Yeah. Well, I just wanted to let you know I'm in your town. I'm stayin' over at the hotel."

Friendly's gaze was intense. He said, "That horse you left with Slye, was it a buckskin gelding? Branded MF Bar on the left shoulder?"

"It was," I said.

"He's down at Peabody's Livery. I brought him back, with a paint horse and a gray, from Slye's this past week. I expect you'll want to claim him."

"I sure do," I said. "I've got a bill of sale in my saddlebags."

The sheriff stood up. "No need. Your word's good."

He came around the desk and shook my hand again. "Thanks for stoppin' by. If there's anything I can do for you, don't be a stranger."

"I won't," I told him. "You're mighty friendly, Sheriff Friendly."

The big man laughed, but there was no laughter in his eyes. I remember wishing his eyes were friendly, too.

Learning that my Rutherford horse was in town was the best news I'd had in awhile. I set out for Peabody's Livery at a brisk clip, completely forgetting my game leg. I had sorely missed the buckskin; I had thought about him nearly every day since I left him behind. I hoped his hoof had healed, and I vowed to see he was properly shod this time.

I have to admit I was more concerned about my horse than I was with the news that Vernal Slye was dead. Killed in a shootout with a range detective, the sheriff said, gunned down for rustling Circle R beef. There were no witnesses to his death, of course, and I figured any story told by the man who killed him had to be taken with a grain— or maybe a whole sack—of salt.

Was Vernal guilty? He had butchered at least one Circle R steer for food; I'd seen the green hide at his corral and had partaken of the beef it contained. But was the man really a rustler or just a hard-luck old boy trying to scratch out a living in the cedar breaks? Maybe Vernal was both of those things, and maybe he deserved his fate. But one thing I knew—getting ambushed by a professional killer had nothing to do with due process of law, and it was a far cry from a trial by jury.

I found Calvin Peabody at his stable, cleaning out the stalls. From personal experience, I knew that kind of work did not incline a man to a cheerful attitude, so I made it a point to be amiable and polite in the extreme.

"Mr. Peabody?" I said. "I came by earlier, but you were on your way to eat lunch. You said the stable was closed."

Peabody leaned on the fork and fish-eyed me. "So?"

"Ian McKenzie left my saddle and bridle here. I'd like to take them off your hands."

The liveryman looked me over. Then he said,

"Yeah. You're like Ian described you, gimp leg and all. Your rig is in my office."

Peabody leaned the fork against the side of the stall. He looked me over again, trying to read me. His eyes traveled from my boots to my belted forty-four to my borrowed cane and came to rest on my newly shaved face.

"You a friend of Ian's?" he asked.

"You could say that. He's a good kid."

I glanced at the office door. "I'm just guessin'," I said, "but I'd say you were a friend of Ian's yourself. Maybe a *special* friend."

That surprised him. "What do you mean?"

"Just that you seem to be a man who'd go the extra mile for a friend. Especially for a good kid who might not have all that many friends in town. Am I wrong?"

His eyes flashed to the office door and then back to me. "No," he said. "You ain't wrong. I like the boy. Sometimes, young folks get so caught up in what *other* people want, they ain't able to follow their *own* wants. Times like those, a friend tries to help."

"I expect so." I smiled and stuck out my hand. "We've howdied, but we haven't shook," I said. "I'm Merlin Fanshaw, from over in Progress County."

He took my hand. He looked me in the eye, and his grip was firm. "Calvin Peabody," he said. "Call me Cal."

Turning, Peabody opened the office door and led me inside. A battered desk, cluttered with papers and receipts, stood at one side, surrounded by an office chair and a file cabinet, as well as sacks of feed, block and sheep salt, barrels and boxes, and rolls of wire and twine. A coal-oil lamp fought for space on the crowded desktop, and a lantern hung suspended from the ceiling.

Across the room stood the divan so recently occupied by Ian and Morgan Rainford. Horse collars, harness, halters, and hames hung from pegs along the wall, and a thin layer of dust seemed to cover most everything. On the opposite wall, near a second door that led outside, a potbellied stove offered the promise of heat on a cold day. And there, on the floor beside the stove, lay my saddle and bridle.

"Sorry about the clutter," Peabody said. "I keep meanin' to clean the place up, but I can't seem to find the time."

I bent over my saddle and removed the saddlebags. "That brings me to the second reason I'm here, Cal. Sheriff Friendly says my horse is a guest here at your equine hotel. Chesty buckskin the sheriff brought in this past week."

Unbuckling the straps, I took Rutherford's bill of sale from the saddlebag and handed it to the liveryman. "Five-year-old buckskin gelding, branded MF Bar on the left shoulder. Is he here?"

Peabody glanced at the bill of sale, frowned,

and then raised his eyes. His expression was a mixture of disappointment and something very like envy.

"So that's *your* horse," he said. "I'm sorry to hear that. I was thinkin' I might claim him myself. Yeah, he's here, in the corral out back."

I followed Cal past the stalls to the big doorway that opened onto the pens behind the barn. The familiar smells brought back memories of working for Old Walt as a stable hand back in Dry Creek. Cal slid the big door open wide, and we stepped out into the sunlight. A moment later, and we were inside the corral.

Squinting, I looked for Rutherford. As my eyes became accustomed to the brightness, I saw him—he was standing near the far side of the corral, along with a half dozen other horses. His eye was wary, and he held his head high, watching us. I had to smile. Rutherford had already begun to work out his strategy.

We had a well-established ritual. I tried to catch him, and he tried not to be caught. If I baited him with a can of oats, he came just close enough to reach the morsels with his lips, neck stretched long and feet poised, ready to flee. If I approached him with a halter or bridle, he'd dance away in mock fright, avoiding me as long as he could.

But if I lacked the patience and time for the contest, I simply walked up on him with my lariat in hand. Seeing me coming with my rope, he calculated the odds and surrendered. That was part of the game, too. When Rutherford saw clearly that the jig was up, he gave in and allowed himself to be captured without further ado.

I stood, admiring him. And then, as if he was glad to see me, too, the buckskin made his way through the other horses and came directly to me at a trot! His nostrils flared, catching my scent, and he rubbed his proud head against me in greeting. I scratched him behind his ears and told him I was glad to see him. "Well," Cal said, "there sure ain't much doubt he's your horse."

I placed my hand on Rutherford's hip bone and crowded him over against the corral. Then, with my other hand, I picked up his nigh rear hoof. To my relief, the corn that had caused me to leave him at Slye's was almost completely healed. "You're lookin' good, old son," I told him. "Now let's put a decent shoe on that foot."

Cal loaned me his shoeing tools, and I took my time fitting and shaping a new shoe, setting it so that it would protect the heel of the buckskin's foot. As I worked, I talked to him, apologizing for failing to supervise the farrier back in Dry Creek. When I was finished, I led him inside the stable and fed him a ration of oats.

"I do believe I've seen everythin' now," Cal said. "A man who apologizes to his horse is a rare thing."

"There's plenty who *should* apologize," I said. "A good horse is a pardner that trusts his owner to care for him. Besides, I like talkin' to horses."

"You're preachin' to the choir," Cal said. "I'm in this business because I like horses better than most people."

I took a good look at the liveryman. His weathered face was cross-hatched with wrinkles, and his nose put me in mind of an Idaho spud, but it was an honest face. My gut told me Calvin Peabody was a man I could trust.

Knowing that he played cupid to the sheepman's son and the cowman's daughter on the eve of a range war made me wonder if he was brave or just crazy, but he obviously believed it was the right thing to do. I decided I liked him.

"Tell you what, Cal," I said. "I figure to be around town for a week or so, maybe longer. How much to board my horse?"

He looked at Rutherford and then back at me. "Make it a dollar fifty a week. Two fifty with oats."

I handed him a gold half eagle. "That's for two weeks. With oats."

"I'll be takin' the buckskin out from time to time," I said. "I'll want him ready when I need him."

"He'll be here."

Stepping out the big front doors onto the street, I turned. Peabody was still watching me. I grinned.

"Talk to him now and then, if you've a mind to," I said. "Rutherford don't say much, but he's a first-class listener."

The day had been warm, but sundown brought a cool breeze in its wake. Twilight silvered the buildings along Main and Trail Streets and softened the hard edges. Merchants locked their shops and went home to their families. Shadows deepened, and lamplight glowed in windows as the first stars appeared. I ate an early supper at the hotel and took a walk up the street to Doc Reynolds's place.

As before, I found the doctor seated on his porch, watching the street. I walked along the picket fence that enclosed his front yard and stopped at the gate. "Evenin', Doc," I said. "I've come to return the cane you loaned me."

"Oh, yes," the doctor said. "It's you, young fibula! Come in and sit awhile."

"Well, maybe for just a minute," I said, entering his yard. As I neared the porch, I saw a black dog of uncertain ancestry lying beside the doctor's chair. The animal struggled to its feet and challenged me with a half-hearted bark. It was an old dog, its coat drab and listless and its muzzle silvered with white hairs.

"Don't be alarmed," said the doctor. "Beware has ceased to be much of a guard dog."

I patted the dog's old head. "Beware?" I asked.

"Yes. Beware, the dog. Or, if you prefer the

Latin, *Cave Canem*. Those words were found written beside a mosaic of a dog at the entrance of a Roman house in old Pompeii. They should have written 'Beware the volcano,' I suppose."

An empty chair and a small table that held a bottle and a glass stood at the doctor's right hand. He indicated the empty chair with a wave of his hand. "Have a brandy with me," he said. "I'll fetch another glass from the kitchen."

Returning with a second glass, the doctor poured two fingers of brandy into it and handed it to me. "I find it awkward calling you young fibula," he said, "but Westerners have curious customs. For example, it's considered bad manners to ask a man's name, but it's all right to *shoot* him for any number of reasons. Thus, curiosity seems a more serious crime than murder in frontier society."

I laughed aloud. "All right, Doc," I said. "My name is Merlin Fanshaw, and I come from Progress County. I'm obliged for the drink."

The doctor raised his glass. "Josiah Reynolds, MD," he said. "To your health."

I had never drunk brandy, but I figured it must be something like whiskey. I gulped mine down in one quick motion and immediately regretted doing so. I felt like I'd swallowed molten lead. The brandy burned all the way down, and I couldn't breathe. My eyes watered, I choked, and I gasped so loud I scared the dog.

"Lordamighty, Doc!" I said when I caught my

breath again. "Drinkin' brandy is like drinkin' fire!"

"Yes. Well, brandy does warm the cockles of the heart, but I think you'll find it more agreeable if you'll sip it slowly."

Doc poured another two fingers of brandy into my glass. By way of demonstration, he swirled the liquor in his own glass, closed his eyes, and breathed in the fumes. Then, eyes still closed, he sipped the brandy and smiled.

I figured if he could do it, *I* could. With more than a few misgivings, I sloshed the contents of my glass around, took a sniff, and sipped carefully. Doc was right; the vapors cleared my head, and the sip warmed me to the tips of my ears.

"So, Merlin," Doc said. "How did you pass your first day in Reata?"

"I met some folks. And I had a reunion with a horse."

"Ah. Which of our local citizens did you meet?"

"The barber. Sheriff Friendly. Cal Peabody, down at the livery."

"Three very different men. Anyone else?"

"I saw someone I'd *like* to meet. Fine-lookin' young lady—Morgan Rainford. She rode up the street on a black Arab filly. It was like she was part of the horse."

Doc Reynolds sipped his brandy and smiled. "Ah, yes. The lovely Morgan. I delivered her, you know. Welcomed her into the world with a slap on her tiny bottom. Since then, I've treated her for colic, chicken pox, measles, whooping cough, and growing pains. Now that she's a young lady, she has, I believe, finally forgiven me for that slap."

I took a sip of my brandy. To tell the truth, I was a mite embarrassed by Doc's comment. I wasn't raised to talk about slappin' ladies' bottoms, even if they were newborn babes at the time. I suppose it was all right, him being a doctor and all, but his comment left a picture in my mind it was hard to get shut of.

We both fell silent for a time. The night sky was filled with stars, more than a man could count. A breeze stirred the leaves of the trees. Somewhere in the darkness, crickets chirped. I don't know whether it was the events of the day or the brandy, but all of a sudden, I felt dog tired and bone weary. "Reckon I'll say good night, Doc," I said, yawning. "Much obliged for the brandy, and the conversation."

"My pleasure, son," the doctor said. "We'll talk again."

I walked to the gate and turned toward the lights of Main Street. My limp was gone completely. Behind me, on the porch, Beware, the dog, was snoring.

NINE

▼

INCIDENT AT THE LONGHORN SALOON

I spent the next week working with Rutherford and getting to know the town better. Mornings, I saddled the little buckskin and rode him out into the countryside. Once away from the town's distractions, I put him through his paces, brushing up on his reining while I practiced making hoolihan catches with my lariat.

It felt good to be in the saddle again, with a sound leg on each side of a good horse. Rutherford seemed pleased, as well; he answered to rein and spur with a quickness that bespoke his willingness to work and to please.

The month was May, and every draw and coulee seemed to hold thickets of chokecherry and wild plum. The aroma of their blossoms perfumed the air, and the rangeland abounded with new grass, wildflowers, and creatures large and small.

Grouse and sage hens flurried from grassy hiding places, sailing away on whirring wings to settle once again. Meadowlarks warbled atop fence posts, and hawks circled overhead in skies of sapphire blue. Out on the open range, calves frisked while their mothers grazed.

Saddle horses stood sky-lined in pairs on sunlit

hills, switching each other's flies away with restless tails.

Far out on the broken country above the creek, pronghorns drowsed in the sunshine while their sharp-eyed lookouts kept watch. Everything seemed right with the world. Surrounded by the beauty of those mornings, I almost forgot the trouble brewing in Meriwether County. Almost, but not quite.

Somewhere out there, a killer hunted men who might or might not be rustlers. Stockmen large and small walked cat-eyed and watchful as they made their daily rounds. Like a prairie fire fed by winds of greed and fear, trouble stalked the county and hatred was its name.

Afternoons found me back in Reata, walking its streets, talking to its citizens, watching, and listening. The town boasted ten saloons, two banks, a newspaper, a hardware store, two or three groceries, a dry goods store, and the two-story Sanchez Mercantile. There was also a jewelry store, a gunsmith, a saddle maker, two barbers, and a blacksmith. Two hotels and three boarding houses offered lodging to humans, while two livery stables provided the same for horses. I counted three churches and a school, a half dozen eating places, and a brewery.

Four of the ten saloons were located west of the tracks and ranged from low dives to one fairly decent drinking place called the Golden Fleece. Most sheepherders, in town after six months or more on the range, did their carousing in that part of town. They spent their money on whiskey and women, and often blew six months pay within a few short weeks. When their debauch was over, the herders went back to their solitary lives and the sheep they cared for. Away from the company of men, they dried up and healed up for another half year, when they'd do it all over again.

I didn't see Haggis during that week, but I did have a chance to visit with Loco John, another of Abel McKenzie's herders. I ran into John by chance at the Golden Fleece. He had just hit town, and he told me he had a room at a high-class flophouse down the street called The Shepherd's Rest.

John had a weather-beaten face that was mostly hair, and his clothes were ragged and stained from his life on the range. Luckily, I caught him before his spree was well begun and asked about the McKenzies and Haggis McRae.

John said the McKenzies were shearing at the home ranch and would be moving the sheep up to Vendetta Canyon when the wool gathering was done. I asked if Haggis would be coming into town. John said he didn't think so. Haggis was that rare bird, he said, a sheepherder who saved his wages and didn't drink.

The barkeep at the Golden Fleece told me the herders he knew were friendly and sociable for the most part. "They ain't like cowpunchers and loggers," he said. "They don't pick fights or tear up saloons. And they're honest to a fault. Sheepherders always pay their debts."

When I asked him why he thought they were different, he said, "They live their lives apart from people. When they hit town, they're glad to see everybody."

On the other side of the tracks, on Main Street, the Longhorn Saloon catered to cowboys and cattlemen. Spacious and well-appointed, the Longhorn boasted a fifty-foot cherry wood bar and back bar, two full-time bartenders, a faro layout, poker tables, and a roulette wheel. Doc Reynolds often spent his evenings there, and I took to meeting him for brandy and conversation.

Civilization had begun to find Reata. Toting guns in plain view was permitted on the streets of town but prohibited in saloons and gambling halls. The ordinance was strictly enforced. Customers entering the Longhorn were required to check their weapons with the bartender before being served.

"The policy has greatly reduced the number of gunshot wounds I treat," Doc told me, "and it has seriously cut into the undertaker's bottom line. Poor fellow had to diversify—he now does carpentry and a little cabinet making on the side."

As a deputy U.S. marshal, I knew I would not be required to check my revolver. Still, my goal was to gather information and to talk freely with all sides of the grazing dispute. I figured I could best meet those goals if folks took me for a drifting cowhand or a small-time rancher, so I checked my gun just like everyone else.

On a Saturday night at week's end, I was sitting with Doc at our usual table in the Longhorn. Spring roundup had ended, and cowboys from the area's ranches were in town to turn their wolf loose. Men were two and three deep at the bar, and the gaming tables were running full-tilt. Here and there, dancehall girls worked the crowd.

A tall, well-built rider with straw-colored hair and questioning eyes approached our table. He was lean-hipped and big-shouldered, and he carried himself like the cock of the walk. His hat was a silver belly Stetson, high-crowned and wide-brimmed, in the Texas style. A red silk handkerchief, tied loose, hung at his throat. His shirt was of white flannel, and a black wool vest topped it. He wore California pants, foxed with buckskin, and his boots were handmade and fancy. He might as well have worn a sign reading "I am somebody."

He spoke to Doc Reynolds, but his eyes were on me. "Evenin', Doc," he said. "Who's your friend?"

Doc smiled. "This is Merlin Fanshaw, Travis. Merlin's from over Progress County way." Turning to me, he said, "Merlin, say hello to Travis Burnett, ramrod of the Circle R."

We shook hands. His smile was friendly enough, but his eyes were cold. "You're a long way from home," he said. "You aim to be around here long?"

"Depends," I said. "I'm still lookin' the country over."

"Circle R could use a line rider, if you're lookin' for work."

"Obliged. I'll let you know."

Burnett's gaze was intense. At last, he said, "You do that. See you around."

"Yeah," I said. "See you."

I watched as Burnett walked to the bar and put a foot up on the rail. The men around him stepped aside and made room for him. He said something, and the other men laughed and glanced my way.

I stood up. "I didn't hear that, Burnett," I said. "Say it again."

The wagon boss turned. "I just told the boys you didn't *look* like a damned snoozer. I hear you came to town with that lamb-lickin' kid of Abel McKenzie's."

"I'm surprised you figured it was any of their business. Or yours."

He wasn't used to being called on his manners. His eyes blazed, and his jaw set. For a moment, our end of the room grew quiet.

Behind the bar, a pair of sheep shears hung from a peg. Burnett nodded at the shears. "See them cutters?" he asked. "Bartender says he'll use 'em to cut the ears off the first damn sheepman that comes in here. Feelings run high against mutton punchers and their friends in this county. I'd hate to see you lose your ears."

Well, I had no intention of losing my ears, or my temper. Ridgeway didn't send me to Meriwether County to go around getting in bar fights. I was all set to shrug off Burnett's implied threat and go back to visiting with Doc when circumstance lit the fuse to the powder keg and everything changed.

The saloon's double doors slammed open with a crash, and a man stumbled into the room—Loco John, the sheepherder I'd spoken to earlier in the week!

He stood, swaying, in the doorway, his eyes wild. His face was flushed and mostly hidden by his bushy beard and tangled hair. His tattered shirt was filthy, and he wore ragged denim work pants held up by galluses. Well-worn brogans covered his feet, their laces trailing.

Raising a trembling hand, John opened his mouth, trying to speak. He took a faltering step and then stumbled unsteadily toward the bar. "Whiskey," he croaked.

The silence broke. Someone said, "Well, I'll be go-to-hell! It's that crazy sheepherder, Loco John!"

"Hoo-ee!" another man said. "Sum'bitch is roostered to a fare-thee-well!"

Loco John had nearly reached the bar when Burnett stepped out, blocking his way. "Whoa now, Shep," he said. "You've come to the wrong water hole!"

Burnett reached for the shears on their peg behind the bar. "Take hold of him, boys," he said. "I'm fixin' to shear me a sheepherder!"

Two of the cowboys grabbed Loco John and spread-eagled him atop one of the poker tables. He struggled, eyes wild and fearful, his face a mask of confusion and dread.

"Hold him down, boys!" Burnett ordered. "It's shearin' time!"

The shears were spring steel, their points sharp as needles. The blades flashed in Burnett's hands, clipping hair and beard. The cowboys laughed and whooped their encouragement. Unable to defend himself, the man stopped struggling and lay still in the hands of his tormentors.

The bartender tried to make himself heard above the din. "Damn you, cowboys! Take this outside!" Burnett and the Circle R hands either didn't hear or heard but ignored him.

The shears nicked the herder's scalp. Bright blood flowed. I thought, *This has gone too far.*

I raised my eyes to the crowd. They reminded me of a pack of wild dogs, savaging a smaller, helpless animal. "Roach his mane, Travis!" someone called out. "Notch his ears!" another yelled.

I was watching the cowboys backing Burnett. Mostly Circle R riders, I figured. Then, suddenly, I saw another man, watching along with the others—County Sheriff Ross Friendly! I caught his eye. Pointing, I mouthed the question, "Aren't you going to stop this?" Ross shrugged and turned his gaze back to the hazing.

Metal slid and sang on metal, the shears flashing. Hair drifted to the floor. Another cut appeared on his head. More blood. I felt myself moving toward the fray.

No, I told myself. *Ridgeway didn't send you to Meriwether County to get involved in bar fights. This is not your concern. Really, it isn't . . .*

. . . The hell it isn't!

Burnett was bent over the herder, his back to me. I took hold of his arm, and he straightened, turning to face me. "That's enough," I said. "Let him alone."

"Get your goddam hands off me! I'm not finished with him yet!"

"Yes, you are. Turn him loose."

Burnett's eyes blazed. "I *figured* you for a sheep-lovin' sonofabitch," he gasped. "You shouldn't have bought cards in this game!"

Jerking free of my grasp, Burnett thrust the shears at my chest! I dodged, felt my shirt rip. I swung from the shoulder, catching the cowman full in the face with my fist. I felt the shock of the blow all the way to my shoulder.

Burnett staggered, fell to one knee. One of the Circle R cowboys stepped between us. He was a big man, with broad shoulders and a fighter's nose. I guessed he outweighed me by a good forty pounds. "Come on," he said. "Try *me*."

My blood was up. "If you think your weight gives you an edge, you're wrong. I'm not impressed much by *bulk*."

Burnett pushed the big man aside. "He's mine," he said. "Let me have him."

Blood flowed freely from Burnett's nose. Deliberate now, he came toward me in a fighter's crouch, his hands up. The Circle R men watched as he approached. Behind them, Doc Reynolds was tending the sheepherder's wounds.

I fixed my attention on Burnett. He circled slowly to my left, his eyes hot and his teeth bared in a hard smile. He swiped his right hand across his nose and mouth, wiping blood away. I turned with him as he moved, waiting. I heard voices from the crowd, egging him on: "Clean his plow, Travis!" "Coldcock the sheep-lovin' sum'bitch!"

Let 'em talk, I thought. *Just as long as they don't decide to lend him a hand.*

When it came, the cowman's move was fast. Burnett suddenly stopped circling and struck out hard with a left jab. I swung my arm up to block his blow, but I was a shade too slow. Burnett's knuckles scraped my cheekbone, jolting me, throwing me off my stride. Following up, he bulled into me, attacking with a flurry of rights and lefts. I covered up, blocking, back pedaling, and waiting out the storm.

My time came. Dropping into a crouch, I saw Burnett's mid-section exposed. I drove a hard right to his paunch, feinted with my left, and threw a second right to his belly for good measure. Burnett gasped; his face went white. I hit him again, just below his rib cage, and stole his breath.

As Burnett's head came down, I caught him with a solid uppercut that snapped his head back. I hit him again with a left to his temple that struck mostly bone and sent a stab of pain streaking up my arm.

I didn't see it coming. Burnett ducked low and slammed a hard right to my ribs. I grunted and nearly went down. Recovering, I choked back the pain. Burnett came swinging again, bringing the fight to me. I jabbed with my left hand straight from the shoulder, once, twice, and then stepped in and struck the cowman with a solid left hook. His eyes closed, blood sprayed from his broken nose, he dropped his guard. Stepping inside the circle of his arms, I caught him with a hard right hand that snapped his head to the side. Around us, I saw the faces in the crowd, saw them yelling, but could no longer hear their words.

My ribs hurt with each breath. My arms felt heavy, as if they were bound with a log chain. Burnett drove at me, trying to wrestle me down. I pummeled his head and shoulders, trying to break his grip, but he locked his arms and threw his weight against me until we crashed together to the floor. He was on top of me, his fingers clawing at my eyes. I struggled beneath him and tried to throw him off.

His arm tightened about my throat, cutting off my wind. My eyes watered; I saw the boots of the onlookers in a blur. Twisting, I caught Burnett in the ribs with my elbow and rolled out of his reach.

Burnett got up quickly. He lashed out with a vicious kick aimed at my groin, but I was a moving target; his boot heel struck my thigh instead.

Again, he tried to use his weight to wrestle me to the floor. He clutched my throat, his fingers choking me, his face tight with rage. I thrust my arms up sharply between his, breaking his grip. I hit him in the belly again and saw him double over. Grasping the back of his head with both hands, I brought my knee up hard into his face.

Burnett groaned and swung a roundhouse blow that caught only empty air. My right fist throbbed with pain, but I hit him with it anyway. The blow caught the cowman solidly on the point of his chin. His eyes crossed. He went back on his heels, and I hit him again with everything I had left. It was enough. Burnett shuddered; his arms dropped to his sides. He sagged. His knees buckled, and he fell face down onto the barroom floor.

The big man who offered to fight me earlier

stepped forward. Two of the other Circle R hands also moved toward me. "You whipped Travis fair and square," the big man said, "but that don't mean you get a pass. When you took on our wagon boss, you took on the Circle R."

I still hadn't caught my breath, but I gasped a reply. "You boys want to be next?" I asked. "Come on ahead then." I was running a bluff, and I'm sure they knew it. I couldn't have whipped a sickly schoolgirl at that point.

Sheriff Ross Friendly spoke up. "That's enough, boys," he said. "This was between Fanshaw here and Travis. Fair fight. It's over now."

Now you speak up, I thought. *Where were you when these boys were tormenting that poor, help-less drunk?*

The crowd drifted away, back to the tables and the long bar, but the hard-eyed stares they cast my way told me I wasn't the most popular man in the room.

Sheriff Ross hooked his big thumbs in his gun belt and looked me over. "Only reason I didn't let those boys take you on is I don't want a U.S. deputy marshal killed in my town," he said. "If that was to happen, there'd be inquiries and investigations and more paperwork than you're worth. And I purely *hate* paperwork.

"But don't go thinkin' you settled anything here. All you did was paint a big bull's-eye on yourself."

TEN

▼

IN THE LION'S DEN

By the time Doc and me got Loco John out of the Longhorn, the sheepherder was quaking like the leaves on an aspen tree, and I wasn't doing all that well myself. I was skinned up and bloodied, my left eye was swollen and nearly closed, and I felt like I'd been run over by a freight wagon. Even my *hair* hurt.

Doc leaned the herder against the saloon wall and raised an eyebrow. "I think I understand now why you chose *me* as a drinking companion," he said. "A man with *your* proclivities needs a doctor on call full-time."

I had reclaimed my six-gun and belt from the barkeep. Now, beneath the pale light of a street lamp, I buckled the weapon in place. "Startin' a fight with the Circle R was the last thing on my mind," I said, "but I couldn't just stand by and let those boys abuse Loco John."

Doc nodded. "Obviously, our *sheriff* could," he said. "But then I suppose not everyone has his gift for hypocrisy."

A lanky cowpuncher stepped out through the swinging doors and came toward us. *Oh, no*, I thought. With my hand near my gun butt, I turned to face him.

"Easy, mister," the cowboy said. "I'm Harve Rawlins. I ain't here to cause trouble. I thought maybe you could use a hand with that feller."

"Why so generous? You boys were havin' fun tormentin' him a short while ago."

"Not me," Rawlins said. "I ride for the Circle R, but I don't hold with Travis Burnett and them other hell-raisers. I had no part of what went on in there."

"You didn't stop it."

Rawlins looked down at his feet. "No," he said. "I didn't stop it."

I pulled in my horns. "Well," I said. "I guess we could use some help gettin' John bedded down. He's stayin' at the Shepherd's Rest, over across the tracks."

"I know the place," Rawlins said. "I'll get my horse."

He walked away along the mounts that lined the hitch rack. A minute later, he came back leading a glass-eyed roan. We lifted Loco John into the saddle and steadied him while Rawlins swung up behind him. "I'll see he gets there all right," he said.

"I'm obliged," I said. "But I still don't know why you're doin' this."

"I'm helpin' him now," Rawlins said, "because I didn't help him *then*."

He turned the roan and rode away with Loco John into the darkness.

News travels fast in a small town. By the following afternoon, it seemed everyone in Reata had heard about my ruckus with Travis Burnett. Nobody said much, but as I left the hotel and made my way across town, I felt I was pretty much the center of attention. Cowhands rode past me, their eyes hard as flint. Merchants watched me from the doorways of shops and stores, curiosity plain on their faces. A homesteader in a hay hat and dashboard overalls paused in the act of loading fence wire on his wagon to nod and smile as I walked by.

I could not have been a pretty picture. My face was puffy and battered, with cuts and bruises galore. My left eye was swole up like a bullfrog's belly, and the knuckles on both my hands were scraped and raw. In spite of all that—or maybe because of it—folks seemed to make a point of watching me saunter along Main Street. Some of them frowned, some looked thoughtful, and one or two even smiled. For the moment, at least, I seemed to be the town's main attraction.

At the livery stable, I found Calvin Peabody scooping up horse apples from the street in front of his barn. He greeted me with a broad grin and leaned on his fork. "No offense, Merlin," he said, "but with that swollen eye and all those cuts and bruises, your face is ugly enough to curdle milk."

"I've been engagin' in fisticuffs," I said. "What's *your* excuse?"

Calvin laughed. "I was *born* ugly," he said. "There's coffee on the stove. Come on in."

Inside the office, Cal filled a cup from the pot and handed it to me. He filled one for himself and sat down on a corner of his desk. Sunlight slanted in through the open door. I sat down on the divan, facing Cal.

"So," Cal said. "You're a deputy U.S. marshal. What brings a federal lawman to Reata?"

"Business," I said. "It was supposed to be *secret* business, but your sheriff let the cat out of the bag."

Cal took a sip from his cup. "I expect you know by now Zack Rainford pretty much owns this county, up to and includin' its sheriff."

"Yeah," I said. "Golden rule. Man with the gold makes the rules. You sayin' Sheriff Friendly is crooked?"

"I wouldn't go that far. Let's just say he's partial to the cattle interests."

"Yes. I expect he is."

I sipped my coffee. Cal did the same. For a time, neither of us spoke. Finally, I asked, "How do I find the Circle R? I believe it's about time I paid Zack Rainford a visit."

Cal snorted. "You'd be about as welcome as a skunk at a picnic! Are you tired of livin' or just crazy?"

"Neither one," I said. "Just bein' neighborly."

Cal shook his head. "Well," he said, "the Circle R ain't all that hard to find. You just take the road north past the cemetery and go another fourteen miles. Some of Rainford's hired guns will likely be on hand to greet you, after which they'll shoot you full of holes and fetch you back here to Reata. As far as the cemetery, anyway."

I laughed. "You sure do paint a gloomy picture," I said. "You've got me dead and buried, and I haven't even left town yet."

At the doorway, a figure blocked the light from outside. "You're right," a soft voice said. "Cal's forecast is a bit bleak. The latchstring is always out at the Circle R. For everyone."

I turned my head. Morgan Rainford stood, framed by the doorway. She was dressed as she was the first time I saw her, in a high-crowned Stetson, white blouse, divided riding skirt, and boots. Her spurs chimed softly as she stepped inside. I stood, doffing my hat. "We haven't met," she said, "but I know who you are. I'm Morgan Rainford."

"Everyone knows who you are, Miss Rainford. I'm Merlin Fanshaw, from over in Progress County."

Her large eyes were blue as snow shadow as she looked up at my battered face. Her gaze was honest and open, with a hint of curiosity. "And you," she said, "are the man who whipped our wagon boss at the Longhorn yesterday."

"Yes, miss," I said. "We had us a slight difference of opinion."

She laughed. "People who were there say it was more like a major disagreement," she said. "Travis Burnett looks even worse today than you do."

Morgan looked into my eyes again—at least the one that wasn't closed. Her smile was earnest. "I meant what I said about the latchstring at the Circle R being out for everyone. If you'd like to talk to my dad, I'm headed for the ranch now. You're welcome to ride along, if you like."

"I'm obliged, Miss Rainford. I'll saddle my horse."

Admiration plain in his expression, Calvin Peabody beamed at Morgan. "I ain't sure which is stronger-willed," he said, "you, or that Arab filly you ride. I suppose you want me to saddle her for you."

"In a minute," Morgan said. "I need to talk to you first about those legal papers of Dad's."

"Go on ahead back, Merlin," Cal said. "We'll join you directly."

I found Rutherford at the far side of the big corral behind the livery barn, socializing with a sway-backed bay, two sorrels, and a strawberry roan. I was stiff and sore from head to foot, and I was in no mood to play catch-me-if-you-can with my durned saddle horse. For a mercy, Rutherford seemed to sense my state of mind. He turned away from his companions and came to me, gentle as any lamb. It was almost as if he knew I was hurting and took pity on me. I was not too proud to accept his charity.

I curried and brushed the buckskin and saddled him. Leading him through the barn's deep shade, I found Morgan waiting for me, already mounted, in the sunlit street. She sat her saddle as if born to it, her shoulders back and her feet thrust forward in the stirrups. The black filly she rode shuffled restlessly, eager to take the road. Stepping up onto Rutherford, I said, "Ready when you are, Miss Rainford." Her smile was my answer. We turned away from the livery barn and rode up the street at a trot.

The road stretched out before us, past the graveyard and the scattered buildings that made up the outskirts of Reata. We passed small homesteads and farms as we rode through a grassy valley marked by stands of cottonwood and willow. Ahead lay rolling hills and plains, rising in the distance to flat-topped buttes standing stark against the summer sky. Morgan set the pace, and we rode at a jog-trot for nearly two miles before easing the horses back to a walk.

She pulled up beside me, her expression serious. "I'm curious," she said. "What business does a deputy U.S. marshal have with my father?"

"I'm here to keep the peace," I said. "Your dad is

an important man in Meriwether County. I figure he can help me."

Morgan bristled. "That's more diplomatic than honest," she said. "Do you suspect my father of breaking the law?"

"You want honesty? All right, I don't know whether he's breakin' the law or not. But I aim to find out."

"Never in my life have I known my father to do a dishonest thing."

"That's more loyal than helpful," I said. "There's trouble in the county. Four men have been killed here in the past two months. There will be more."

"Rustlers!" Morgan said. "The cattlemen have a right to protect their holdings."

"By bringing in a hired killer? That doesn't do much to keep the peace."

"If you're talking about Griff Tallon, he's not a hired killer; he's a stock detective."

"You can call jimsonweed a rose bush, but that doesn't make it one. A man accused deserves to face his accusers in court, not some hard-eyed ambusher out on the plains."

Morgan frowned. "Sheriff Friendly doesn't seem to have a problem with our hiring Tallon."

"It has been said that Sheriff Friendly is partial to the cattle interests."

Morgan's blue eyes flashed. "What about you? People say *you're* a friend of the sheepmen! They say you stayed with one of Abel McKenzie's herders for a time—and it was Ian McKenzie who brought you to Reata."

Morgan's voice was angry, her words clipped, but her tone softened when she spoke Ian's name.

"I take people as I find them," I said. "I'm a friend to law abidin' folks and an enemy to law-breakers and spoilers. I've worked for cowmen, and some are among my closest friends. I never was around sheepmen much until lately, but Abel McKenzie's herder Haggis took me in when I needed help. He's a good and decent man. Abel is hot-headed and proud, but I like him. I like Ian, too. I suppose a lot of people do."

Morgan looked away, toward the distant buttes. She said nothing, but I knew she was thinking about Ian. When at last she spoke again, her voice was gentle and without anger. "Yes," she said. "I'm sure they do."

Morgan turned toward me and looked hard into my eyes. "I saw you," she said quietly. "That day you came to town with Ian. You were watching us."

Her frankness caught me off guard. "I . . . I never meant to," I said. "I was looking for you. I met Cal Peabody on the street. He said nobody was at the livery barn, but I saw you go inside just minutes before. I looked in the office window . . ."

"And you saw me with Ian. There aren't many places we can be together, but Cal is a good friend. He lets us meet in his office sometimes."

"How long . . ."

"How long have we been in love? A year, maybe longer. We've known each other since we were kids. We went to school together. Ian was a shy, quiet boy. I liked him, but I had no romantic feelings for him. We were just friends.

"After graduation, I went back east to what mother calls a 'finishing school.' Good name for it—it almost finished *me*. I missed the ranch, the people, my friends . . . and I couldn't wait to come home.

"I'd been back less than a week when I ran into Ian in town. He was the same as I remembered, but somehow *not* the same. Ian had become a man. I can't explain it, but when our eyes met and he smiled that shy smile, something happened to me, deep inside. Ian says it happened to him, too."

Remembering Pandora, I said, "I guess that's how it is sometimes."

"Yes. Something else changed while I was back east getting 'finished.' Our families, my dad and Abel McKenzie, became deadly enemies. Made it a bit difficult for Ian and me to share our happiness."

"Except with Cal Peabody. Does anyone else know?"

Again, Morgan's clear blue eyes found mine. "Only you," she said. "Are you going to keep our secret?"

Keeping the peace in Meriwether County was

more than enough for me to deal with. I had no wish to become involved in anybody's secret romance. Still, as I met Morgan's earnest gaze, I knew what my answer would be. Ian and Morgan hadn't asked for the growing feud between their families. They deserved whatever chance for happiness they could find. "Yes," I said. "I will."

Morgan smiled a shaky smile. The proud daughter of Zack Rainford seemed defenseless and vulnerable. When she spoke, her voice was so soft I could scarcely hear her. "Thank you," she said.

There was nothing more to say, and we had the good sense not to keep saying it. Morgan slacked her reins and touched the filly with her spurs. The animal broke into a trot once again, stepping smartly away up the road. Rutherford followed suit, but I held him to a length behind. It's only common courtesy to let a lady have time alone with her thoughts.

For nearly three more hours we followed the road through some of the finest livestock country I've ever seen. Native grasses grew thick on the hills and slopes, rippling in the wind like water in a pond. Spring-fed streams cascaded down coulees and draws, providing water for the herds that occupied the range. Wild plum, chokecherry, and cottonwood trees offered shelter and shade. There was no need to ask Morgan if the cattle I saw all around us were Rainford stock. Even at a distance, the

Circle R brand stood out plainly in the late afternoon light.

A short time later, the road made a turn, and a wide gate framed by two log uprights and a ridgepole stood tall at the roadside. Suspended from the ridgepole by chains was a wrought iron replica of the brand: an R inside a circle. Beyond the gate, a wagon road crossed the plain and ascended a low hill. I kicked Rutherford into a trot, rode past Morgan, and stepped down to open the gate. Swinging it wide, I led the buckskin through behind me and held the gate for Morgan. She said nothing but favored me with a slight smile as she rode through.

Drawing rein, she waited while I closed the gate and mounted again. Then she said, "The home ranch is just over that second hill. We'll be there in ten minutes."

Morgan hesitated. "I'm sorry if I was cross back there," she said. "I know you're just doing your job. But so is my father. People in this county look up to him as a leader. He does his best to meet their expectations."

I held my tongue. "Yes," I said. "Everybody does what they think is right."

As we reached the crest of the second hill, everything changed. One minute we were riding together uphill with only grassland and distant mountains in view. Then, all at once, we were looking down at an orderly collection of buildings that made up the Circle R's headquarters. A narrow stream, bordered by willows, red alder, and cottonwood trees, set the barn and outbuildings off from two houses I guessed were the residences of the Rainford family.

The older of the two houses was a low, sod-roofed place, built of log and graced by mature trees and a lilac hedge. It had apparently once been the main residence, but now a new, two-story frame house stood just across the way.

The new house sported a gable roof with a turret on one corner, twin chimneys, a handsome bay window, and a long, covered porch. The house was gussied up by all manner of fancy woodwork and painted at least six different colors. It stuck out like a sore thumb among the weathered log structures that made up the ranch complex.

"The new house was mother's idea," Morgan said. "It's called a Queen Anne. Dad says it looks like a wedding cake surrounded by beef jerky and beans."

Beyond the houses, a wide plank bridge spanned the stream and led to the barn and pole corrals, a bunkhouse, a blacksmith shop, a cook shack, and a scatter of other buildings.

In the round corral behind the barn, a rough-string rider worked at gentling a bronc. Another man perched on the corral's top rail, watching, and—I smiled—no doubt offering advice. In a pasture beyond the corrals, three men on horseback cast long shadows as they rode in off the range. Over at the bunkhouse, riders squatted on their boot heels and leaned against the building's uprights, smoking and talking as they waited for the supper bell.

As we came down the hill, I saw a woman watching us from the porch of the new house. She was slender, fair-haired, and pale, and she wore a stylish, high-collared suit with a bustle that a person might expect to see in town but which seemed out of place on the ranch.

"Speaking of Mother," Morgan said. "That's her there on the porch. Come and meet her."

We drew rein. "Good evening, Mother," Morgan said. "This gentleman has come to see Daddy. His name is Merlin Fanshaw, and he's new in the county. Merlin, this is my mother, Melissa."

I doffed my hat. "Pleased to meet you, ma'am."

Melissa Rainford smiled a polite smile. Without appearing to, she sized me up like a lawyer looking for a loophole. It seemed to me her cool blue eyes took in all of me there was to see, from my tousled hair and bruised face to my belted forty-four and scuffed boots.

"My husband will be along directly," Melissa said. "The family takes its meals here at the house. You really must join us for supper."

I gave Morgan a sideways glance. Her eyes danced with mischief, but she restrained her smile.

Caught off guard, I felt like a man walking a tightrope. I was a complete stranger to Zack Rainford, except for what Sheriff Friendly might have told him and what he might have heard about my fight with Travis Burnett.

I had come to his home as a lawman to question him. I was there to confront him, to ask hard questions about his feud with Abel McKenzie and his hiring of Griff Tallon. And now his wife had invited me to join the family for supper!

I stammered, trying to find a way out of my quandary. "I . . . I appreciate your invitation, ma'am, but I wasn't . . . that is, you weren't expectin' me. I don't . . ."

She smiled again. "I insist, Mr. Fanshaw. Put up your horse and come inside. Morgan will show you where you can wash up."

I recalled Calvin Peabody's words: "You'll be about as welcome as a skunk at a picnic."

Right then, I felt more like a snake in the grass.

Eleven

▼

Storm Clouds Gather

Having delivered her invitation, Melissa Rainford turned and went back inside the house. Morgan smiled. "Mother doesn't take no for an answer. At least she never has with me. Looks like you'll be joining us for supper."

"Looks like it," I agreed. "I need to take care of my horse."

Morgan nodded at a patch of tall grass beyond the house. "There's good feed over there," she said. "I guess your horse will be staying for supper, too."

I led Rutherford over to the grassy patch and hobbled him. Loosening the cinch, I slipped the saddle and bridle off, and turned him loose. The buckskin looked like he wanted to lay down and roll, but he merely tossed his head and fell to grazing.

Morgan stroked her filly's neck. "I'll take Sheba down to the barn. There's a mud room at the rear of the house, off the kitchen. You can clean up there."

"Are you . . . comin' back?"

Her laughter was like music. "Don't worry," she said. "I wouldn't leave you to face the family dragons all by yourself."

I watched Morgan ride away toward the cluster of outbuildings below the bridge, and then I walked around to the back of the house.

The mud room turned out to be a sort of catch-all space, filled with hats, coats, and saddle slickers hung from pegs, gum boots, and catch ropes sharing space with brooms and mops, and a wash stand that held a bucket, basin, and towel. I took off my spurs, hung my hat and gun belt on a peg, and did what I could to make myself presentable. As a final touch, I took my deputy's star from my pocket and pinned it to my shirt front. I was dead certain Zack Rainford wouldn't welcome my presence at his supper table, but at least I'd be flying under my true colors.

Melissa Rainford saw it first. She came through the kitchen to the mud room just as I gave up trying to comb my hair. I watched as she fixed her keen-eyed gaze on me again, this time taking in the nickel-plated star on my chest. She offered no comment but simply said, "Please . . . come into the dining room. My husband and Morgan are waiting."

She turned, leading the way. I took a deep breath and followed. As we entered the dining room, I saw that the table was set for four, and that Morgan and her father were already seated. I had just a moment to take in the scene, and I made the most of it.

Zack sat at the head of the table, reading a newspaper. He was a good-looking man in his early forties, clean-shaven and dark-haired. His face was ruddy, his forehead white where his hat blocked the sun's rays. Morgan was seated at her father's left. The other two places were set and waiting, one across from Zack and one across from Morgan. Melissa Rainford indicated I was to sit opposite her husband and then took her place across from her daughter.

Zack looked up from reading his newspaper and saw me. His eyes widened and then went hard. He dropped the paper and started to rise from his chair, but Melissa touched his arm and said, "We have a guest for dinner, dear. Morgan brought him from Reata to see you."

"I'm Merlin Fanshaw, Mr. Rainford," I said. "I didn't mean to break in on your family time. Your wife . . ."

Zack Rainford was not glad to see me. He did not offer to shake my hand. "I know who you are," he said.

"I told Mr. Fanshaw the latchstring here is out to everyone," Morgan said. "That's true, isn't it, Dad?"

When his answer came, it came through gritted teeth. "Yes," he said. "That's true. Welcome to the Circle R."

The meal turned out to be a boiled New England supper, with pandowdy for dessert, and we pretty much ate it in silence. It was a mighty toothsome meal, and I told Mrs. Rainford I thought so. She said, "Thank you." Other than that, it was quiet as a grave in that dining room.

When supper was over I rose to help clear the table, but Mrs. Rainford would have none of it. "Thank you, Mr. Fanshaw," she said, "but our hired girl Lucy will attend to the dishes. You came to speak with my husband. I'll bid you gentlemen good evening."

Morgan followed her mother out of the room, and I was left alone with Zack. He said. "I keep an office down at the old place. Get your hat."

I collected my hat, spurs, and gun belt from the mud room and walked behind Zack down the slope to the ranch house. Above the distant mountains, round and ripe as a peach, a full moon flooded the land with light. Dark shadows deepened beneath the cottonwoods. Somewhere in the distance, coyotes celebrated moonrise.

We stepped up onto a broad veranda at the front of the house. Zack opened a door and disappeared into darkness. I waited as he lit a lamp, and then followed him inside.

Zack's office was a man's room, built of log and memories. Massive and solid, a heavy oak desk stood facing the doorway. Filing cabinets filled the space behind the desk, under a fly-specked map of Meriwether County. Mounted heads of elk, deer, and antelope decorated the walls, and Navajo rugs of red, gray, black, and white gave color to the floor's oiled wood.

High on the wall beside the desk hung the framed portrait of a man I remembered from my long-ago visit to the Circle R. Straight-backed and proud, Zeb Rainford looked out from the canvas as if he was seeing all the way to the farthest corner of his range. He wore a high-crowned hat, and he held the symbols of his empire, a braided leather *reata* and two branding irons—one a circle, the other an open R—in his strong, long-fingered hands.

Zack sat down behind the desk and nodded. I took a chair facing him and waited for him to speak. He placed his clasped hands before him on the desk. They were like the hands in the portrait. A simple gold band on the third finger of his left hand winked lamplight.

"You're sure as hell long on nerve," he said. "You used my daughter to get yourself invited to the Circle R and my wife to intrude on a family supper."

"Morgan heard me talking to Cal Peabody at the livery barn. I told Cal I wanted to meet you. Morgan said she was on her way home. She told me everyone is welcome at the Circle R and said I could ride along."

Zack scowled but said nothing.

"When we rode in, Morgan introduced me to your wife. Mrs. Rainford insisted I join your family for supper."

"By god, you'd have had a different welcome if you'd eaten down at the cook shack. The boys are pretty hot about the way you worked Travis Burnett over."

"Are you?"

The cattleman lowered his head. He looked down at the desk top. "No," he said. "I guess not. Burnett is a top hand, but he's got a mean streak. Sometimes he goes too far."

For a moment, Zack was silent. Then he looked up and said, "All right. You're here. State your business, and state it plain."

"All right," I said. "I'm here to look into the killings of four men and to try to head off a range war. Is that plain enough for you?"

"Too plain by half. If you're talkin' about Davis, Shubert, Spengler, and Slye, all four of those men were cow thieves, caught in the act. They were rustlers, and they paid the price."

"Maybe they were rustlers and maybe they weren't. Your range detective didn't give them much chance to tell their side."

"Who says cow thieves deserve a chance?"

"Law says so. Law says they deserve a judge and jury."

The cattleman smiled a bitter smile. "We brought Pete Davis to trial a year ago. Tried him by a jury of his peers. Trouble is, they were *his* peers, not mine. His friends found him not guilty, and he left the courthouse laughin' at me. He probably butchered one of my steers on his way home that night.

"I lose cattle every year to drought, winter kill, and wolves. Those are losses a cowman has to live with. But my losses to thieves are now greater than 5 percent a year, and I'm *not* prepared to live with *that*."

Zack stood and walked over to the portrait. "My old man started this outfit back in '65. He picked

157

up worn-out oxen from emigrant trains and raised beef to feed the miners in the gold camps. Later on, he brought longhorns up from Texas. He built this spread with guts and sweat, and he backed it up with a gun when he had to.

"I was born and raised here. This place is part of me. When Dad died, I made myself a promise. I won't tolerate a cattle thief, and I won't be crowded off my range!"

"Times have changed," I said. "Nowadays the range belongs to everyone: homesteaders, small ranchers, and sheepmen. They have rights, too."

Zack's eyes narrowed. "So they tell me. Over the years, sodbusters and squatters moved in here and settled. They plowed up the ground, and they fenced off the water holes. Now I hear Abel McKenzie is movin' his sheep to Vendetta Canyon and onto grass and water the Circle R has used since my dad's time.

"That range is ours! If Abel wants water, let him *buy* water—he's not puttin' his damned sheep where my cattle drink!"

"I've met Abel McKenzie," I said. "He strikes me as a reasonable man. Seems to me you two could work all this out if you wanted to. I understand you used to be friends."

A shadow seemed to pass over Zack's face. Silent again, he toyed nervously with his wedding ring. At last he said, "*Used* to be, but no more. That time is gone."

He turned back to his desk and slumped heavily into his chair. "*Long* gone," he said.

Zack stiffened. He leaned forward, his stare hostile. "And now, deputy," he said, "unless you have a specific charge you want to make, I expect you'd best get on back to town. You *can* find your way, can't you?"

I got to my feet. "You bet," I said. "And when I need to, I can find my way back *here*."

Outside, moonlight softened the land's hard edges. I found Rutherford standing knee-deep in grass where I'd left him, and I spoke to him quiet-like so as not to spook him. "Evenin', old son," I said. "We've outstayed our welcome, and it's time we found our way back to town."

Rutherford nickered, like a man clearing his throat. I took off the hobbles and saddled him. Drawing the cinch taut, I swung up onto his back. As I left the ranch, I looked up again into the southern sky. *That surely is some moon*, I thought. *A man could read a newspaper by its light.*

The ride back to Reata was uneventful, and the hour was late by the time I turned Rutherford onto Main Street. Lamplight burned low in the lobby of the hotel, but most of the town's shops and stores were shuttered and dark. I rode the buckskin past the Longhorn and the barber shop to the end of the street, and drew rein at Peabody's Livery. A smoky lantern hung from a nail inside, but the office was closed and I saw no sign of Peabody's night man.

I unsaddled Rutherford by the lantern's light, wiped him down with a grain sack, and led him into a stall. I forked a flake of hay into the manger, poured him a ration of oats, and high-heeled it back up the moonlit street.

When I entered the lobby of the hotel, I found the desk clerk sprawled in an overstuffed chair, reading a dime novel. Recognizing me, he stood up and moved back around behind the front desk. He handed me my room key and bade me good night. I wished him the same. Then I climbed the stairs, unlocked the door to my room, and stepped inside. Still thinking about my visit to the Circle R, I shucked my boots and got outside my clothes.

I was asleep before my head hit the pillow.

In my dream, I stood with Morgan atop a high and grassy hill. Just over our heads, close enough to touch and big as Rainford's barn, hung a silver moon, flooding the world with light. We stared together at the great shining ball, struck speechless by its wonder.

As I studied the moon's surface, I was surprised to see the faint outline of a door, barely visible in its brightness. Across the top of the door was painted the word "Private." Looking at Morgan, I broke the silence. "How," I asked, "can we get inside?"

Morgan bent down and picked up a stick from the ground. "Here," she said, handing me the branch. "Reach up and strike the door four times."

Somehow, the stick became a cane as I touched it, like the one I borrowed from Doc Reynolds. I stretched my arm high above my head and rapped on the moon door sharply—once, twice, three times, four. The knocking echoed with a hollow sound, but the door didn't open. "Try again," said Morgan. Again I knocked—one, two, three, and four! Still the door failed to open.

In my dream I knocked no more, but I still heard the sound of knocking: *Rap! Rap! Rap! Rap!* The hilltop faded. Morgan disappeared. The moon grew pale and vanished. Only the sound of the knocking remained.

I awoke to find myself tangled in my bedclothes, no longer asleep but not yet fully awake. Someone was in the hallway, knocking on my door. "Merlin!" said a voice, "Wake up, lad—it's daylight in the canyon!"

I sat up, rubbing sleep from my eyes. Placing both feet on the floor, I got out of bed. Slipping my forty-four from its leather, I held the gun behind me as I padded to the door. *Cuidado,* Ridgeway had cautioned. *No point in taking chances*, I thought.

"Who is it?" I mumbled. "Who's there?"

"It's me, Abel McKenzie," the voice said. "It's

six thirty in the mornin' and time you were up and earnin' your keep."

I opened the door. Abel grinned a greeting, mischief in his manner and a twinkle in his eye. He looked the same as when I saw him last, same feisty grin, same freckles, same ginger-colored hair. "I see you've picked up the townsman's ways," he said, "sleepin' the day away. Get your pants on and I'll buy you breakfast."

I had a notion to reply that it would be hard to sleep away a day that had scarcely begun, but I thought better of it. Abel was wide awake, and I was not; I was not prepared for a battle of wits. "Come in," I muttered. "I never turn down a free meal."

I slid the revolver back into its holster and splashed water on my face at the wash stand. Abel glanced quickly at the weapon, his expression suddenly serious, and then he looked at me and grinned. "That's a good policy," he said. "It's a rare occasion when a Scotsman offers to buy."

We were out on the street before sunrise, walking together across the tracks to the combination saloon, barber shop, and café called the Golden Fleece. The café part of the enterprise was nearly empty at that hour, with only a tattooed cook and a gray-faced waiter behind the counter. In a corner near the back, a sheepherder with a bad case of the shakes sat alone, drinking—and spilling—coffee from a china cup. "Hey, Shep!" the waiter called, "try an' get some of that Arbuckle's *inside* yourself. I just mopped the damn floor."

Abel and me found a table near the front and sat down together. I said Abel looked the same as before, but that's not entirely true. There were lines about his eyes I hadn't seen before and an edgy set to his jaw that I didn't recall. Most telling of all, he now wore a revolver buckled about his waist in an open holster. During our brief acquaintance, Abel had not struck me as a gun-toter, but there he was, and there the gun was. The weapon looked to me like a Smith and Wesson Schofield.

The waiter shuffled over to us, a coffee pot in hand. Cups were on the table, and he filled one for each of us without asking. "Mornin', gents. What can I bring you?"

I took a quick look at the bill of fare. "You have any side pork?" I asked.

"All you want."

"Bring me a double order," I said. "And three eggs over easy."

Abel nodded. "Same for me, but I'll have my cackle berries on the sunny side."

The waiter wrote down our orders and walked back to the kitchen. Across the table, Abel studied me in silence, a slight smile on his lips.

"Well," I said, "how've you been? Did you get your sheep sheared?"

Abel's smile faded. "Finished a week ago.

Trailed both bands to summer range up on the mountain."

"Vendetta Canyon?"

"That's right."

"How's that workin' out?"

Abel shrugged. "About like I expected. Night riders tryin' to spook my herders. Ridin' through the sheep. Runnin' 'em off the bed ground. Somebody *hung* one of the good ewes from Haggis's band."

"*Hung* one of your sheep?"

"From a box elder tree. There was a note pinned to the carcass: 'Keep your woolly maggots out of Vendetta Canyon or we'll hang you next.'"

I lowered my eyes. In my mind's eye I saw again the body of the faithful sheepdog, Robbie, hanging upside down from a cottonwood branch. I saw the gaping wound, the blood that matted the animal's fur and pooled on the ground below. Haggis McRae and me had searched for and found the dog, but the magpies and flies had found it first.

When I spoke, my voice sounded strained and tight. "Somebody in Meriwether County seems to take pleasure in hangin' helpless animals."

"And men," Abel said.

I sipped my coffee. Abel looked across the table at the badge pinned to my shirt front. "You never told me you were a lawman."

"I guess it just never came up."

"Not until you drew cards in Travis Burnett's

game last week. I heard about how you cleaned his clock. I wish I could have seen that."

"You didn't miss much. I got lucky."

"Just the same, I'm obliged. That's the second time you've stood up for one of my herders."

"How *is* Loco John?"

"A mite goosey since those Circle R boys worked him over. He hasn't quit me yet, but he's scared of the night riders."

"Did you tell the sheriff about the raids?"

Abel's answer was a scornful smile. "I have a feelin' he already knows," he said quietly.

The last thing I expected to do was defend Sheriff Ross Friendly. "All right," I said. "Friendly does tend to favor the cattlemen some. But he is the duly elected sheriff of the county. You need to let him know about the night riders."

Abel's face turned red. "I can handle those sons o' bitches myself."

"Through hired guns like Bill Packer and Al Wilson?"

"If it comes to that."

"It will come to that. It came to that when you hired them. Call off the dogs and settle your feud with Rainford. The last thing this county needs is a war."

"I thought you were on my side."

"I'm on the law's side. I'm just a poor, hard-workin' deputy, tryin' to keep the peace."

Abel's jaw took on its stubborn set. "It's too late

for buryin' hatchets with Rainford," he said. "Twenty years too late."

The waiter showed up with our orders and set them before us. I was hungry when we walked in, but somehow my appetite had gone.

How had Ridgeway put it when he gave me the assignment? "Storm clouds are gatherin' over Meriwether County."

Ridgeway was right. Two days later, the storm struck.

Twelve

▼

Starting for the Mountain

Abel and me spoke no more of night riders and hired guns, or of range wars and taking sides. We simply fell to eating, and scarcely another word passed between us. I knew he was disappointed in me. I had stood up for his herder when the Circle R riders were abusing him. Because I had, Abel believed I was on his side in the range dispute. I had tried to make it clear that as a lawman, I could take no side but right. Still, news of the raids up in Vendetta Canyon troubled me and called me to action.

Abel used his last bit of bread to sop up the gravy in his plate, wiped his mouth with his napkin, and pushed back away from the table. "It was good to see you again," he said, "but I need to pick up supplies and get back to the home place. I'll be tendin' my camps tomorrow."

"Much obliged for breakfast," I said. "Take care of yourself, Abel."

There was just a hint of bitterness in his reply. "I reckon I'll have to," he said. "It don't look like anyone *else* wants the job."

Abel gave me a parting wave and turned north on Trail Street. I watched him go until he was small in the distance, and then I headed up the street on a mission of my own.

I found Sheriff Friendly behind his desk at the courthouse, drinking coffee and sorting through his mail. He looked up as I walked in. "Good mornin', deputy," he said. "What can I do for you?"

"I just had breakfast with Abel McKenzie. He says he's havin' trouble with night riders up at Vendetta Canyon."

The sheriff took a sip from his cup. "That don't exactly surprise me," he said. "McKenzie moved his sheep onto prime Circle R range. I'd be surprised if he *wasn't* havin' trouble."

"The way he sees it, open range is for everyone."

"Way the Circle R sees it, McKenzie is a trespasser and a spoiler."

"How do *you* see it, Sheriff?"

Friendly shrugged. "Meriwether County has been cow country for a long time. Cattle were here first."

"*Buffalo* were here first. *Indians* were here first. Those night riders are breakin' the law."

I didn't mean to, but I guess I lit his fuse. The sheriff jumped to his feet, his face red. "Damn you, Fanshaw! You don't come into my office and lecture *me* about the law! I was a peace officer when you were still messin' your didies—both you and Abel McKenzie are damned *troublemakers!*"

"I meant no offense," I said. "I came here because you *are* the law in this county. I figured you'd want to know about the trouble before things get out of hand."

Friendly was still on his feet and still riled. "All right. You've let me know. Why didn't McKenzie tell me himself?"

"I asked him that. He said he figured you already knew."

"You're wastin' my time, deputy. Get the hell out of my office!"

I kept a check rein on my temper. "You bet," I said. "No point in wastin' any more of *my* time."

Back at the hotel, I took pen in hand and wrote a preliminary report to Marshal Ridgeway. I told him of my encounter with Vernal Slye and of being ambushed at the rockslide. I wrote about my time at the wagon with Haggis McRae and about my dust-up with Griff Tallon. I wrote of meeting the McKenzie family. I described the situation in the county, confirming the information Ridgeway had given me, and I gave an account of my meetings with Sheriff Friendly and my visit to the Circle R.

I made no mention of my fight at the Longhorn or of what I'd learned about the secret romance between Ian McKenzie and Morgan Rainford. I told myself that neither the fight nor the romance had any present bearing on my assignment, and thus need not be mentioned. Besides, I'd promised Morgan I'd keep her secret.

I wrapped up my report with an account of the dispute over the range out at Vendetta Canyon, and I told Ridgeway I would follow up reports of night riders and raids against McKenzie's camps. Finally, I gave my address as general delivery, Reata. I signed my name and mailed the letter.

Come evening, I had supper at the hotel and walked down to the Longhorn for a beer. It was a quiet night at the saloon, with only a handful of customers standing at the long bar. The oil lamps were turned low, except one that lit a poker game on the far side of the room. Beneath its yellow light, four townsmen and a stone-faced dealer went through the motions of a low-stakes stud game.

Now that my status as deputy marshal was common knowledge, I did not offer to check my gun with the barkeep. A couple of Circle R riders were among the drinkers at the bar when I stepped up beside them, but though their eyes were hot and their shoulders cold, neither man made a hostile move. I paid for my beer and turned away to find a quiet place.

It was then I saw Doc Reynolds, sitting alone at his usual table. Beware, his dog, lay sprawled at his feet like an old coyote pelt. Doc raised his brandy glass, inviting me with a wave of his hand to join him.

"It's been some time, Merlin," he said. "I thought perhaps you came to your senses and left the county."

I pulled up a chair and sat down. "I did take a short trip out of town day before yesterday," I said. "But I couldn't stay away. I guess I missed your friendly face."

Doc swirled the brandy around in his glass and inhaled the vapors. He ignored my jest. "You certainly are the talk of the town. Seems *everyone* knows about your recent trip to the Circle R."

I smiled. Doc Reynolds loved being in the know. More to the point, Doc hated *not* being in the know. The look on his face was one of complete indifference, but he didn't fool me. I knew he was dying to learn the details of my ride with Morgan Rainford and my visit to the ranch.

As a lawman, I knew Doc to be a good source. Through him, I had received a flood of information about people and events in Meriwether County. But I knew, too, that information is a two-way street. If I wanted to keep the flood coming, I needed to prime the pump.

"I just figured it was time I had a talk with Zack Rainford," I said. "I asked Cal Peabody the way to the ranch. He told me I'd be crazy to go there, that I wouldn't be welcome. Morgan Rainford overheard our conversation. She said the latchstring at the Circle R was out to everyone. She said she was just leaving for the ranch and invited me to ride along. I told her I was obliged, and we took the road north.

"When we got to the ranch, Melissa Morgan asked me to join the family for supper. I had my misgivings, but she wouldn't take no for an answer. When Zack found me at his table, he didn't like it much, but he bowed to the womenfolk. Supper was tasty, but the atmosphere was frosty as a February mornin'. Somehow, we all managed to get through it. Those Rainfords are proud, but they're long on manners.

"After supper, I talked with Zack awhile and rode back here. That's all there was to it."

Doc looked at me over the tops of his spectacles. "That's not what Travis Burnett says. He was in here an hour ago, telling everyone who'd listen that you're courting Morgan Rainford."

"That's a lie," I said.

Doc sipped his brandy. "You have to understand Travis," he said. "He's not the brightest star in the sky, but he's ambitious. He aspires to be a cattle baron, and he's willing to do whatever it takes to reach his goal. What it takes, in his estimation, is to marry a certain cattle baron's only daughter.

"Therefore, when he learned you not only rode out to the Circle R with the object of his affection but had supper with her family and a private chat with her father, he lost what little composure he has. The green-eyed monster now possesses him entirely."

"He's a durned fool," I said. "What makes him think Morgan would take an interest in him?"

"Delusion, plain and simple. But it goes farther than that. He took liberties with Morgan one day last fall, and she rebuffed his advances with a rawhide quirt. By the time his welts healed, Travis had convinced himself she was just playing hard to get."

I decided to find out just how much Doc Reynolds knew about Morgan. "Girl as pretty and rich as Morgan must have suitors aplenty," I said.

"Yes, one would think so. The prevailing opinion is that she does have a special beau, but no one seems to know who he is."

I took a drink of my beer and put on my best poker face. *I know*, I thought. *For once I'm one up on you, Doc.*

First thing the following morning, I made a beeline for Peabody's Livery. Cal Peabody was busy renting a buggy to a customer when I got there, so I walked back to see if I could catch Rutherford. I expected the usual run around, and I was thinking

I should have brought my lariat along, when the buckskin surprised me again. He came across the corral sweet as pie, as though he'd never played hard to get in his life. What's more, he didn't so much as turn a hair when I bridled him and led him back inside the stable. Who knows what goes on in the mind of a horse?

By the time I had Rutherford combed and curried, Cal's customer had set out on his buggy ride. Cal walked back to the stall where I was saddling the buckskin and asked, "Takin' him out, are you?"

"Yeah," I said. "Figured I'd ride up into the War Bonnets for a few days. You wouldn't have a pack horse I could rent, would you?"

Cal thought about it. "I've got that gray the sheriff brought in from Vernal Slye's place. You need a pack outfit, too?"

"No. Just a horse I can pack my blankets on."

"Treat yourself. I'll lend you my own outfit. No charge."

"Why so generous?"

The liveryman shrugged. "Hell, I don't know. Maybe because you're a good customer. Maybe because I'm a poor businessman. Maybe because you beat hell out of that blowhard from the Circle R. Or maybe just because I like you."

I grinned. "All right," I said. "I'm not proud. Throw in a pack saddle and a couple of panniers. Like you say, I'll treat myself."

Calvin was as good as his word. While I went up

the street to check out of the hotel and buy some groceries for my expedition, Calvin caught up the gray horse and gathered the pack saddle, panniers, ropes, and pads he thought I'd need. When I got back with my groceries, I found he had set me up with a good camp outfit, too—coffee pot, skillet, Dutch oven, and eating tools. He even offered to lend me his bedroll.

"I don't need your bed, Cal," I said. "I can make out fine with just my saddle blankets and pads."

"Yeah, you can if the weather doesn't change," he agreed. "But it can turn cold and wet up on that mountain. I'd hate to see a promisin' young feller like you freeze his . . . freeze his *ears* off."

"You fuss over a man more than my old granny," I said. "I'm no greenhorn, you know. I've heard the owl and seen the elephant. And I haven't froze yet."

"Then there's no point in startin' now," Cal said. "Take my damn bed."

Cal offered to help me pack the gray gelding, but I drew the line. "No," I said. "I won't have help when I'm in the mountains, and I need to practice throwin' a one-man hitch. It's been a while."

Back when I was just a shirt-tail kid, my pa showed me how to throw a diamond hitch, but Pa was a great one for doing things the easy way. He taught me how to tie the hitch *before* it's thrown over a pack, and that system sure does simplify things. All I have to do when I unpack is unhook from the cinch and set the pre-tied diamond aside until it's time to pack again.

The gray horse was no greenhorn, either. He stood steady while I worked the ropes and tightened the load, and I had the uneasy feeling he knew more about packing than I did. He sure was built like a pack horse, with a short back, thick body, and strong, sturdy legs.

"If this pony hasn't been packed plenty and frequent," I told Cal, "I'll eat my hat. And I wouldn't say that if I wasn't sure. I rely on my hat for shade."

When all was ready, I slid my Winchester into its scabbard and untracked Rutherford. Taking the gray's lead rope in my left hand, I stepped up onto the buckskin.

"Much obliged until you're better paid, Cal," I said. "I'll be back in a week or so."

The liveryman looked thoughtful. "Uh . . . you wouldn't happen to be goin' near Abel McKenzie's place, would you?" he asked.

"I might. Why?"

Cal produced a sealed envelope and tapped it against the fingers of his left hand. "This letter's for his son, Ian. Important business, I'm told. Do you suppose you could take it to him?"

I took the letter. The envelope was addressed in flowing script simply "To Ian."

"Make sure no one else sees it," Cal said. "Give it to Ian personally."

"Don't worry," I told him. "And when you see Morgan, tell *her* not to worry, either."

I didn't wait for his reply. Turning the horses away, I left Cal behind me. It was enough that he knew *I* knew.

With the gray in tow, I rode Rutherford across the NP tracks and onto the road leading south. A few miles out, I met a family of homesteaders bound for Reata in a weathered farm wagon. A grim-faced granger in dusty black drove the team, while his wife sat demurely in faded gingham and a sun-bonnet on the spring seat beside him. Behind them, in the wagon box, two curious youngsters watched wide-eyed as we met and passed.

The morning grew warmer. Clouds gathered and towered above the mountains. Overhead, a red-tailed hawk rode the rising currents, hunting. The land changed from plains to rolling hills, and I no longer saw travelers on the road. Recalling my ride to Reata with Ian McKenzie, I looked for and found the place where the trail to the sheep ranch joined the main road. I turned my horses off onto the trail and let my mind drift.

I thought some about Ian, and about Morgan Rainford. By every standard I could think of, their romance seemed ill-starred and hopeless. Their fathers, by all accounts the best of friends in their youth, were now sworn enemies, headed for a showdown over grass and water. Reata was a fair-sized town by Montana standards, but it wasn't big enough to hide their secret for long. Maybe Doc Reynolds still didn't know, but Cal Peabody did, as did I. It was only a matter of time before their love affair became general knowledge, and it was not likely to be well-received by either Abel McKenzie or Zack Rainford. It may be true, as Shakespeare wrote, that the course of true love never did run smooth, but what lay ahead for Ian and Morgan promised to be a rocky road indeed.

It was nearly noon when I turned my horses across the bridge and up the lane to McKenzie's. Shaded by cottonwood and alder, the ranch house lay long and low under the summer sun. Inside the picket fence that bordered the yard, a young boy watched my approach. His ginger-colored hair was a tousled mop, and his blue eyes were guarded and cool. Freckles rioted across his face. He looked to be about ten, and I guessed him to be Ian's younger brother Keith. I drew rein at the fence and grinned.

"Howdy," I said. "I'm Merlin Fanshaw—friend of Ian's. Is he at home?"

The boy's face brightened. "I've heard about you," he said. "You're the deputy marshal from Dry Creek, ain'cha?"

"That'd be me, all right. You must be Keith."

Behind the boy, the screen door to the house opened and Teresa McKenzie stepped outside. Shading her eyes against the brightness, she looked up at me from the doorway. "Hello,

Merlin," she said, smiling. "Get down and come inside. You're just in time for dinner."

Teresa McKenzie wore a low-necked blouse of white cotton and a full skirt beneath an apron of blue-checked gingham. A small gold cross hung by a chain at her throat, and the sleeves of her blouse were short. Her long dark hair was drawn back and done up in a single braid at the back of her head in the Mexican manner.

"Thank you, ma'am," I said. "I had an early dinner back in Reata. Truth is, I'm on my way up the mountain and I thought I'd stop by and see if Ian is home."

She stepped outside, letting the screen door close behind her. "I'm sorry," she said. "Ian and Abel are both up above Vendetta Canyon, tending the sheep camps. Is there something I can do?"

"No," I said. "I'm headed up that way myself. I expect I'll run into them."

"They planned to make camp at Red Rock Springs, this side of the canyon. Just follow the main trail up until it forks at Cabin Creek. Then take the right fork down across Black Elk Meadows until you reach the springs. Ian and Abel will either be there or out with the herders. I can draw you a map, if you like."

"Cal Peabody gave me a general picture of the area," I said. "I believe I can find my way."

Teresa smiled her bright smile. "*Vaya con Dios,*" she said. "Go with God."

"That's the only way to travel," I replied. Tipping my hat, I turned Rutherford and the pack horse up to the mountain trail above the house. Behind me, Teresa and young Keith watched from the front yard until they were small in the distance.

Thirteen

▼

To Make Amends

The trail to Vendetta Canyon wound up through timbered hills and open parks toward the granite peaks that crowned the War Bonnet range. Aspen groves shimmered on the hillsides, their leaves a-patter with a sound like rain. Wheatgrass bent with the breeze. The heat of early afternoon eased its grip on the day, giving way to cooler air and the medicine smells of pine and sage. Shadows grew longer. Blue as wood smoke, fool hens pecked nervously under spruce trees, and mule deer browsed the ridges as I rode Rutherford up the switchbacks.

The packhorse led easily, without fuss or foolishness, and I was glad I'd brought him. Ever since I was a kid I had loved summertime in the mountains, and I was looking forward to making camp and scouting the country on horseback.

Out of nowhere, I thought of Griff Tallon. I was all but certain it was his bullet that killed Vernal

Slye's pinto at the rockslide, and nearly killed me. Tallon was a manhunter and no mistake, but I didn't believe he had targeted me personally. I was convinced he simply mistook me for Vernal.

But he had killed others. If ambushing me was a mistake, he soon corrected it. He killed Vernal later, and gunned down three other men he also claimed were rustlers. Tallon was a loner by all accounts, a solitary man who wandered the range land away from the company of other men, "coyoting the rim rocks," as Vernal said.

I recalled the showdown at Haggis's wagon, when I stood up to him with my forty-four in hand. I remembered his cold eyes as he left the camp and his words to me: "Another time." Maybe he hadn't intended to take my life at the rockslide, but that didn't mean he hadn't changed his intentions since then.

I heard the wagon coming on the trail ahead. I had just stopped at Cabin Creek to give the horses a breather when the clatter of shod hooves and the rumble of wagon wheels came clearly to me from just beyond the rise. I waited in the shadows, my eyes on the crest of the hill, and watched as Abel and Ian McKenzie came into view.

It was just as it had been the first day I met them. Father and son sat together on the wagon seat, Abel at the reins and Ian at his side, a Winchester carbine in his hands. Water barrels occupied the wagon box behind them, and the bay team plodded in tandem, the rich red-brown of the horses' hides shining in the late afternoon light.

I rode out of the trees, my right hand raised in greeting. Abel reined up sharply, his eyes wary and his mouth set in a hard, thin line. Ian half rose from the spring seat, bringing the rifle to bear. "Don't shoot," I said. "It's me, Merlin!"

"Fanshaw?" The way Abel said my name made it sound like his recognition of me was at war with his suspicion of who I *might* be. "What the hell are you doin' up here?"

I lowered my hand and urged Rutherford forward. "Takin' the mountain air," I said. "Figured I'd sleep out under the stars for a night or so."

Abel set the wagon brake. He was clearly glad to see me but too proud to show it. "Be careful you don't wind up sleepin' under the *sod*," he said. "There seem to be some night riders in these mountains who don't much like sheep."

I grinned. "I don't much like *work*, but I've had to get *used* to it. I expect the same will happen to the sheep haters."

"By god, I hope you're right," Abel said, "but I don't see much sign of it."

"Riders chased Haggis's sheep off the bed ground two nights ago," Ian said. "He shot the hat off one of them. Silver-belly Stetson, size seven and a quarter."

"Good for Haggis," I said. "How is he?"

"He's all right," Abel said. "Those damn cowpunchers have done their best to try to scare him, but the big highlander doesn't spook easy."

I thought about Abel's other herder, Loco John. He struck me as a timid man, one who might not do as well under hazing. He'd been terrified the day Travis Burnett took the sheep shears to him. "How's John holdin' up?"

"Not good," Abel said. "It wouldn't take much to make him run."

"I'll pay him a visit," I said. "It might help him to know he's got a friend up here."

Abel nodded. "It might at that. John is camped above the east wall of Vendetta Canyon, maybe three miles from Red Rock Springs. Haggis is about six miles beyond that."

"We tended both camps," Ian said. "Dad and I are headed back down to the ranch."

The sun had set as we talked. Suddenly, the warm, late light left the mountain and twilight took its place. Overhead, sundown stained the clouds, and darkness began to move in. I looked up at the sky. "Guess I'd best find me a place to camp," I said. "Night's comin' on."

"You'll find a good spot about two miles back," Ian said, pointing. "Good grass and plenty of wood. There's a clearing in a patch of lodgepole. Cabin Creek runs right through it."

I stood in my stirrups and stretched my neck, looking in the direction Ian was pointing. "I can't make it out from here," I said. Dismounting, I looked up at Ian. "Would you mind walkin' up the trail with me a little? We should be able to see the spot from the top of that rise."

Ian looked a little puzzled, but he nodded. He handed the Winchester to Abel, put a foot on the wagon wheel's hub, and stepped down to the ground. "Sure," he said, "but it's not that hard to find."

While Abel waited, Ian and me walked back in the direction he and his dad had come from. At the crest of the hill and out of earshot of the wagon, Ian pointed to the clearing. "Right over there," he said. "See? I told you it wasn't hard to find."

I grinned. "By golly, it sure isn't. I'll bet I could have found that spot all by myself."

Ian frowned. "Then what . . ."

I reached inside my coat and took out the letter Cal Peabody had given me. "A crotchety old stableman with a nose like an Idaho spud said I was to give you this if I saw you," I said. "Well, I see you, so here's your letter."

Ian took the envelope and glanced sharply at me. He still looked puzzled, but he obviously recognized Morgan's handwriting. "What . . . what's this?" he asked.

"Well, if I was to guess, I'd say it was a love letter from your sweetheart. But I don't know for sure. I haven't read it."

Ian glanced quickly back at Abel, and then looked at me. "I . . . I don't know what you mean . . ."

"It's all right," I said, smiling. "You and Morgan have friends you don't even know about."

Gratitude showed clearly on his face. "How did you find out?"

"I saw you two together at Peabody's that day you drove me into town. Then, a few days ago, Morgan told me everything. Your secret's safe with me."

"I don't know what to say. Thanks, Merlin."

"That's what Morgan said. You're welcome."

Darkness was falling fast. We walked back down the trail to where Abel waited, still sitting in the wagon. "I was about to give up on you two," he said. Looking at me, he said, "If you're sure you can find that clearing, Ian and I need to get down off the mountain. There's home cookin' and soft beds waitin' for us."

My horses were grazing on the grass beside the trail. I picked up the buckskin's reins and the pack-horse's lead rope and swung into the saddle. "Never let it be said I kept good men from their hearth and home," I said. "See you boys."

The first stars began to appear as I broke out of the timber and onto the meadow. I unpacked the horses, gathered rocks for a fire ring, and laid out my borrowed bed roll. Minutes later, I was eating warmed-over beans I'd brought from town and enjoying my own company. The horses grazed on the meadow's tall grass, shuffling at the end of their picket ropes. My campfire was a spot of comfort in a cold land, and everything seemed right with the world.

Except I knew it was not. Proud men were on a collision course. Lives were at risk. Riders raided the sheep camps, growing bolder each day. Both Abel McKenzie and Zack Rainford had gunmen on their payrolls, and it was only a matter of time before someone was killed. The situation in Meriwether County was a powder keg, and I could smell the smoke from its burning fuse.

I thought about Morgan and Ian. I liked them both, and I sympathized with the dilemma they faced. The feud between their families demanded their loyalty, while their love for each other made demands of its own.

They had found a solution of sorts, a way to live with the problem that was at best temporary and at worst dangerous. Morgan and Ian simply kept their romance a secret, known only to a few trusted allies. Cal Peabody, at the livery barn, was one of those allies. Now, without intending to, I had become one. All my life I'd been a seeker, longing to know more. That night, for the first time, I wished I knew less. I wished I didn't know what I knew about Morgan and Ian.

My campfire burned down to ashes and a handful of glowing coals. Overhead, stars glittered like cold fire. In the morning, I would ride the high country. I would visit the camps of Loco John and Haggis McRae. I would offer them hope and let them know they weren't alone against the men who scattered their sheep and threatened their lives.

I tossed the dregs of my coffee on the dying coals, shucked my boots and hat, and crawled between the soogans of my bed roll. Thinking about Morgan and Ian led me to thoughts of Pandora, and I wondered if she was Mrs. Johnny Peters yet. At last, I closed my eyes and drifted off to a restless and fitful sleep.

I came awake with a start. My heartbeat was fast as a rabbit's and loud in my ears. Holding my breath, I lay perfectly still, listening. The wind had picked up. Cold on my face, it sighed through the bunch grass and stirred the lodgepole branches at the edge of the meadow. I stared up into darkness, possessed by dread.

What had awakened me? I could recall neither dream nor sound, and yet I felt some great threat lurked nearby, just beyond my reach. I breathed in, smelling the dew-wet canvas of my bed tarp, the damp earth beyond, and my own fear. Slowly, I reached my hand beneath the war bag that served as my pillow and touched the familiar grips of my holstered forty-four.

"I wouldn't do that, deputy."

I froze. The voice was harsh, the words curt and

clipped. It was the voice of a man unaccustomed to speaking, but I had heard it before. I sat up in my bed.

"Keep them hands where I can see 'em," said the voice. "I ain't here to kill you, but I will if I need to."

I believed him. "Who are you?" I asked.

"We met a while back, at the Scotchman's wagon. You pulled a pistol on me. I told you there'd be another time."

"Tallon," I said.

"That's right. Light a fire, and we'll talk. And don't try nothin'. I got cat's eyes; I can see near as good in the dark as in the light."

I could make him out then, a shadowy figure huddled maybe ten feet away. I sensed rather than saw the gun he pointed at me. Groping in the grass around my fire ring, I found the kindling I'd set aside for my morning fire. Stacking it loosely in the ashes, I fanned the sleeping coals with my hat until they glowed and burst into flame. Then I added more wood and watched the fire burn a hole in the darkness.

Tallon crouched in the meadow grass, a long-barreled Colt trained on me. "Ain't here to do you no harm," he said. "Quite the contrary, like the lawyers say." His laugh was a hoarse chuckle.

In the firelight, Tallon's face was without expression. His eyes were alive, though. I don't know if they really were cat's eyes, but they seemed to take in every move I made.

"What do you want with me?" I asked.

Beneath his black moustache, Tallon's mouth turned down at the corners. "I'm good at my trade," he said. "I don't make many mistakes. When I do, I try to make 'em right if I can. I made a mistake with you."

"You mean when you tried to kill me at the rock slide? You almost got it done."

His eyes narrowed. "I took you for Vernal Slye. You rode out from his place, on one of his horses. I never meant you no harm."

"No harm done," I said, sarcastic as I knew how. "You killed the horse, I broke my leg when it fell on me, and I got knocked cold when my head struck a rock."

Tallon nodded. "That's why I'm here. I owe you, deputy."

He wore the flat-brimmed black hat and the canvas duster that were his trademarks. He gestured with the Colt. "Give me your pistol," he said. "Pass it to me with two fingers . . . by the barrel."

I calculated my chances and didn't like the odds. Reaching beneath my war bag, I did as he directed.

"Now," Tallon said. "Give me your handcuffs . . . and the key."

The muzzle of Tallon's Colt studied me with its cold, dark eye. I tried to keep a cool head. I didn't much like being ordered about in my own camp, but Tallon had the drop on me. Men had threatened to take my life before, but Tallon killed for a living. Meek as a lamb, I handed over my cuffs and their key.

"All right with you if I put my hat on? I don't feel dressed without it."

Tallon nodded. "Go ahead."

"What now?" I asked.

"Now," he said, "I save your life."

False dawn came to the meadow. Gray light pushed at the gloom. Tallon walked behind me up to the tree line. Once there, he stopped at a sturdy pine and told me to sit down with my back against its trunk. "Put your hands out behind you," he said, "one hand on each side of the tree." When I did so, he shackled my hands together with the cuffs.

"I'll come back later and turn you loose," he said. "Meantime, just set still and abide."

I tried to keep my voice steady. "Don't seem like there's much else I *can* do," I said. "What's this all about?"

Tallon was silent for a moment. Then he said, "I figure you're up here to visit McKenzie's sheep camps. That right?"

"That's right. I aimed to ride over first thing this morning. Why?"

Again, Tallon paused. When he spoke, his voice was flat and without expression. "I can't let you do that. Come sunup, a hard rain is goin' to fall on them sheep and their herders," he said. "King

Death is comin', and hell is comin' with him. If you're in either of them camps, you'll be a dead man."

A cold rock seemed to turn over in my belly. I had no reason to doubt Tallon's words. He was telling me raiders were coming to strike the sheep. Haggis McRae and Loco John were in deadly danger, and I could neither warn nor help them. My heart was pounding again. "Tallon," I said. "You've got to turn me loose. We can still stop this thing, you and me . . ."

Tallon shrugged. "No," he said. "Nobody can stop it now." He turned his face to the east. Above the trees and the granite peaks, pale light stained the sky. "I did what I came to do," he said. "We're even now."

I flexed my arms and strained against the handcuffs. Pain stabbed upward from my wrists, but the cuffs held fast. Tallon turned and walked back toward my little camp. In the gray light the canvas tarp that covered my bed looked like a white rock in the meadow grass. The fire had died, and a sudden gust of wind scattered ashes into the cold morning air. I scooted around on my butt, watching the man walk away. "Damn you, Tallon," I shouted. "Don't leave me like this!"

He made no answer but continued to walk across the clearing toward my tethered horses. His own saddled bay stood ground-tied near the others, and I saw him pick up its reins as he walked toward

Rutherford and the pack horse. As I watched, he freed them both from their picket ropes. Then he swung up onto his bay and rode out at a trot, driving my horses before him.

FOURTEEN

▼

FIRE ON THE MOUNTAIN

Shackled to the tree with my own handcuffs, I fought to free myself. With my back to the pine's trunk and my hands locked behind me, I twisted and strained until my wrists bled. I had to admit Tallon knew how to put irons on a man.

He had crept into my camp under cover of darkness. He had handcuffed me to a tree to protect me, according to some strange code of his own. Because he had ambushed me by mistake back at the rockslide, he now thought to make amends by saving my life.

Foolishly, I struggled against the restraints. According to Tallon, Loco John and Haggis McRae would soon be under attack by the cattlemen and their raiders. That knowledge made me desperate, and in a near panic, I tried even harder to pull free of the cuffs. At last I gave up. I stopped struggling. I cleared my mind and remembered that I knew a better way. In fact, I had planned for it!

I leaned back into the tree and allowed my muscles to relax. My breathing slowed and returned to normal. I recalled Ridgeway's lecture back in Dry Creek on being watchful, and blamed myself for getting caught napping. All right, Tallon had taken me by surprise. Nothing I could do would change that. But lawmen have their own tricks, and I'd picked up a few.

Some officers carry a second gun or a hidden knife. I do neither of those things, but I had acquired another habit. Beneath my hat band was a second key to the handcuffs. When Tallon marched me to the tree line, I'd asked if I could take my hat, and he had allowed it. Now, my hat lay on the ground beside me, beneath the pine. I twisted around the tree, groping blindly. My fingers touched the brim, felt inside the band. *Slowly,* I told myself, *take it easy . . .*

Where *was* it? Could I have lost it somewhere? The key *had* to be there!

And then I felt it! Taking the key from beneath my hat band, I prayed I wouldn't drop it in the grass. Carefully, I felt for the lock, slipped the key in, and turned it. The lock opened! My left hand was free!

Moments later, I was running back to where I'd camped the night before. My cartridge belt and six-gun lay in the blankets beneath my bed tarp, and I buckled the weapon about my waist with hands still numb from the handcuffs. Scanning the meadow before me, I saw no sign of Rutherford or the gray. Tallon had taken no chances; I remembered him driving my horses before him as he rode away.

At that point, I nearly threw in the towel. According to Abel McKenzie, the nearest sheep camp was three miles beyond Red Rock Springs—and Haggis's camp was six miles beyond that. I knew there was no way I could make it in time to warn the herders or help them unless I got mounted and rode like the very devil.

I stared across the meadow in the direction Tallon had taken. My horses were gone, I knew, but I stood watching anyway. I watched with a desperation born of need, as if I could bring the horses back by sheer force of will. But the meadow was empty and silent. Shadows of the pines reached out across the sunlit clearing. I saw nothing.

And then, just as I was turning away, I caught a glimpse of something on the other side of the meadow—movement! I held my breath. There! At the edge of that aspen grove—*Rutherford!*

The buckskin stepped out into the sunlight and stopped. He raised his head, looking at me. *Please, big horse,* I thought, *come to me. This one time, come easy.*

As if he read my thoughts, Rutherford tossed his head, pawed the ground with a forefoot, and then crossed the meadow toward me at a quick-footed trot. I could have kissed the old renegade!

He lowered his head when he reached my side,

and I caught him by his halter and led him to the fallen log that held my saddle and bridle. Seconds later, I was mounted astride the buckskin and riding hard on the trail to Red Rock Springs.

Rutherford struck out at a high lope, sweeping to the top of the rise and then dropping down the other side in a series of stiff-legged hops that rattled my teeth and spine. I felt his muscles ripple and flex beneath me, and I narrowed my eyes against the wind of our passage. Then, at a sharp zigzag in the trail, Rutherford faltered, turned back on himself, stumbled, and nearly fell.

Off balance, he dropped his head, and I feared his body—and mine—would quickly follow. I pulled hard on the reins, bringing his head up and forcing him to throw his forelegs out before him. The big horse righted himself, got his bearings, and continued his dash down the mountain.

Ahead, the trail snaked down in a series of switchbacks that led to a shadowed valley. Above the valley's floor, a grassy meadow nestled on a broad bench at the foot of a densely wooded mountain. Thick as dog hair, the trees rose to a ridge topped by columns of rock that thrust above the forest and towered over the meadow. The rocks glowed brick-red in the morning sunlight, and I knew I was looking at Red Rock Springs.

Breaking out onto the meadow, I spurred the big

horse past the site of McKenzie's camp, noting the rock fire ring and the flattened square of grass where his wall tent had stood. Beyond, a fast-flowing stream dashed through willow and elk brush at the meadow's edge. I rode across the stream and found the trail again, angling up a long hill from the valley floor.

Rutherford didn't hesitate. He was lathered now, his breath huffing like a bellows, but he carried me up that steep trail at a run and fought my attempts to slow him down.

A mile farther on, I finally managed to stop the big horse, and I forced him to stand so he could catch his breath. Ahead, the trail widened and became a grass-grown wagon road. Tracks from what I guessed were McKenzie's wagons were plain in the road, and I knew I must be within a few miles of Loco John's camp. And then, as I waited for Rutherford's breathing to come back to normal, I suddenly caught my own breath.

Fifty feet beyond, another road joined the road I followed. Dismounting, I led the buckskin to the junction and froze. Fresh tracks of what must have been at least ten shod horses showed clearly in the rocky soil. *Night riders!* And they had come this way ahead of me!

I turned Rutherford uphill and swung into the saddle. Leaning forward over his withers, I touched his flanks with my spurs, and he took the trail again. The wind shifted, coming down the mountain from above. I caught the familiar smells of sagebrush, pine, and . . .

Smoke! The acrid smell stung my nostrils and set my heart to pounding. Somewhere up ahead, fire burned uncontrolled. The smell of smoke seemed to grow stronger as I rode, thicker and more pungent. I raised my eyes from the trail to the ridge top. Now I could see the smoke clearly, billowing against the sky, blocking the sun, dirty brown in the morning light.

I slid my Winchester from its boot and jacked a shell into its chamber. Ahead, the ground began to level out. I remember thinking I should be able to see Loco John's camp soon. Rutherford made a final push, and suddenly I was on top and in the clear.

The scene struck me like a hammer blow. A sheep wagon burned fiercely in the freshening breeze, roaring flames devouring its running gear, wagon box, and sideboards. The canvas top had burned away from the hardwood bows, leaving only tattered remnants that fluttered bat-like in the flames, and fire dripped from the wagon to the blackened earth beneath it.

The grass had burned over an area of maybe three acres, and I saw the charred bodies of dead sheep by the score scattered across the hilltop. They lay singly and in groups, some on their sides, some on their backs, spindly legs thrust out from swollen bodies like sticks. At the wagon, a gust of wind pushed the smoke aside and I saw what I believed was Loco John's saddle horse, dead on its side and steaming.

Rutherford caught the scent and danced backward in a panic, eyes wide and nostrils flaring. The big horse was lathered and wet from our headlong ride, and his feet jittered nervously in the blackened grass. I dismounted, stroking his neck and talking to ease his fear. Leading him upwind of the fire, I tied him to a sagebrush shrub and walked back toward the wagon.

As I came near the burned area, something at its edge in the high grass caught my eye. Drawing nearer, I found the still, dead body of a sheepdog, its silky fur matted with blood. The dog had been shot twice through the body with a large-bore gun of some kind. Once would have been enough.

I turned back toward the wagon but couldn't get close because of the heat. Explosions sounded above the fire's roar, and I guessed Loco John's canned goods were bursting from the heat. Smoke stung my eyes and set them to watering, but I wiped them with my bandana and covered my nose.

Thirty feet from his wagon, I found Loco John. He lay face down in the ash and embers of the grass fire, his hair and beard singed and his skin charred by flame. In his hands he clutched a rusted old Stevens rifle. Perhaps, I thought, he'd had the pluck to use it. If he did, he was badly outmatched; the rifle was more fit for firing at coyotes and sage hens than at armed men, and it was a single-shot. When I turned him over, I found a single bullet wound high in his chest. His sightless eyes were wide open and staring, their last view perhaps of his killer. John had died where he fell. He could not have suffered much.

I remembered his helplessness the day Travis Burnett and the Circle R boys took the shears to him at the saloon. I recalled Abel McKenzie telling me of the man's fear when the riders taunted and tormented him by night.

Now, Loco John was dead. He had been a gentle man, a caretaker of sheep. He had not been a brawler or a man to provoke others. His offense, in the eyes of his killers, was that he herded sheep on a range claimed by cattle. He was a victim of ignorance and hate in of a war that was not his own.

Kneeling in the hot ash, I lifted his body onto my shoulders and carried it to a level place away from the burned area. There, I laid him on his back, closed his eyes, and covered him with loose rock to keep the coyotes and magpies away. I would come back for him later, but I had urgent business to attend to. I strode quickly to my tethered horse and swung into the saddle. Haggis McRae's camp was still six miles away.

The trail was faint and grass grown, but clear enough. It stretched out before me across open meadows and timbered hillsides, and Rutherford covered the ground with a will. The memory of Loco John, dead on his belly in the ashes, haunted me, and I rode like a man possessed, fearful of what I might find at Haggis's camp.

Along the way, I saw scattered sheep, in groups of two or three, staring stupidly as I passed. No longer tended by herder and dog, they grazed bewildered along the ridges and in the brush-filled coulees. I recalled the dead ewes and lambs of John's band and wondered how many sheep the raiders had killed. There had been no time to investigate, but I told myself I'd go back after I learned Haggis's fate.

Rutherford kept up his headlong pace, pushing even beyond what I asked of him. There was no quit to the big horse, and I knew he'd run until he dropped if I asked him to. "Easy, big son," I said, easing him back to a trot. "Go easy."

The need for hurry was no less than before, but riding the buckskin into the ground would benefit no one. From that point on, I switched him back and forth from a trot to a lope, and in that manner, we covered the miles.

I kept my eyes focused on the hilltops, watching for a glimpse of Haggis's wagon and the sheep in his care. I both expected and dreaded to see the rising plume of smoke that would tell me his camp, too, had been set ablaze. As the miles passed, and the sky remained clear, I held my breath and dared to hope.

The trail ahead turned upward through thick stands of pine, breaking out suddenly onto a grassy hill. Haggis's sheepwagon stood on a broad bench fifty yards below the hill's crest, its canvas top stark white in the sunlight. A dozen sheep lay bloodied and dead in the high grass along the bench. The wagon's door stood wide open.

I rode to the wagon at a lope. Bullet holes riddled the canvas and the wagon box. Also punctured by gunfire, the water barrels beside the wagon stood in mud, still leaking water. I leaned forward in the stirrups and looked inside. Sunlight stabbed in through the bullet holes, crisscrossing the wagon's dark interior. Pots, pans, and canned goods were strewn across the floor. Quilts and blankets lay bunched and twisted atop the empty bed. But there was no sign of Haggis. Where *was* he?

I turned Rutherford away from the wagon, searching for the herder's body among the dead sheep along the slope. Looking up to the crest of the hill, I saw an outcropping of rock, shaded by twisted pines. It was a spot that commanded a view of the bench land and the wagon, and I remember thinking it would be a prime location for a bush-whacker. Again, I recalled Ridgeway's *Cuidado* lecture. The marshal would be pleased, I thought. I was finally learning caution.

Suddenly, in the darkness of the pines above, I saw the flash of sunlight on metal! I jerked the reins, turning Rutherford sharply to the right. I felt the wind from the bullet brush my face, heard the gunshot shatter the stillness. I pulled my Winchester from its scabbard, throwing myself from the saddle. My heart pounding, I lay in the grass, staring up at the outcropping.

The second shot I expected didn't come. Instead, I heard a voice that banished my fear and left relief in its place—Haggis's voice! "So, ye damn puggie," it said. "Have ye come back t' finish your bloody work?"

I laid my Winchester in the grass and raised my hands. "Don't shoot, Haggis," I called out. "It's me, Merlin—Merlin Fanshaw!"

There was silence in the shadows beyond the rocks. Then the big Scot stepped out into the light, his rifle at the ready. "Laddie?" Haggis said. "Why didna ye cry out? I might have shot ye!"

I got to my feet. "Can't argue with that," I said. "If your bullet had come a half inch closer, we wouldn't be havin' this conversation. I'm glad you're all right, pardner. I was worried about you."

Haggis swung down toward me, a broad smile on his face. He carried his rifle in his left hand, and he walked with the bold stride I recalled, and yet it was not quite the same. There was something different, a halting in his pace . . . and then I saw it— a blood-stained bandage tied about his left thigh. Haggis was not *entirely* all right, after all.

"I'm fine, laddie," he said, grasping my hand with his. "One o' them damn bushwhackers had a wee bit o' luck. Got me in the leg, but 'tis a clean shot, in one side and out the other. Man, it's good t' see ye."

Guilt fell on me like a weight. I told myself I should have pushed on instead of making camp back at the meadows. I should have been with Haggis and Loco John when the raiders came. I should have . . .

"I'm glad to see you, too," I said. "Sorry I missed the party. I should have been here to help."

"Wheesht, laddie," Haggis said. "Ye couldna hae known! They came like the coyotes, before dawn. They came t' butcher an' burn."

His blue eyes searched my face. "What about John? Is he . . ."

"He's dead," I said. "The raiders killed him. Killed his horse and dog, too. They set fire to his wagon and scattered the sheep. Like I said, I should have been here."

"A man does what he can," Haggis said. "Ye're here *now*, Merlin."

We sat together in the grass, and Haggis told me about the raid. "They wore hoods," he said, "feed sacks with eye holes cut out, to hide their faces. But they were the same bunch as came before. They rode the same horses and made the same threats. But this time, they came t' kill.

"When I saw the smoke and heard the shootin', I knew they'd struck John's camp. I figured they'd soon be hittin' mine. I caught up ma Jimmy horse and ma dog Tip and took 'em up yonder to the rocks. I tied 'em out of sight back in the trees an' settled down t' wait."

Haggis paused. When he spoke again, there was sorrow in his voice. "The gunfire stopped. Smoke darkened the sky. Minutes later, the riders came, scatterin' the sheep and shootin' up my wagon. Some of the riders shot the sheep, too. Others carried axe handles. They rode among the sheep, brainin' the puir creatures with their damned clubs! That's when I decided t' do some shootin' myself.

"I didna shoot t' kill, mind ye, but I fired over the riders' heads and at the feet of their horses until the damn cowards grew nervous. They fired back, an' a bullet struck ma leg. They couldna see me, back in the trees. They couldna tell if I was one man or ten, and I held the high ground. They killed a few more sheep, scattered the rest, and rode away down the mountain. I lost some of ma flock—but I saved ma horse and ma dog."

"And your life," I said. "I'm mighty glad about that, my friend."

The big herder's smile was wistful. "Och," he said. "Ye're nae so glad as *I* am, laddie."

FIFTEEN

▼

BEARER OF BAD NEWS

Leading Rutherford, I walked with Haggis back up to his stronghold in the trees. Haggis had tied his sheep dog Tip to a low branch, and the dog tugged against the rope that held him and begged to be freed. Haggis obliged and then turned to untie his horse as well.

"I need to get down the mountain and let Abel know what's happened up here," I said. "I'll have to let the sheriff know, too."

Haggis nodded. "Aye. Abel told me ye're some kind o' peeler—a deputy U.S. marshal, is it?"

"That's right. I was sent here to head off a range war. Looks like I'm a day late and a dollar short."

Haggis stood, his mouth a grim line as he looked at the dead sheep dotting the hillside. "Poor beasties," he said. "It's monstrous wicked t' kill a puir creature for no purpose but hate."

Leading our horses, we walked together down to his wagon. "Those boys sure shot up your livin' quarters," I said.

"Aye," Haggis said, "but it doesna take a sharp-shooter t' hit a wagon."

I nodded. "Do you want to ride down to McKenzie's with me?"

"Nae. I have Tip and ma Jimmy horse. I need t'gather what sheep have survived, both from John's band and my own."

"What about your leg?"

"It's all right. What canna be changed must be endured, as ma mother used to say."

"Do you have enough grub? Those raiders even shot up your water barrels."

Haggis looked in through the wagon's open door. "There's plenty grub for a week or two," he said. "And there's water galore on this mountain."

I reached into my saddlebags and took out my spare box of cartridges. "Take these," I said, handing Haggis the box. "Your rifle is a Model '73, like mine. You just may need a few extra forty-fours."

Haggis shook his head in protest, but he took the cartridges.

"One more thing," I said. "Ian told me you shot a hat off the head of one of the raiders earlier this week. Do you still have it?"

"Aye. 'Tis in the grain box at the back of ma wagon. D'ye need it?"

"You never can tell. It might be evidence."

Haggis led his horse over to the riddled sheep-wagon and opened the grain box. Reaching inside, he took out a rumpled silver belly Stetson and handed it to me. A neat, round bullet hole marked its high crown. "I dinna ken who wore this," he said. "The man was masked, like the others. But he seemed t' be in a terrible hurry. He rode away and left his bonnet behind."

"Yeah," I said, grinning. "Maybe he was tired of it."

I pushed the hat into my saddle bag and got ready to mount Rutherford. "By the way," I said. "If you didn't shoot to kill, how do you explain your shot comin' so close to him?"

Haggis's face was expressionless. "Sometimes," he said, "I shoot t' come *close*."

When I reached the meadow where I'd spent the previous night, I hid my camp outfit in the trees and struck out on the trail down the mountain. I kept an eye out for the gray packhorse as I rode but saw no sign of it. Turning my mind to the job ahead, I told myself I'd make a more thorough search later.

No man likes to be the bearer of bad news, and I dreaded having to tell Abel McKenzie about the raids and the death of Loco John. I had no idea how many sheep from the two bands had been slaughtered, but I knew Haggis would provide an accurate head count once he had time to gather the strays.

I felt sorry for Abel, of course. One of his herders had been killed, together with his horse and dog. Haggis, his other herder, had been wounded while defending McKenzie property. Abel's sheep had been clubbed, shot, and scattered. One of his sheep wagons had been burned and the other riddled by gunfire. I liked Abel McKenzie, and I sympathized with the man, but I have to admit I blamed him, too.

Abel had deliberately provoked Zack Rainford by moving sheep onto grazing land the cattleman claimed. Abel had defied the warnings. He had pushed himself into the heart of the Circle R's summer range. Bull-headed and reckless, he seemed to be spoiling for a fight. Well, now he had one.

I rode Rutherford down through the aspen groves above McKenzie's home ranch just at sundown. Darkness had already settled in across the valley, and lamplight shone soft in the windows of the house and bunkhouse. I topped the last rise and pulled up at the gate that set the ranch buildings off from the pasture. I was about to step down and open the gate when I heard a voice, hard-edged and close at hand. "Hands up, mister," the voice said. "Who are you, and what do you want?"

Even in the fading light, I recognized Abel's hired gun, Bill Packer. He stood on the other side of the fence, a short-barreled carbine in his hands. Just seeing the man raised my hackles. It seemed to me that bringing in gun-hands like Packer by either side was more likely to cause trouble than prevent it. "Merlin Fanshaw," I said. "I'm here to see Abel. Open the durn gate."

Packer lowered the carbine. Opening the tight

wire gate would take two hands. That meant he would have to set the rifle down for a moment, and it was clear he didn't like the idea. After a brief hesitation, he propped the weapon against a fence post, pushed hard with one hand against the upright while he slipped the fastener with the other, and opened the gate. I rode through, and he closed it again. "Sorry, Fanshaw," he said. "I didn't know it was you."

"Well," I said. "Now you do." I touched Rutherford with my spurs and rode on down to the main house. The front door opened, and Abel himself came out to meet me.

"Merlin," he said. "Get down and come inside. You're just in time for supper."

I stepped down off Rutherford and stood at the buckskin's shoulder. It had been a long ride, and it felt strange to be standing on solid ground again. "It's good to know I'm finally in time for somethin'," I said. "I'm afraid I've got some bad news."

Abel's blue eyes narrowed. "In that case, you're just in time for something else—a drink before dinner. My boy Keith will take care of your horse."

Abel ushered me into the sitting room and showed me to a chair. Ten-year-old Keith watched curiously from the kitchen as his father approached him. "Take Deputy Fanshaw's horse down to the barn, son," Abel said. "Cool him out and grain him. There's a good lad."

I heard the screen door bang as the boy left the house. Abel disappeared into the kitchen and returned with a bottle and two glasses. He placed the glasses on a side table and filled each one half full. "I'm obliged," I said, "but I have to tell you, I never cared for whiskey all that much."

Abel nodded at the glasses. "Maybe you never had the right whiskey," he said. "This is single malt Scotch, and it's two years older than Keith." He raised his glass in salute and took a sip. I lifted my glass and did the same. The whiskey went down smooth as silk, warming my belly and straightening out the kinks. It had a faint smoky taste, and it helped prepare me to deliver my bad news. I took a deep breath.

"Raiders struck your camps at sunup this morning," I said. "Loco John is dead, and so are his horse and dog. The raiders killed and scattered your sheep. I don't know yet how many are dead. They burned John's wagon, too—all that's left is ashes and the iron tires.

"Afterward, they hit Haggis, but he heard them coming and took up a position in the trees above his camp. The raiders shot and clubbed the sheep in his band. They shot up his wagon. Haggis fought 'em until they rode out, but the raiders managed to put a bullet through his thigh.

"I asked him if he wanted to come out with me, but he said no, he'd stay there and gather the sheep that are still alive. He's a good man."

Abel was silent for a moment. Then he asked, "Did he recognize any of the riders?"

"No. He said they wore masks. Feed sacks, with eye holes cut out."

"Doesn't matter. We know they were Circle R riders—Zack Rainford's men."

I was suddenly tired of all the finger-pointing and hate. "We *don't* know that," I said. "You *think* you do, and you may well be right. But you weren't there. You don't *know*."

Abel's mouth was a grim, hard line. "You're a lawman," he said. "You rely on evidence—on confessions, witnesses, and such. I don't need to. I've known Zack Rainford for over twenty years, and I know he ordered those raids to get at me."

I finished my whiskey and set the glass down on the side table. "And I'm saying again, you *don't* know," I said. "But you're right, I am a lawman. Tomorrow, I'll tell the county sheriff what I just told you. I'll take him and maybe the coroner back up on the mountain with me, and we'll look for evidence. We'll question Haggis, take his statement. We'll bring John's body back down.

"What I *won't* do is jump to conclusions. And I won't tolerate anyone takin' the law into his own hands. No strikin' back. No gettin' even. No durned eye for an eye and tooth for a tooth. All that ends here, Abel. Do you understand me?"

"Aye. I understand well enough. It's you who don't understand, Merlin. Sheriff Ross Friendly is

Zack Rainford's man, bought and paid for. It's likely he knows all about the raids and that he knew about them before they happened. Hell, he may have been one of the masked raiders himself!

"Vendetta Canyon is open range. I have as much right to run sheep up there as Rainford has to run cattle. And I have a right to defend my men and my property, any way I have to."

"Not if you go outside the law," I said. "If you break the law, you come against me. Don't make me arrest you."

Abel's face was flushed, and it wasn't from the whiskey. His voice was tight, and his eyes glittered like blue ice. I listened as his breathing slowed; watched as he relaxed and unclenched his fists.

When he spoke again, he seemed to have taken hold of himself. "I appreciate you comin' to tell me about John and Haggis," he said. "I respect your position, and I admire straight talk in a man. All right, I'll give you a chance to deal with the situation your way. I'll hold off—for *now*."

Abel's wife Teresa appeared in the kitchen doorway. She wore the blue-checked apron I remembered, and her straight, dark hair shone in the lamplight. She smiled, and I stood up, my hat in my hand. "It's good to see you again, Merlin," she said. "Are you gentlemen ready for supper now?"

Abel raised an eyebrow. "*Are* we?"

I grinned, and we were friends again. "I am if *you* are," I said.

• • •

A stranger, watching as we shared supper that evening, would not have suspected there was anything amiss in our lives. By unspoken agreement, we said nothing about the raids on the camps and the losses in human and animal life that had been the result.

Teresa seemed to sense that *something* was wrong. She cast an anxious glance at Abel as we sat down at the table, searching her husband's face for information, but he was a book that declined to be read. He would tell her later, I knew, when they were alone, but he chose not to discuss it until then.

We spoke of ordinary, trivial things. Ian was not at home; he had gone to Reata for supplies. Ten-year-old Keith had seen a black bear that afternoon in a serviceberry patch down by the creek. The McKenzie daughter, fifteen-year-old Ginger, informed us of the arrival of a new litter of sheepdog puppies. Abel spoke of the weather, and of wool prices. I complimented Teresa on an excellent meal.

I spent the night in a borrowed bedroll down at the bunkhouse, where I slept but little and was up and dressed well before sunup. When I stepped into the barn, I found Rutherford none the worse for wear and eager to go, despite the hard way I had used him the day before. Sweat had matted his hair, and I combed and brushed him by lantern light until he shone like a new penny. Then I saddled him, blew out the lantern, and led the buckskin out under the stars.

To the north, the Big Dipper lay at an angle just above the far mountains. Stars glittered overhead, unconcerned about range wars and human plans. I breathed in the cold air, swung into the saddle, and set Rutherford out on the road to Reata.

Sheriff Friendly wasn't hard to find. When I rode up to the courthouse that morning, I found him standing on the building's front steps, entertaining a couple of local cowhands. I didn't know either of the men by name, but I remembered seeing them at the Longhorn with riders from the Circle R. The sheriff was apparently telling some kind of humorous story. He gestured and grinned in a comic manner, swinging his arms and rolling his eyes, keeping the men laughing.

Dismounting, I loose-tied Rutherford to the hitch rail and started up the steps toward the men. Looking past the cowhands, the sheriff saw me and his face changed. His grin faded, and he frowned as though he smelled something bad. Sheriff Ross Friendly was not happy to see me.

Seeing Ross's face, the men stopped laughing and turned to see what he was looking at. It was clear they recognized me. Like Ross, their expressions changed from good-natured to hostile. I kept coming, and they stepped aside.

"Fanshaw," Ross said. "What can I do for you, deputy?"

"I need to talk to you, sheriff."

"Later. As you can see, I'm talkin' to *these* fellers at present."

"And I don't mean to bust in. But it's important. I need to talk to you now."

The sheriff's jaw jutted out like a bulldog's. His face grew flushed, and his voice took on a hard edge. "I don't guess you heard me, deputy . . . I said *later*."

I stood my ground. "*Now*, sheriff," I said.

The cowhands turned away, looking back over their shoulders. It was easy to see I wasn't the most popular man in Reata right then. I didn't much care.

Ross's face went from red to purple. His eyes flashed, and his voice shook. "All right, god-dammit!" he said. "Come on . . . we'll talk in my office!"

Inside, Ross led the way along the corridor, his boot heels pounding the floor as if he was trying to tromp holes in it. When we strode through the doorway of his office, Ross's lanky deputy looked startled and dropped the dime novel he'd been reading as though it was on fire. Ross marched to his desk and stood behind it. "Now," he snapped, "what's so goddam important that it couldn't wait?"

"I just came down from Vendetta Canyon," I

said. "Night riders raided McKenzie's sheep camps at sunup yesterday."

Bob slumped into his swivel chair like a sack of oats dropped from a freight wagon. "Is *that* all?" he snorted. "Hell, them raids been goin' on for a week or more! Some of the boys are just hoorawin' them snoozers. Can't say as I blame 'em!"

I had not come to make things easy for Ross Friendly. I said, "Difference is a man got *killed* this time. Raiders gunned down Loco John, his horse, and his dog. Burned his wagon, and clubbed and shot his sheep. Then they hit Haggis McRae's camp, but Haggis managed to fight 'em off. Even so, they shot up his wagon and put a bullet through his thigh. They killed sheep from *his* band, too."

Ross's deputy looked nervous. He flashed a sideways glance in his boss's direction and seemed to hold his breath. Ross's frown deepened, but he didn't move. I waited for his reply.

When it came, it came late. "Why," Ross said, "that is a hell of a note. If what you're sayin' is true, somebody is guilty of some serious crimes."

"Like murder, assault with a deadly weapon, willful destruction of private property, and arson," I said.

Ross tapped his fingers on his desktop. He shook his head, his expression somber. "You did right to come tell me about this, deputy," he said. "I'll need to ride up there and look into the matter."

"I'll go with you," I said. "I expect we'll want the county coroner, too."

"Yes," Ross said. "I'll fetch him. How soon can you be ready to go?"

"Soon as I can saddle a fresh horse."

Ross got to his feet. He fished his watch out of his vest pocket and snapped open its cover. "How about if we meet back here in an hour?"

"I'll be here."

I found Cal Peabody seated on a bench in front of his livery barn, whittling on a piece of pine with a jackknife. I rode Rutherford up to him and drew rein. Cal and me had acquired an easy way with each other since our first meeting. He looked up, his eyes shaded against the sun, and said, "I thought you were up on the mountain."

"No," I replied. "I'm right here in front of you."

Cal shrugged. "I'll take your word for it. What can I do for you?"

I dismounted. "I need another horse," I said. "I've about wore this one out."

"So it appears. What happened to the camp outfit and the packhorse I loaned you?"

"I left 'em up on the mountain. *Lost* the durn packhorse, I'm sorry to say."

Cal shrugged. "He always *was* pretty lost," he said. "If you find him, fetch him on back."

Cal seemed to sense there was more to the story. He waited, studying my face. I met his gaze.

"There was some trouble up there," I said. "Masked riders raided both McKenzie sheep camps yesterday. Shot and clubbed sheep. Burned a wagon. Loco John is dead. Haggis McRae's been wounded. I'm ridin' back up today with the sheriff and the coroner."

"If you can find another *horse*," Cal said. "One that ain't played out or lost."

"That about sums it up."

Cal closed his jackknife and stood up. "Well," he said. "I do have a sorrel mare out back. She tends to be a camp staller of sorts, but a touch of the spur usually gets her attention. Would you ride a mare?"

"I'd ride a nanny goat if that's all you had. I need to get back up the mountain."

Cal looked thoughtful. "Wish I *did* have a nanny goat. I'd like to see you a-settin' tall in the saddle."

Together, we walked out back, and I cinched my rig on the mare. She was a touch whey-bellied, but she seemed steady and calm and she had a deep chest and good legs. A quick glance at the other horses in the corral told me Cal had given me the best he had.

"Much obliged, until you're better paid," I said. "With luck, I'll bring her back in one piece and maybe the packhorse, too."

"I'll see you then," Cal said. Again, he assumed a thoughtful look. "About that letter I sent with you last time . . ."

"I delivered it. Seemed to make the recipient mighty happy."

Cal nodded. He was silent while I untracked the mare and stepped up into the saddle. As I turned her away, Cal chuckled and said softly, "We sure are an unlikely pair of cupids, ain't we, Merlin?"

I couldn't argue with that.

Sixteen

▼

THE SCENE OF THE CRIME

The sorrel mare gave me to understand she would just as soon remain in town as carry me up a mountain, but I touched her with my spurs to remind her she was the horse and I was the rider. With a great sigh, she set her own wishes aside and protested no further.

I had not eaten since the previous evening, and my belly was doing a little protesting of its own. I pulled up in front of the Uptown Café and tied my female companion to the hitch rack out front. Inside, I took on a double order of ham, eggs, and biscuits and left feeling like a bull snake that swallowed a rabbit.

When I arrived at the courthouse, I found Sheriff Ross Friendly dressed for the trail in shotgun chaps and sporting a red silk bandana the size of a bath towel. A handful of curious onlookers provided an audience, and the sheriff was in rare form that morning. He played to the crowd, giving his hapless deputy orders and strutting around big as all outdoors and twice as windy. The deputy (who I learned went by the name of String Bean) had hitched a pair of bay work horses to a farm wagon and was busy loading bed rolls, a chuck box, and some tarpaulins and tools when I rode up.

Sheriff Ross saw me coming and swelled up like a bullfrog. "There you are," he said. "Good thing you got here on time. We're about ready to ride out."

"Good thing I waited for you then," I said. "Where's the coroner?"

Ross nodded toward the Sanchez Mercantile across the street. "That's him now," he said.

I turned in the saddle as a townsman in a black broadcloth suit and top hat walked up. He carried an overcoat and a small case like a medical bag, and he was nearly as tall and gangly as String Bean. He seemed pleasant enough, but his eyes were hidden behind dark-colored spectacles, and his skin was as pale as the moon.

"This here's Leviticus Glick, county coroner and owner of the local mortuary," Ross said. "Leviticus, say hello to Merlin Fanshaw. Fanshaw is a U.S. deputy under Chance Ridgeway. He's the one who found the body."

Glick walked up to where I sat my saddle atop the sorrel mare and looked up. He held out his hand, and we shook. "It's a pleasure to meet you, deputy," he said. "Ross has told me much about you."

"I'll bet he has," I said. "Good to meet you, too, Leviticus."

String Bean climbed into the wagon seat and took the reins. He reached down and helped the coroner up beside him. Then I heard hoofbeats from beyond the wagon and here came Sheriff Ross, astraddle of a blocky piebald gelding that seemed to have more colors than a calico cat. "Let's go, boys," he said. "We're burnin' daylight."

We lined out along the road to McKenzie's like a sad parade, with Sheriff Ross Friendly leading the way. String Bean and Leviticus Glick followed in the wagon, and I brought up the rear.

Now, I have to confess I liked it that way. I had no wish to spend the day riding side by side with the sheriff of Meriwether County. Our previous conversations had produced more heat than light, and they tended to leave me grouchy and depressed. Besides, I needed time to sort out my thoughts.

I had told no one about my encounter with Griff Tallon on the night before the raids. The mysterious bounty hunter handcuffed me to a tree that night—in order to keep me away from the attacks on the camps, he said. He said he did so to protect me and to make amends because he had fired on me by mistake back at the rockslide. Just before he left me, he said, "I did what I came to do. We're even now."

I wondered: Could I have made a difference if I'd been with Loco John and Haggis? There was no way to know. You can bet I'd have tried, but whether I'd have been successful or not was anyone's guess. Ridgeway sent me to head off a sheep and cattle war, but now the war had begun. Stopping it would not be easy, I thought, and it might not even be possible.

Whatever the reasons, I had failed in my assignment. Fate and hate had dealt the cards, and I had come up with what appeared to be a losing hand. My thoughts were bringing me no peace of mind. I might as well have rode up front with Ross.

It was a quarter to three when we turned off the road and onto the bridge that led to the McKenzie ranch. At the house, Abel's old sheep dog Rascal struggled to his feet and barked half-heartedly to announce our coming. Having fulfilled his obligation as watch dog, at least in his own estimation, he then sat down beside the gate and watched us turn up toward the house.

Al Wilson, one of Abel's two hired guns, stepped out from behind the house and walked to the gate. He carried a Winchester carbine and wore a Colt's Peacemaker on his hip. Sheriff Ross drew rein and puffed himself up, to look imposing, I suppose.

"Howdy, boys," Wilson said. "I work for the McKenzies. Can I help you fellers?"

I spoke first. "Howdy, Al," I said. "I'm Merlin Fanshaw. You remember me; I'm a friend of Abel's and Ian's. Are they at home?"

Wilson took a second look and recognized me. "Yeah," he said. "I remember you. You're a deputy marshal, ain't you?"

"Like I said, I'm a friend of the McKenzies."

"They ain't here."

The screen door opened, and Teresa McKenzie stepped outside. Ten-year-old Keith, her youngest boy, stood just behind her in the doorway, looking grown up and serious. The sun was low in the sky, and Teresa shaded her eyes with her hand against its brightness. "Mr. Wilson is right," she said. "Abel and Ian have gone up to our camps on the mountain."

She turned toward Ross Friendly, and her face seemed to harden. She nodded, taking in the deputy and the coroner in the wagon. "You've heard, apparently. We had some trouble up there yesterday . . ." Her voice faded, and she added, "Sheriff." The way she said the word made it clear she was no friend of his.

Ross didn't meet her eyes. Instead, he shifted in his saddle and looked at the ground. "Yes'm," he said. "We're headed up there to investigate the matter."

Teresa looked at the coroner. When she spoke

again, her voice was thick with sarcasm. "And to bring our herder's body down. I know it will be a comfort to his soul just knowing Sheriff Friendly is on the job."

She looked at me then, and her smile was warm and honest. "I'm glad you're going with these men, Merlin. Abel and Ian will be glad to see you."

Turning to go back into the house, Teresa stopped briefly at the open door. "Good afternoon, gentlemen," she said, and went inside. Keith stood for a moment, watching us. Then he turned and followed his mother, closing the door behind him.

Wilson cradled the Winchester in the crook of his arm and nodded toward the rising mountains above the ranch. "The road lies yonder," he said. "I reckon you know the way."

"Yes," I said. "I reckon we do."

When we reached the clearing where I'd camped the night before the raid, I picked up the bed roll, panniers, and pack saddle I'd borrowed from Cal Peabody and loaded them into the wagon. Sheriff Ross grumbled some about having to stop for my camp outfit, but I ignored him. As much as he pretended to be the leader of our expedition, he depended on me to take him to the site of the raid and to Loco John's body. When push came to shove, he was following me instead of the other way around, and we both knew it.

All through that afternoon, I kept an eye out for the pack horse Tallon had driven off, but saw no sign of it. As the sun dropped toward the edge of the world, I gave up the search and turned my attention back to the road.

Daylight was fading fast by the time we reached the switchbacks that led down to Red Rock Springs. I left my chosen place at the rear of our procession to join Ross at its head, while String Bean eased the wagon down the rocky trail behind us. Below, in the valley, a campfire burned bravely in the gathering gloom. On the broad meadow where Abel and Ian had made their camp the week before, a wagon stood beside a wall tent. In the high grass, a work team and two saddle horses grazed.

Approaching the meadow, I rode out ahead of the others and drew rein. "Hello, the camp," I called. "It's me, Merlin. All right to ride in?"

Abel McKenzie stepped out of the shadows beside the parked wagon, his Winchester at the ready. Ian stood behind him, also holding a rifle. "Aye, come ahead," Abel said. "Who's that behind you?"

I turned in my saddle, looking back. "That's Ross Friendly on the patch-work plow horse," I said. "His deputy and Leviticus Glick are in the wagon. I told you we'd be comin' up."

Anger twisted Abel's face. "You told me. And I told *you* I don't need that two-bit peace officer *or* the coroner."

"Ross Friendly is the county sheriff. This is a matter for the law, Abel."

"The law? In this county, the law belongs to my enemies. The law belongs to Zack Rainford. The damn *law* can go to hell!"

"*I'm* the law, and I don't belong to anybody. As for Ross, he has a job to do, whether you like him or not."

Ian placed his hand on his father's shoulder. "Dad," he said. "We can't set things right by doing wrong. Tell them they can come in."

Abel frowned. Red-faced and tense, he gave me a stubborn glare. Then he let his breath go out in a long sigh. His shoulders slumped as he turned away. "You tell 'em," he told Ian. "I can't right now, but you do it."

Ian walked out to where Ross, String Bean, and Leviticus waited with the wagon, and invited them to come in to camp. He offered them beans and coffee and told them they could roll out their blankets near the wall tent. Meanwhile, Abel walked away into the darkness, and I went with him.

"It's not my way to be less than hospitable," he said, "but Ross Friendly has proved he's the cowman's friend too many times for me to trust him. Hell, he might even have been *in* on the raid!"

"You don't know that," I said. "As sheriff, Ross is here to investigate John's death. That's all."

"Maybe he's just here to go through the motions.

Maybe he already *knew* about John's death. Maybe he was *with* those masked sons o' bitches when they killed John!"

Abel stopped walking. We were out in the high grass of the meadow where the picketed horses grazed. Behind us, Ian and the others hunkered around the campfire.

"There's too many 'maybes' in your thinkin'," I said. "A man needs to deal with what he knows, not what he suspects."

"By god, you are plain spoken," Abel said. "All right. I'll put a check rein on my temper while they're here . . . but make no mistake, I'm mad as hell about all this!"

"I'll be plainer spoken still," I said. "I figure you're also mad at yourself."

Abel spun around to face me. "At myself?" he said. "Why would I be mad at myself?"

"You moved your sheep and your men up here in spite of the warnings. You put a chip on your shoulder and dared the cowmen to knock it off. Well, they took your dare. Now the chip's on the ground, and the fat's in the fire."

"Damn it, Merlin—I had every *right* to move my sheep up here! I have a right to defend myself, too!"

I spoke plainly once again. "Before you got stubborn about your rights," I said, "Loco John was alive."

The silence between us was sudden, and cold.

Instantly sorry, I caught my breath. "I . . . I'm sorry, Abel," I said. "I didn't mean that."

Abel shook his head. My words had hurt him, but he waved my apology away. "No," he said. "You're right. It was my pride that got John killed and Haggis wounded. I knew the danger, but I pushed ahead anyway."

He turned to me, and his face was close in the darkness. "But I didn't break the law," he said. "I didn't club my sheep or burn my wagon. And it wasn't *my* bullet that killed John."

"You're right, Abel. Forget what I said, if you can."

It was too dark to see his smile, but I could hear it in his voice. "Forget what?" he said.

Abel and Ian slept inside their tent that night, while Ross, String Bean, Leviticus, and I made our beds out under the stars. Beneath us, the land seemed to sleep as well, as a soft breeze sighed through the pines and drifted across the meadow. Overhead, stars crowded the sky, appearing close enough to touch. Thoughts of the feud between Abel McKenzie and Zack Rainford busied my mind and kept me awake long after the others fell asleep.

My friend Orville Mooney once remarked that sleep is like a woman. "Pursue her and she'll run from you," he said. "Turn away, and nine times out of ten, she'll come your way."

I don't know whether that's really true of sleep

or not. I remember thinking I had enough on my mind without worrying about falling asleep. I don't recall what else I thought, because about then is when I dozed off. I didn't wake up until sunup.

Morning dawned cloudy and overcast, with a hint of rain in the air. Low-hanging clouds drifted like smoke through the pines and hid the mountain peaks. The cold air found its way through my shirt and jacket and chilled me to the bone. It must have been the same with the others because I heard teeth a-chattering and saw men drawing as close as they could to the cook fire.

Abel and Ian served up a breakfast of venison stew, biscuits, and coffee, which helped us all to begin the day on a friendly note. However, I did notice that the sheriff and Abel didn't have much to say to each other. Instead, they walked watchful and stiff-legged around each other, like town dogs in a strange neighborhood.

Afterward, we rode up the trail up to where Loco John's camp had stood. The death smell was heavy as we broke out of the trees and onto the bench. Ravens and magpies flew up as we approached, then settled back upon the burned and swollen carcass of John's saddle horse. Other birds fed on more than a score of dead sheep that lay scattered across the slope.

The remains of the sheepwagon lay in a jumble

of charred wood, ashes, and iron. I stepped down onto the scorched earth and showed Ross where I'd found John's body. Then, with Ian's help, I removed the rocks I placed over the corpse and stood back.

"I found him there," I said, pointing, "not far from his wagon. He'd been shot point blank in the chest. I carried his body away from the fire and covered him with these rocks."

Ross held his fancy bandana over his nose and mouth and turned away. I couldn't blame him. John's appearance hadn't improved any since I saw him last, and the stench of death was strong. It didn't seem to bother the coroner, though. Leviticus dropped to one knee and examined the body. "Yes," he said. "Cause of death was apparently a gunshot to the heart. Large caliber bullet. I'd say forty-five or forty-four."

I showed them the single-shot rifle I'd found beside his body. "It looked like he was tryin' to fight back against his murderers with this," I said. "He was out-gunned and outmatched."

Ross cleared his throat and squinted. "Now you don't know he was murdered," he said. "You weren't here when it happened. Maybe somebody had to shoot him in self-defense. Hell, maybe he shot himself."

Abel had been standing near me, his face tight as he looked at the body of his herder. I had to give him credit; he had been as good as his word. He'd tried hard to control his temper and to hide his dislike of Ross Friendly. But the sheriff's words were too much. Abel looked at him as though he couldn't believe his ears, and exploded.

"And *maybe* he died of old age or the goddam German *measles*," he said, "but I *doubt* it!"

Abel was red-faced and so mad he trembled like a tuning fork. I don't know what would have happened if Ross hadn't backed off some, but as luck would have it, he did.

"I . . . all I'm sayin' is . . . we don't know what happened for sure," he said. "There were no witnesses."

Abel choked but held onto his self control. "We probably could find ten or *twenty* witnesses in the Circle R bunkhouse," he said, "but I doubt if they'd be all that much help."

I stepped between the two men. "All right," I said. "That's enough. Let's get John's body down to the funeral parlor in town. Leviticus can call a coroner's inquest and determine the official cause of death."

We wrapped the body in a canvas tarp and lifted it into the wagon. I walked the ground with the sheriff, pointing out the horse tracks and the bludgeoned sheep. We even found a bloody, broken axe handle in the grass away from the burned area.

Later, we found Haggis. The big Scot had combined the remaining sheep from his band and John's into one and was holding them on water at

Vendetta Creek. He walked with a limp, but he assured me his bullet wound was healing nicely. Ross questioned him about the raid, and Haggis was straightforward and direct. He related the story as he'd told it to me, and the sheriff made a few notes. Abel and Ian started back down to their camp, and Ross, String Bean, and Leviticus moved out for Reata.

I spent another hour or two with Abel and Ian and then rode the sorrel mare out on the trail back to town. Other than that, the day was unremarkable, except . . .

As I approached the clearing where I'd camped the night before the raid, I saw a horse on the ridge ahead, silhouetted against the sky. Drawing nearer, I saw that it was tied to a tree by the side of the trail, as if someone had left it for me to find.

It was the gray pack horse Cal Peabody loaned me—the same one Griff Tallon drove off the morning of the raid!

SEVENTEEN
▼

WHAT THE DOCTOR ORDERED

Back in Reata, I helped Leviticus Glick deliver the corpse of Loco John to the funeral parlor and bade a grateful good-bye to Ross. I say *grateful* because I was happy indeed to be free of the man's company. Reluctantly, Ross agreed to meet with me again after Leviticus completed his examination of the body. He said he would attend a coroner's inquest when one was called, but he didn't say he was looking forward to it.

Ross seemed irked at John for getting himself killed, and annoyed with me for reporting the killing. I figure he was caught between the demands of his office and his need to curry favor with the cattle interests. Straddling a fence has to be uncomfortable at best.

I returned the borrowed gray pack horse, camp outfit, and bedroll to Cal Peabody and turned in the sorrel mare. I said nothing about how I found the missing gray, mainly because I didn't understand all I knew about it myself.

The gray had been tied to a low-hanging branch beside the trail, where I'd be sure to find it as I rode back down the mountain. As to *who* tied it there, I had no idea. I thought Haggis might have found the horse while he was rounding up the scattered sheep, but he had said nothing about it when I spoke to him. Neither had Abel or Ian, and I was sure they would have if either of them had found the animal. By process of elimination, I had a pretty fair idea who *hadn't* done it, but no real notion who *had*.

Except that Griff Tallon, the mysterious stock detective, kept coming to mind. The bounty hunter had handcuffed me to a tree to save my life because, he said, he had mistakenly tried to *take* my life. He had driven off my buckskin and the gray to make sure I couldn't reach the scene of the raid on McKenzie's camps.

Maybe, I thought, his strange sense of honor led him to bring back the missing gray. It wasn't much of a theory, but it was the only one I had.

The raids and the killing of Loco John were the talk of the town. The local newspaper, after the manner of small-town papers everywhere, published the story on its front page after everybody in Reata had already heard about it. Men stood shoulder to shoulder at the bars in the saloons, expounding on the Vendetta Canyon raids and arguing their own points of view. At the barber shop, gents who came in for a shave and a haircut engaged the proprietor in hot debate. And wherever I walked in town, curious eyes followed.

I checked back into the hotel that evening and took my personal gatherings up to my room. Once there, I put pen to paper and wrote a three-page report to my boss, U.S. Marshal Chance Ridgeway. I described the events that had occurred since my last report and assured him that I had the situation well in hand. I remember reading back over what I'd written and wishing I was as sure of myself as I sounded.

Of course, I did leave out a few things. For example, I made no mention of getting myself shackled to a tree on the night of the raid, and I sort of neglected to tell him how Cal Peabody and me were playing cupid to the cattleman's daughter and the sheepman's son. I was not exactly an old hand at the peace officer trade, but one of the first things I'd learned as a deputy was that a good report doesn't have to include *everything*.

When I finished my letter, I took it down and left it with the desk clerk to be sent out with the morning mail. I planned to have my supper in the hotel dining room and then look Doc Reynolds up. I knew Doc would be eager to hear the news from the horse's mouth, so to speak. I also knew he would—as always—be a good source of local news and gossip.

The dining room was nearly empty when I walked in. The waiter was a youth named Harold, and he seemed as glad to see me as if I was his rich uncle. A minute after he showed me to a table, I knew why.

"Deputy Fanshaw," he said, "it's good to see you again, sir—mighty good!" He handed me the bill of fare and stood by. "Exciting days in Meriwether County," he said. "I expect you're mighty busy investigating the killing and all."

"Some," I said. "We're waiting for the coroner's jury."

"What was it like up there on the mountain? That sheepherder . . . all those dead sheep . . . it must have been terrible!"

"Uh, yeah. I believe I'll have me a T-bone steak this evenin', and some fried spuds. You can bring me . . ."

"I heard night riders killed his horse, too . . . and his dog!"

"A cup of coffee, black. And a slice of pie. Apple, if you have it."

"Is it true they burned his wagon, too?"

I shoved the bill of fare into his hands and looked him in the eye. "Harold," I said. "I tend to get mean and cranky when I'm hungry. Killed a waiter down in Cheyenne because he was slow gettin' my order to me. I'd hate for that to happen again."

His laugh was a kind of nervous chuckle, like he figured I was joking but wasn't altogether sure. He shuffled in place for a pace or two and then made a bee-line for the kitchen.

Twenty minutes later, he brought my order and left me alone with it. I cleaned up the steak, spuds, and pie, paid my bill, and walked out onto the street.

The Longhorn Saloon was doing good business when I walked in that night. A dozen men—ranch hands, teamsters, and townsmen—lined the cherry wood bar.

Near the stove, a slick-haired gent in shirtsleeves pounded out melodies on a piano that I first believed was seriously out of tune. After listening to the man play for a while, I changed my mind. The piano wasn't out of tune; *he* was.

Another six men bucked the tiger over at the Faro table, while dance hall girls watched the play like wolves above a water hole. They glanced up as I walked to the bar, but I tipped my hat and passed them by.

Catching the barkeep's eye, I asked, "Doc Reynolds been in tonight?"

"Haven't seen him," the bartender said. "I expect he's over at his house."

"I need to pay him a call," I said. "Give me a bottle of that brandy he drinks."

The bartender produced a dusty bottle from the back bar and placed it before me. "Three dollars," he said. "You sick or somethin'?"

"No," I said. "Just payin' him a visit."

The barkeep nodded. "Like the two Irishmen I heard about," he said. "Pat and Mike, their names were. Seems Pat asked Mike to come see his new cabin, and Mike said sure, he would. 'That's foine,' says Pat, 'Me cabin is the last house on the street. Just walk right up and ring the doorbell . . . with your nose.'

" 'Ring the doorbell with me *nose*?' says Mike. 'And why would I do such a fool thing as that?'

" 'Why, surely you're not comin' *empty-handed*,' says Pat."

I took the brandy and headed for the door. "That's a good one," I said, but it wasn't.

Lamplight shone from inside Doc Reynolds' house as I turned in at his gate and made my way up to his front door. I rang the doorbell (though not with my nose!) and waited. A moment later, I heard footsteps inside and the sound of the latch being thrown. The door opened a crack, and then wider as Doc recognized me. Beware, his dog, pushed his way to the forefront, growling and slobbering and wagging his tail. Covering all the bases, I suppose.

"Evenin', Doc," I said, showing him the brandy. "I come bearing gifts."

"Gifts are always welcome," he said. "So are you. Come in."

I hung my hat on a peg inside the door and waited while Beware sniffed my boots and my crotch, after the manner of dogs everywhere. Apparently, I passed inspection; the dog gave me two lazy wags in recognition and ambled off to follow his master.

"If that dog's eyesight gets any worse, you're going to have to buy him some spectacles," I said.

"Beware has long since ceased to earn his keep," Doc replied, "but he still goes through the motions. He pretends he's a watch dog, and I pretend I don't know how old and worthless he is. It's a symbiotic relationship."

Doc showed me to a chair in his sitting room and fetched a pair of brandy glasses from the kitchen.

Uncorking the bottle, he poured two fingers of brandy into each glass and sat down in a wing chair across from me.

"I guess you've heard the news about the raid on McKenzie's sheep camps," I began.

"Indeed," Doc said. "The killing of Loco John is particularly unfortunate."

"I expect Loco John would agree with you."

Doc swirled the brandy in his glass about and inhaled the vapors. "You were there?"

"Just after the raid. Seventy-five, maybe a hundred sheep were dead. So were John's horse and dog. His wagon was burning, and I found John himself face down in the ashes of a grass fire. He'd been shot through the heart."

Doc nodded. "What about the other herder, Haggis McRae?"

"Raiders hit his camp, too, but Haggis managed to fight them off. He took a bullet through the thigh, but he doctored himself. He's stayin' up on the mountain with his sheep and John's."

I took a sip of the brandy Doc poured me, felt it warm me all the way to my vitals. I said, "We brought John's body back to town today. The coroner plans to convene an inquiry. I expect you'll be hearing from him."

"I may be jumping to conclusions," Doc said, "but in my expert opinion, being shot through the heart just might be the cause of death."

Doc looked owlishly at me over the top of his

glasses. "How is Abel McKenzie taking all this?" he asked.

"He blames Zack Rainford but says he won't strike back . . . at least not yet."

Doc shook his head, a slight smile on his lips. "Abel and Zack. Once the best of friends, now deadly enemies."

Sprawled on his side at Doc's feet, Beware's legs jerked fitfully, as if chasing rabbits in a dream. Doc finished his brandy and then reached for the bottle to refill his glass. "Did I ever tell you how they came to *be* enemies?" he asked.

I held my breath. Doc was about to tell me exactly what I hoped to learn. I shrugged. "I don't believe so," I said. "How did they?"

"The answer to that goes back nearly twenty-five years," Doc said. "Montana was mostly Indian country then. Except for a few trappers and traders, about the only white men here were prospectors, hoping to strike it rich. They lived in rough camps like Bannack and Virginia City, and they were a single-minded bunch. They had neither the time nor inclination to do much more than work their claims, and they paid for what they needed in nuggets and dust.

"Of course, the main thing they needed was food. Flour and salt, bacon and beans, potatoes and pork all came in by freight wagon from Fort Benton on the Missouri and up from Salt Lake over South Pass. The country was rich with game, but the gold-seekers had little time to hunt. Meat in the camps was scarce and costly.

"A few men saw their opportunity. Granville Stuart brought in some lame oxen from Idaho, fattened them on the good Montana grass, and sold them as beef to the miners. Nelson Story brought a herd of longhorns up the trail from Texas. As the territory grew, other cattlemen came. One of those cattlemen was Zeb Rainford.

"Zeb moved his operation here to what was to become Meriwether County, and prospered. The town grew up to serve his Circle R ranch and the other outfits that followed. Zeb and a partner opened the Cattlemen's Bank, and then the hotel. The railroad came. Santiago Sanchez opened his mercantile here. Ran it until he passed away two years ago."

Doc fell silent. He sipped his brandy, and seemed to be gathering his thoughts. At last, he placed his glass on the table between us and continued his account.

"Zeb had a son, Zack, when he came into this country, and Zack was truly his father's son. He grew up knowing cattle and horses, and he soon became a good judge of men.

"Abel McKenzie was eighteen years old, one year younger than Zack, and a top hand. Old Zeb hired him, and Abel and Zack became friends. They rode broncs and worked cattle together, they drank and raised hell together in the saloons and gambling halls, and they led the young ladies of the county on a merry chase.

"They made everything they did a contest. They were friends, and they were competitors. They were like brothers, and they were rivals. In the end, that quality is what ended their friendship."

"A woman?" I guessed.

Doc nodded. "A beautiful and enchanting woman. Teresa, eldest daughter of the late Santiago Sanchez. You've met her, I believe."

I sat bolt upright in my chair. "Teresa . . . Teresa *McKenzie*?"

Doc smiled, pleased by my surprise. "The same. Teresa was something quite apart from the others. Both Abel and Zack ardently courted the lady. In the end, she chose Abel.

"Abel and Teresa eloped and were married by a priest at Fort Owen. Zack never forgave them."

Doc swallowed the last of the brandy in his glass and looked up. "Abel quit the Circle R—or was fired, no one seems to know for certain. That same year, Teresa's father offered to back his new son-in-law in the sheep business, and a feud began.

"Ian was born the following summer. Ginger and Keith followed at five-year intervals. I delivered all three."

"What about Zack?" I asked.

"Old Zeb passed away later that same year. Zack turned his back on his wild ways and set about managing the Circle R. He met his wife Melissa in

Chicago while on a business trip. She came back here with him, and he built her that grandiose mansion they call home."

"And Morgan?"

"The lovely Morgan was born eight months later. I delivered her right there in that house. She had a few of the local gossips counting on their fingers."

I grinned. "Nothing worse than a gossip," I said.

Doc took my meaning but chose to ignore me. Blushing, he said, "Well, there may be a *few* things worse."

Back in my room at the hotel, I thought about Ian and Morgan and their troubled romance. When I was a kid, back in Dry Creek, a preacher gave a fire-and-brimstone sermon one night at a camp meeting. He commenced to work up a sweat, thumping the pulpit and preaching in a loud voice about sin. It seemed he was pretty much *against* it.

Well, that gospel-sharp scared hell out of me, which I suppose was pretty much the whole idea. He commenced to read from the scriptures about how the Almighty was going to visit the sins of the fathers on their children unto the third and fourth generation, and like I say, it spooked me some. I knew some of the things my pa had done, and I sure wasn't looking forward to sharing his punishment.

Of course, I didn't understand those scriptures at the time—I'm not sure I do now—but I have come to see how a father's sins *can* affect his children, and how those children sometimes do have to pay a penalty.

It seemed to me that Ian McKenzie and Morgan Rainford fit that picture, and they sure had my sympathy. Caught between their love for each other and their loyalty to their parents, they were locked in a situation that could only cause them pain.

Looking back on it, I guess I became a lawman in the first place because I saw things that were wrong and I wanted to help make them right. What I didn't know then was how *many* wrong things I'd see once I became a peace officer and how *little* I'd be able to do to make them right.

My boss, U.S. Marshal Chance Ridgeway, would tell me not to get involved with the people but to simply investigate and enforce the law. The law, he'd say, will make things right. Ridgeway had little use for emotion in connection with the job, and no use at all for indulging in sympathy for either victim or lawbreaker. If the law said people should fly, Ridgeway would simply arrest everyone who couldn't get off the ground. "Feelin's can confuse a man," he told me once. "Society don't need confused peace officers."

He was right, of course, or mostly right, anyway. In the morning, I would saddle Rutherford and ride out to the Circle R. I would confront Zack Rainford and bring the power of the law to bear on the growing trouble. I would forget about Ian and Morgan and their romantic problems. I would set my feelings aside and simply represent the law.

That's what I'd do, all right.

Sure it was.

Eighteen
▼
Official Business

Morning dawned cold and moody. Storm clouds scowled above the town and hid the rising sun behind a blanket of gray. I stood at the window of my hotel room, looking down at the windblown street, and let my thoughts ride ahead of me to the Circle R and my meeting with Zack Rainford.

Rainford would not be glad to see me. He had made it clear on my previous visit that he had nothing further to say to me about rustlers, range detectives, or his feud with Abel McKenzie. I was neither welcome nor wanted at his ranch. Still, he would be expecting me. He knew I'd be coming, and he knew why.

I locked the door to my room behind me and took the stairs down to the lobby. A moment later and I was walking into the wind on my way to Peabody's Livery.

I believe my horse Rutherford must have made a solemn vow to keep my life interesting. Just when

I thought he had developed some sense and had quit his catch-me-if-you-can game, he took it up again. When he saw me coming toward him across the corral, he watched until I was within arm's reach before he threw his head up and pranced briskly away to the pen's far side. He did that twice more before I lost my patience and went to fetch my catch rope from the forks of my saddle.

When I stepped back into the corral, I walked toward the buckskin with the coils of my rope in my left hand and the loop dragging behind me. Wary as a deer in lion country, Rutherford watched me come toward him. I watched his feet dance in the dust as he made ready to do his quick shuffle-and-dash.

But this time, I was ready for him. When I was about fifteen feet away, he suddenly threw up his tail and bolted for the opposite side. Turning with him, I rolled out my loop in front of him and sunk my boot heels into the soft corral dirt.

The noose closed about his front feet and burned through the honda. The rope drew tight. The horse's own motion dumped him hard. I was on him in a flash. Before he could get up again, I threw a half-hitch around both his forelegs. The buckskin struggled to his feet, hobbled by my catch rope, and I left him to fetch my saddle and bridle.

The busting did him no harm, and I believe he got the message that I was no longer amused by his game. As I brushed the corral dirt from his back, I expected him to be sullen and ornery, but he fooled me again. Rutherford turned meek as any of McKenzie's lambs and made no fuss about the saddling or the rough handling. I think he was more embarrassed than anything.

With an eye on the clouds, I added my yellow slicker to the blanket roll I carried behind the cantle of my saddle, led Rutherford outside, and closed the corral gate behind me. Playing safe, I untracked the buckskin, but he seemed to have truly reformed. I stepped up into the saddle, and we swung up Main Street to the city's center.

When we reached the Sanchez Mercantile, I drew rein and dismounted. The hat Haggis had given me was still in my saddlebag, and I took it out. Tying Rutherford to the hitch rack, I opened the front door.

Inside, the store was dark and quiet. The smells of its offerings were many and varied, blending together in a mix that would have confused a bloodhound. I smelled coal oil and leather, coffee and new cheese, pickled fish, lye soap, plug tobacco, and spices.

A counter for groceries occupied the right-hand side of the room, while floor-to-ceiling shelves and a dry goods counter took up the left side. Brooms, buckets, and cooking pots hung from the rafters, and barrels, kegs, and crates seemed to fill every available inch of floor space. A potbellied stove stood at the room's center, surrounded by chairs in a rough circle.

I heard a rustle at the rear of the store and saw an aproned clerk walking toward me out of the gloom. The man was of medium height, with thinning hair and skin as white as chalk. I saw his glance settle briefly on my badge before he raised his eyes and smiled.

"Howdy, deputy," he said. "What can I do for you today?"

"I need a box of cartridges for a Winchester 73," I said, "and your professional opinion."

"Why, sure," the clerk said. "The cartridges will run you seventy cents a box. My opinions are free."

I showed him the Stetson. "I found this hat up on the mountain the other day," I said. "I wonder if you can tell me if it came from your store."

The clerk took the hat from me. Carefully, he smoothed the nap of the brim and re-shaped the crown with his fingers. "Five-inch brim," he said. "Six-and-a-half-inch crown. Yes, this is one of ours. This hat sells for eight dollars. It's one of our finest."

He smiled a sly smile. "We don't offer this model with bullet holes," he said. "The customer generally has to provide those himself."

"In this case," I said, "they were provided *for* him. Any idea who might own that particular sombrero?

The clerk hesitated. He looked down at the floor. "I . . . always like to help the law," he said, "but a man in business . . ."

He shrugged, handing the hat back. "I really couldn't say, deputy."

Then he smiled his sly smile again. "But I sold a hat just *like* that one this week. Travis Burnett, cow boss of the Circle R, bought it. He didn't say what happened to his old one."

As I was paying him for the cartridges, I said, "Much obliged, friend. You really should start *chargin'* for your opinions."

Outside, the wind blustered like a bully. Dust clouds chased each other up the street and spattered like birdshot against the buildings. I narrowed my eyes against the grit, stuffed the hat back into my saddle bag, and untied the reins that held Rutherford to the hitch rack. Backing the buckskin away from the boardwalk, I swung into the saddle and rode north out of town on the road to the Circle R.

The gloomy skies matched my mood. Thunder rumbled, and I figured a storm might break out at any minute. I kept watching the clouds as I rode, until my nerves were tight as fence wire and I was jumpy as a sack full of grasshoppers. Finally, I could stand it no longer. I reined up, loosed my saddle strings, and slipped into my slicker.

"All right," I said, looking up at the clouds. "Do your worst. I'm ready for you now."

At that point, I expected rain or maybe hail to fall, or that a lightning bolt would maybe smack me, but nothing happened. Within minutes, the wind died down and the clouds opened and allowed blue sky to show through. Sunshine lit up the land, and the storm threat passed.

I win, I told the clouds. *Most bluffs don't hold up when they're called.*

Maybe so, the clouds seemed to reply, *but I sure made you put on your slicker, didn't I?*

At the hilltop overlooking the house and ranch buildings of the Circle R, I stepped down to give Rutherford a breather. Taking out my field glasses, I studied the scene below for a time.

Everything was as I remembered it. The Rainford family home stood proud and out of place in all of its Queen Anne glory. The sod-roofed house where Zack Rainford kept his office slumbered in the shade of willow trees and lilac hedges. Across the stream lay the barn and corrals, bunkhouse, cook shack, and blacksmith shop. There were no horses in the corrals, and although I watched for several minutes, I saw no sign of people.

I was about to put the glasses away and ride on down to the ranch when I saw movement beyond the outbuildings. A figure on horseback was coming down from the upper pasture. Even at that distance, I recognized Morgan Rainford.

She was mounted on the high-stepping filly she called Sheba. She was dressed in men's work clothes, but no man ever looked as good in them as she did. She turned in at the barn and stepped down. Standing close beside her mount, she allowed the animal to drink from a watering trough just outside the corral. I watched as she pressed her face against the filly's proud neck, communing silently with the animal. Morgan's shoulders shook; I realized she was crying.

I lowered the glasses. I had meant to use them only to get the lay of the land. Somehow, watching Morgan when she didn't know she was being watched seemed wrong, almost indecent. I felt my throat tighten. There was something so sad and woebegone about Morgan that I felt melancholy, too.

Swinging back into the saddle, I turned Rutherford down the hill. At the barn, Morgan was leading her filly inside.

As I approached the gate that led to the ranch complex, a hard-eyed man on a black horse rode up to greet me. He wore a belted revolver at his waist and carried a Winchester carbine across the forks of his saddle, pointed my way. His face held the same expression it might have if he'd been looking at a rattlesnake.

"What's your business here, mister?" he asked.

I turned to let sunlight reflect off my deputy's badge. "*Official* business," I said. "You lettin' me in or do I have to ride back to the courthouse and get a warrant?"

The hard-eyed rider backed his horse up a pace or two, but I knew that didn't make us friends. He lowered the Winchester. "Come ahead," he muttered. "Zack said you might show up."

I rode Rutherford through the gate. "Zack is quite a prophet," I said.

Leaving the rider behind, I rode past the house and turned down toward the outbuildings. Just as I was approaching the barn, Morgan came back outside. She looked up, recognized me, and smiled.

"Hello, Merlin," she said. "I guess I've been . . . expecting you."

Her eyes were red, her features clouded by sadness. She closed the barn door behind her and looked up at me. "Dad is in his office over at the old house. He's been expecting you, too."

"I'm sorry I couldn't be here under different circumstances. How are you, Morgan?"

Her smile was shaky. "Sometimes I feel I was born under an evil star. When I heard about the raid up at Vendetta Canyon . . . and that sheepherder's death . . ."

She bit her lip. "Come," she said. "Let's go see Dad."

Zack Rainford was working at his desk when Morgan opened the screen door and led me inside. Seeing me, he rose halfway to his feet and then eased himself back into his chair. He nodded. "Fanshaw," he said.

I returned his nod. "Hello, Zack. I guess you know why I'm here."

"I know it isn't to bring me good news," he said.

"I'm here to ask questions," I said. "Whether that brings good news or not will depend on your answers."

Morgan sat down in one of the chairs that faced her father's desk. Zack glared at his daughter, but Morgan held her head high and met his gaze. A moment later, it was Zack who looked away. He turned back to me.

"I'll answer one of your questions before you ask it," he said. "I had nothing to do with the raids on McKenzie's camps or with the death of that sheep-herder."

"Are you sayin' the men who *ride* for you weren't involved?"

Zack glanced up at the portrait of his father on the wall above his desk. He lowered his eyes. "I'm sayin' *I* wasn't involved.

"I was away on business," he said. "Didn't hear about the raids 'til yesterday. When I did, I called Travis Burnett in and asked my own questions. He said he'd been up on the mountain with some of the boys and that they'd pestered the herders some.

"He said things got out of hand. One of the herders came at them with a gun. The boys defended themselves, and the herder went down."

"Ten men killed *one* man . . . in *self-defense?*"

Zack made a wry face and got to his feet. "Damn you, deputy! You don't cut a man much slack, do you?"

"About as much slack as your cowpunchers cut Loco John," I said. "On your orders or not, Circle R men clubbed and shot nearly a hundred sheep. They killed Loco John's dog and his horse. When he tried to fight back, they *murdered* that old man!

"Then they burned his wagon and went on to raid Haggis McRae's camp. They put a bullet through his leg, but McRae is a different breed of cat. He ran your punchers off with a Winchester!

"Now I need to ask your men some questions, but except for that gunman you've got guardin' your gate I don't see any. Where are they?"

It was Morgan who answered. "Some of the boys are riding line north of here. Travis and a crew are branding slicks over on Sage Creek. They'll be back tonight."

Zack spoke up. "You can stay until then. Ask your questions. As for the man you met at the gate, his name is Cotton Smith. Yes, he's drawin' fightin' wages. If I know Abel McKenzie—and I do—he'll strike back at me any time now for that raid."

"He gave me his word he'd hold off till after I talk to you."

"Abel's a hot-head," Zack said. "You can't trust him—or that damned *kid* of his, either!"

Morgan's face tightened. She got to her feet. Walking quickly to the screen door, she went outside and let the door slam shut behind her.

Zack looked startled by her sudden departure. Frowning, he stared after Morgan as if asking himself, "What did I say?"

I knew, even if Zack did not. I thought: *Maybe you don't trust Abel's son, but your daughter does. She hopes to share her life with him.*

I turned back to Zack, but before I could say anything, Morgan exclaimed from the porch outside, "The *barn!* The barn's on *fire!*"

NINETEEN

▼

WHERE THERE'S SMOKE

I was on my feet in an instant. Zack froze in his chair, confusion on his face, as if unable to grasp the meaning of his daughter's words. As for Morgan, she was already off and running. "*Sheba!*" she cried.

Following her outside, I cleared the porch in a bound. Ahead of me, Morgan raced toward the burning barn. Smoke billowed from the hayloft. Flames broke through the shingled roof. The barn was fully ablaze; fire danced and roared through the weathered building with a sound like a locomotive chuffing up a grade. Above the gusts of sound, the high-pitched whinnies of frightened horses inside sent a chill down my backbone.

I had tied Rutherford to the corral near the watering trough, but I saw in a glance he had pulled free. Backing up a few jittery steps at a time, the buckskin stared wide-eyed at the blaze. Morgan ran past the animal to the barn's door, shouting *"Sheba! I'm coming!"*

Morgan fumbled with the latch and swung the door open. Smoke and flame exploded out into the morning. Morgan swayed with the force of the gust and then forced herself to enter the inferno the barn had become. I called out, *"Morgan! Wait!"* but she either didn't hear me or chose not to heed my warning.

Through the barn's open door, I saw that the fire was spreading. Burning hay dripped down from the loft like molten gold, and the beams and stalls of the barn's interior writhed in rippling shades of red, yellow, and orange. Morgan vanished into the smoke and heat; I could see her no longer.

I caught one of Rutherford's reins and halted the buckskin's retreat. Holding the saddle horn with my left hand, I loosed the strings that held my slicker and blanket roll. I rushed to the stock trough and thrust the blanket into the water, holding it down until it was thoroughly soaked. When I lifted it out again, it was heavy as lead and dripping. I gathered it into my arms and turned back to the barn.

Zack Rainford had been close behind me; now he stood twenty feet from the barn, shielding his face from the heat. The roar of the fire drowned out all sounds, but I saw that Zack was shouting his daughter's name: *"Morgan! Morgan!"*

I ran past him to the barn's open door. Crouching there, I peered inside. The sharp, sour smell of burning wood caught in my throat and stung my eyes. My vision was hindered by the smoke, but I thought I could see Morgan back among the stalls with the horses. Covering myself with the blanket, I dashed inside.

Boards and burning hay tumbled down from the loft. The barn groaned and trembled; my face tightened from the heat, and my clothes burned against my skin. A blazing timber fell with a crash, narrowly missing me. I pushed on.

Suddenly, I saw shapes coming toward me through the smoke! I ducked inside a stall as one horse, and then two, clattered past, racing toward the door behind me. Another timber fell. Overhead, the flooring of the loft seemed to shift and sway.

Another horse was coming! Again I stepped aside, watching the frightened animal rush by. It was Morgan's filly, Sheba! But where was Morgan? Suddenly, my foot struck a heavy object on the barn's floor. I tripped and fell headlong. My eyes watered as I groped the floor with my hand— a body! *Morgan!*

Smoke shifted and eddied; in that moment, I saw her clearly. She lay, limp and still, on the dirty straw. Quickly, I covered her with the blanket, bent down, and lifted her in my arms. Using the uprights of the stalls as a guide, I carried her back toward the open door.

Behind us, the floor of the loft collapsed. Embers flew, dancing in flurries around us. Then, through the smoke, I saw the dim square of light that was the barn door! Holding Morgan close, I ducked my head and rushed toward the opening.

Zack was waiting just outside. He reached out to help carry his daughter just as I stumbled through the doorway. Together, we ran until we were well away from the dying barn.

I wiped my eyes and looked around. Behind us, fire gusted and roared like a furnace. Flames leaped from the barn like demons breaking out of hell. Carried by updrafts, shingles from the roof soared into the sky, and smoke cast a shadow over the barnyard.

We knelt together in the short grass, Zack holding Morgan. Lifeless as a fallen sparrow, with her long, dark hair tangled and matted about her face, she lay limp and unmoving in his arms.

People were coming—the hired gun riding hard from his post at the gate and an older man, bare-headed and balding, jog-trotting from the ranch's cook shack.

Racing down from the house came Morgan's

mother, Melissa. She lifted her skirts above her shoe tops as she ran, her pale face tense with fear.

"Morgan . . . honey," Zack said, "*Breathe*, sweetheart."

Melissa dropped to her knees beside him, her hand trembling as she touched Morgan's face. "I saw the fire from up at the house," she said, raising her eyes to me. "And then I saw you carry Morgan out of the barn. What happened? Is she . . ."

"Her filly was inside," I said. "When Morgan saw the barn was burning, she rushed inside to save Sheba."

Morgan groaned. Her body stiffened. Seized by a spasm of coughing, she turned in her father's arms. Her eyelids fluttered and opened. Clutching my sleeve, she asked, "*Sheba* . . . is she . . ."

"She's fine, Morgan," I said. "You saved her. Sheba and two others."

Tears welled in Melissa's eyes. Zack cleared his throat and said, "That was a mighty brave thing you did, sweetheart, but reckless. You scared your old dad."

"You'd . . . have done . . . the same," she said, "but I'm sorry I worried you." She sat up, looking at her stained, charred clothing and her blackened hands and arms with a kind of wonder. "The heat and the smoke . . . I couldn't breathe. How . . ."

"Deputy Fanshaw went in after you," Zack said. "He brought you out."

Morgan's blue eyes met mine, and she smiled a

wistful smile. "Grateful," she said, "but Dad's right. I was reckless. Sorry I put you at risk, Merlin."

Her smile was payment in full and then some. "That's what friends are *for*," I said.

Morgan struggled to her feet, but she was clearly in some pain. She moved slowly and in that careful way folks do when they're hurting. Zack reached out to steady her, but she pushed him away. She closed her eyes. "Feeling . . . light-headed," she said. "My skin burns."

Melissa took charge. "Come, dear," she told Morgan. "We'll take you up to the house. Lucy will draw you a nice, warm bath. Then we'll see to those burns."

"No argument now," Zack said, sweeping her up in his arms. "Things have come to a pretty pass when a father can't carry his little girl." This time, Morgan didn't resist. Together, the Rainfords turned, walking uphill toward heir house.

Zack looked back at me. "Wait for me," he said. "I want to talk to you."

"Take your time," I said. "I'll see if I can run in those horses Morgan rescued."

I found Rutherford standing in good grass by the creek, but he was so intent on watching the fire he'd forgotten to eat. The buckskin stared, his eyes wide and his ears pointed at the blazing barn. He looked like he'd rather be anywhere but there.

I picked up his trailing reins. "Easy, big horse," I said. "That fire isn't comin' after you."

He nickered, a low rumble deep in his throat, as if to say he wasn't so sure of that. Back at the barn, the balding man and the hired gun were wetting down the corral posts with buckets of water from the creek. I stepped up into the saddle and turned Rutherford away to look for the horses Morgan had freed.

They hadn't gone far. I found them at the tree line beyond Zack's office. All three—a long-legged sorrel, a chesty bay, and Morgan's jet black filly—were nervous and smoke-stained, but they seemed none the worse for wear. Slow and easy, I rode Rutherford around behind them and turned them back toward the barn lot.

A round corral stood well apart from the burning barn. Used by rough string riders as a place to break broncs, the corral stood empty and bare. Working them slow and easy, I herded the horses inside, stepped down, and closed the gate.

More riders were coming over the hill above the ranch. They came at a high lope, two and three at a time, drawing rein at the burning barn. Some dismounted, talking and gesturing to each other, but the fire was unstoppable. All anyone could do was stand back and watch it burn itself out, and in the end, that's what they did.

I saw Zack leave his house and start down the

hill. At the barn, his hired gun saw him, too. Swinging into the saddle, he rode up to meet Zack. They two men spoke briefly, and then Zack continued down toward his office and the *pistolero* rode out in the direction of the Circle R's south gate.

I was waiting on the porch when Zack arrived. "How is Morgan?" I asked.

Zack looked worn. "She has some painful burns. I don't believe they're serious, but I'm no doctor. My wife and the hired girl are tending her."

He looked out toward the south hills. "I sent a man to fetch Doc Reynolds," he said. "Doc will know what to do."

Zack was silent. He stood tall, his eyes on the hills above the ranch. Then he turned and looked directly into my eyes. "There's no way I can thank you for what you did," he said. "I owe you a debt I can't pay."

He looked away again, back toward the hills. "That girl is my life, Fanshaw. I'd like to think I'd have gone in after her if you hadn't, but the truth is, I don't know. Guess I never *will* know for sure. Anyway, you saved my daughter's life, and I'm beholden."

"You give me too much credit. I was just in the right place at the right time."

Again, Zack fell silent. Then he said, "Do you think Abel McKenzie's men started the fire?"

I took the time to think about it. "Not on his

orders. Abel is stubborn, hot-headed, all the things you said. But he told me he wouldn't seek revenge for the Circle R's raid on his camps, and I believe him."

Zack looked across the creek to the smoldering ruins of his barn. "*Somebody* set that fire," he said grimly. "If I find out Abel had anything to do with it . . ."

"One man is dead already because of your feud," I said. "I'd say it's high time you and Abel worked out your differences face-to-face."

"You don't know what you're asking."

"Maybe not, but I am asking. Are you turnin' me down?"

Zack's shoulders slumped. He shook his head. "No. After today, I can't refuse you anything. Tell Abel I'll meet him. We'll talk."

Zack met my eyes, his expression grave. "Do you still want to question my men?" he asked.

"That's what I came for."

Over at the bunkhouse, cowpunchers stood talking in groups of two and three. One or two leaned against the supports that held up the bunkhouse's weathered board awning. Others squatted on their boot heels, smoking. They looked at each other. They looked at the dying flames and smoke. Always, their eyes turned across the flat to Zack and me.

"Looks like most of the boys are in from work

now," Zack said. "Come on. I'll go over there with you."

We walked across the lot, past the blazing heap of blackened timbers and log that had been the Circle R's barn. Smoke rose in great clouds above the ashes. Barring rain, it would rise for days.

As we neared the bunkhouse, the men grew silent. Travis Burnett looked at his boss and nodded. His eyes flashed to me and returned quickly to his boss—not quickly enough to hide the rage and hatred he held for me, though.

I recognized several of the men from the Longhorn Saloon, but the only one I knew by name was Harve Rawlins, the cowpuncher who had helped me with Loco John after my fight with Burnett. I nodded. Harve returned my nod and then looked quickly away.

Zack regarded the rubble where the barn had stood and smiled a rueful smile. "Well, boys," he said, "it looks like we might have to find another place to keep the horses."

Tension lifted. A few of the punchers grinned, but no one spoke. Then Travis broke the silence. "How'd the fire start, boss?" he asked. "Was it somebody from McKenzie's outfit?"

"We don't know. Cotton Smith was on guard, but he didn't see anyone."

"By god, I *know* it was those damned mutton punchers," Travis said. "It'd be just *like* them sneaky bastards!"

I'd had enough. "Well," I said, "if it *was* them, at least they didn't *kill* anybody.

"We brought Loco John's body down from the mountain this week," I continued. "There'll be a coroner's inquest. I expect some of you will be asked to testify about how the man died."

Travis scowled. "Hell, I'll tell you right now! We was hoorahin' them snoozers some—just havin' a little fun—and that crazy sheepherder came out of his wagon with a rifle! Went to shootin' at us!"

"So you boys gunned him down and burned his wagon. Killed his horse and dog, too. That about cover it?"

Travis caught himself. He'd said more than he meant to. His bluster turned sly. "We don't know nothin' about all that," he said. Turning to the others, he asked, "*Do* we, boys?"

No one spoke. Travis had called my bet, and I was holding a busted flush. Without hard evidence or an eyewitness, I could do nothing. Haggis had seen the riders, had exchanged shots with them, but they had been masked. The men couldn't be identified, and they knew it.

"Thanks for your time, boys," I said. "I'll see you at the inquest."

Walking with Zack back down to his office, I tried to throw a check-rein on my temper. Every peace officer has times when he absolutely *knows* a suspected criminal is guilty but can't prove it. Well, that afternoon was one of those times for me.

I was dead certain Travis Burnett led the raids on the sheep camps and that he was involved in the killing of Loco John. But the only real evidence I had—the hat Haggis had given me—only proved Burnett was there. He had already admitted that. Building a case against Burnett and the Circle R riders was proving as difficult as herding cats.

TWENTY

▼

CASUALTIES OF THE WAR ZONE

I was three miles from Reata when I saw the horse and buggy coming my way. Cotton Smith, Zack's hired gun, rode with the rig, his black horse lathered and hot. I pulled over to the roadside as the carriage approached and saw it slow and then stop. Cotton drew rein and nodded in greeting.

Doc Reynolds peered at me from beneath the carriage top. "Young Fanshaw," he said. "How is Morgan?"

"I guess that will be for you to tell us," I said. "Her mother and Lucy, the hired girl, are taking care of her now."

Doc nodded. "Melissa has a cool head and a mother's heart," he said. "And Lucy comes from a long line of nurses. Morgan is in good hands."

"Better hands when you get there," I said. "That's what Zack thinks."

Doc slacked the reins and the buggy began moving again. "My patient awaits," he said. "See you later, young Fanshaw."

It was a quarter past nine the next morning when I rode Rutherford across the bridge that led to the McKenzie place. Shadows still lay cool and soft along the creek, but sunlight flooded the house and outbuildings. Abel's old sheepdog walked stiffly out to greet me, barking as he came.

"It's only me, Rascal," I said. "How've you been, dog?"

I don't know whether Rascal caught my scent or recognized my voice, but his wagging tail told me he remembered me. He barked once more and then flopped down beside the gate.

Drawing rein at the picket fence that enclosed the front yard, I waited for a word of welcome before dismounting. On a low hill beyond the house, Al Wilson sat his pale horse, watching me through field glasses. As Rascal had done, Wilson recognized me. The gunman lowered the glasses, waved, and resumed his patrolling.

Suddenly, the front door of the house banged open and Teresa McKenzie dashed out. "Oh, Merlin," she said. "I'm *so* glad you're here! *Por favor* . . . Please, you must talk to Ian. He respects you—maybe he'll listen to you!"

I was startled. Teresa McKenzie had never struck me as an excitable woman. Always, she had seemed confident and in control of her feelings. She stood, her eyes wide and troubled, looking up at me. Nervously, she wrung her hands, twisting them together in the folds of her apron.

I stepped down from the saddle and turned to face her. "Uh, why, sure," I said. "What's wrong, ma'am?"

It was Ian who answered my question. He appeared in the doorway behind Teresa, holding the door ajar. "I just told Mother I'm going away, Merlin. I'm leaving Meriwether County."

Teresa's eyes pleaded with me. I looked at Ian. When I finally thought of something to say, it sounded lame even to me. "Uh . . . I'm sorry to hear that," I said.

"Please," Teresa said, turning back to her son. "Can't we go inside and talk about this? I'll make some coffee, and we can all . . ."

"I'm sorry," Ian said. "My mind's made up."

"It's been a long ride from town," I said. "I could use a cup of coffee."

Ian hesitated. "All right," he said. "Come on in."

Back inside the house, Teresa busied herself at the kitchen stove. Ian's eyes were as troubled as Teresa's had been. "I was in town yesterday," he said. "Cal Peabody told me Doc Reynolds came by earlier for his horse and buggy. Doc said there'd been a fire out at the Circle R."

Ian slumped to a seat at the kitchen table. "He . . . he said Morgan was burned in the fire."

I sat down across from him. "Yes," I said. "I was at the Circle R when it happened." Briefly, I told Ian what I knew of the events of the previous day. "I don't believe Morgan is badly hurt," I said. "Some minor burns. Smoke and heat. I'm sure she'll be all right."

"That's not exactly the point," Ian said.

"What is the point?" Teresa asked.

"The point is, this isn't Morgan's war and it's not my war. It's a feud between my dad and Zack Rainford. It's pointless and stupid, and it has to end!

"Last week, Loco John was murdered. Haggis was attacked. Our sheep were shot and clubbed to death by masked men. Now, someone has burned the barn at the Circle R and Morgan has been hurt. She could have been killed!

"I've been a loyal son. I've made Dad's cause my own, even though I don't really believe in it. Well, now I'm taking up my own cause. I'm going to marry Morgan Rainford and take her as far from here as we can get!"

Teresa looked stricken. "*Marry* Morgan Rainford? But . . . I didn't know . . . Ian, you *can't* marry Morgan!"

"I'm sorry, Mother," Ian said, "but I can't do anything else. Morgan is . . . well, Morgan is my life."

"Have you talked to your dad?" I asked.

"He's up on the mountain with Haggis and the

sheep. I was just heading out to tell him when you showed up."

"Maybe I'll ride with you, if it's all right. Zack Rainford told me he's willing to meet with your dad and try to work things out. That's good news."

Ian shook his head. "Come along if you want, but I don't believe such a meeting will ever happen. Even if it does, I can't see Dad and Zack reaching an agreement on anything. I'm tired of waiting for things to change. So is Morgan. We have plans of our own."

Teresa stood at the stove, her arms folded tightly across her chest. Tears brimmed in her dark eyes as she looked at her son. "Ian," she said. "Please, wait."

Ian's hands gently grasped Teresa's arms. He looked down into her upturned face, and his voice was softer than before. "Don't take on so, Mother. Everything will be all right."

Then he turned away, striding across the room and out the front door. Hoping to reassure her, I smiled at Teresa before I turned to follow Ian, but I don't know if she even saw me go. I glanced back as I reached the doorway. Teresa stood with her face in her hands, weeping softly.

We left the ranch and turned our horses up the steep trail that led to Abel's camp at Red Rock Springs, but you couldn't really say we rode together. Ian gave no sign he knew I was there.

Instead, he fixed his eyes on the trail ahead, pushing his horse at a rapid clip until the animal was sweated and gasping for air.

At first I said nothing, not wishing to intrude on Ian's mood, but I finally drew the line. My horse Rutherford was deep-chested and tough, but as the miles went by, even he was beginning to labor. It was time to let our ponies breathe, and I said so.

"Hey, Ian," I said. "Let's rest these horses. If we keep pushin' 'em this way, we'll soon be afoot."

Ian turned in the saddle. He seemed surprised, as if he had forgotten I was with him. He turned off the trail and drew rein.

"Sorry, Merlin," he said. "I guess my thoughts were somewhere else."

"Morgan really will be all right."

Ian looked out across the hills with haunted eyes. When he spoke at last, his voice sounded strained. "I hope so. It's eating me up inside, knowing I wasn't there—*couldn't* be there—for her."

His eyes met mine. "But I'm glad *you* were. You've been a real friend to us both."

I shrugged. "I haven't done all that much. But I do wish you well. You and Morgan have a hard row to hoe."

Again, Ian turned his eyes to the timbered hills. There was a naked longing in his gaze that was painful to see, and I knew his heart and mind were reaching all the way to the Circle R.

My question was more for Ian than for my information. "Are you sure you need to leave right now?"

Ian raised his horse's head and touched its flanks with his heels. "I'm sure," he said grimly. "We'd do it *sooner* if we could."

We found Abel at his Red Rock Springs camp, loading supplies into his wagon. Two other men were there with him, new men. They both wore six-guns at their waist, and neither man appeared to be any sort of ranch hand. Clearly, Abel was taking no chances on a second attack. He raised his eyes from his work as we rode in, smiling in recognition.

"Merlin," he said. "Ian. Welcome to the war zone."

I reined Rutherford to a stop and stepped down. "War zone? Have you had more trouble with night riders?"

Abel shook his head. "No. And, by god, I don't intend to! I hired a new herder to take John's sheep, and I've brought in some men to help keep the peace."

"You know how I feel about that," I said. "I'm not sure bringing in more gunhands helps keep the peace."

Abel looked at Ian and then at me, trying to read our faces, waiting for us to tell him the purpose of our visit. Ian dismounted, his expression grim. He didn't meet his father's eyes.

271

"There's news," I said. "Someone burned the Circle R's barn yesterday. Zack Rainford thinks you did it."

"I didn't."

"That's what I told him. But he's edgy. His daughter went into the fire to save her horse. She almost didn't make it out."

"Morgan?" Abel said. "Is she all right?"

"Minor burns. Smoke. That's it, as far as I know. But it was a near thing."

Abel spoke to me, but his eyes were on his son. Ian stood tensely beside his horse, his mouth a thin, tight line. "What else?" Abel asked.

"I told Zack the feud needed to end. I asked him if he'd meet with you one on one—try to settle your differences. He said he would. Now I'm askin' you."

Abel frowned. Anger reddened his face. "I'll think about it," he snapped. "But I wouldn't hold my breath, if I were you."

He turned to Ian. "What about you, son? Have you got bad news for me, too?"

Ian met his father's eyes. "I guess you'll think so. I've already told Mother. The truth is . . . I've asked Morgan to marry me, and she's said yes. We're leaving Meriwether County as soon as we're able."

Abel's ruddy face turned white. I watched his eyes widen in surprise, saw him try to get a handle on the news. When he spoke again, his voice was steady. He seemed to choose his words with care. "You've asked . . . Morgan Rainford . . . to *marry* you. I didn't *know* . . . That is, how long . . ."

"Almost a year now. At first, we both tried to break it off, stay away from each other. You and Zack are enemies. We both tried to be loyal to our families. But it was no use."

"Aye. So, you love her, then?"

"Yes, Dad. I . . . I guess I do."

Abel looked at his son, almost as if he was seeing him for the first time. "You're a man now," he said. "I've been so caught up in my own concerns, I never noticed. Been still thinkin' of you as my boy."

"I'm twenty, sir."

"Twenty. Imagine that. And what about Morgan? She'll need Zack Rainford's permission, and he'll never . . ."

"She's eighteen. Under the law, Morgan is a woman grown. She doesn't need her parents' consent."

"Doesn't she want it?"

"She doesn't *need* it."

Abel looked at me then. His eyes pleaded for help, but all I could offer was sympathy.

"I was twenty once," Abel said quietly. "You say you're leavin' the county. You needn't, you know. You could . . . That is, this is your home, yours and Morgan's."

"Not any more. You said it yourself, Dad. The

county is a war zone. Morgan and I need to find a place of our own, where we can make a new start."

Abel swallowed hard. He reached out a work-hardened hand and gripped his son's shoulder. "Give me a bit o' time, lad," he said. "A few weeks. Then you can go with my blessing."

Ian looked at me, his eyes pleading for help as Abel's had. I felt trapped, caught in a family problem that was none of my business. I met Ian's eyes and nodded.

"All right," Ian told his father. "Two weeks."

TWENTY-ONE
▼
TERESA'S STORY

I decided to spend the night on the mountain and return to Reata the next day, but as it turned out, I didn't see much of Abel and Ian after that first afternoon. Ian agreed to stay on for two weeks and help move the sheep camps, and Abel announced his intention to take the lambs down to the railroad corrals at Reata for shipping at summer's end. He would, he said, herd his bucks and ewes to pastures near the home place during the coming fall and winter.

The hired guns seemed to spend most of their time patrolling the high meadows, watching for riders who might threaten the herders and their flocks. Occasional sightings of Circle R cowboys were reported, but there were no more raids. Whether this was due to the presence of the gunmen or to a change in policy by Zack Rainford, the truce was welcomed by Abel and his herders. And by me.

Haggis McRae was camped on a high meadow above Vendetta Canyon, and I rode up and paid him a visit. His wounded leg was healing nicely, and I complimented him on his recovery.

"I've been braggin' on you over in Reata and I think Doc Reynolds is gettin' jealous," I said. "You fixed my busted fibula and now you've healed your own bullet wound. Next thing you know, you'll quit nursin' McKenzie's woolies and hang out your shingle as a doctor.

"I can see it now," I said. "There you'll be, livin' in the city, wearing a stiff shirt and a claw-hammer coat, healin' babies of whoopin' cough and treatin' spinster ladies for the vapors."

The big Scot blushed like a schoolboy, and his grin was as wide as his face. "Whisht, laddie," he said, "Dinnae be daft! I couldna dwell in a town— there's nae room there for a man to swing his arms!"

We shared a supper of stew and scones, and I filled Haggis in on the news of the day. I told him about the pending coroner's inquest into the death of Loco John, but I didn't offer much hope we'd find John's killer. I said that even though Travis Burnett and the other Circle R riders admitted taking part in the raid, it wasn't likely anyone would be indicted for his murder without an eyewitness.

Haggis offered me a bed in his wagon, but it was a warm, clear night. I said I'd rather bed down outside under the stars. I heard once that even on the clearest night, a man can see only about three thousand stars without a telescope, but I don't believe it. That night on the bench above Vendetta Canyon, the stars seemed to number in the millions, and I marveled once again at their beauty and their mystery.

Thoughts of Pandora came unbidden. Remembrance of our times together passed through my mind in a stately parade and left the hollow ache of loss in their wake. I heard the restless jostling of sheep settling in for the night. I heard Rutherford's shuffle as he grazed in the darkness. I breathed in the odors of earth, crushed grass, and sagebrush. And finally, I slept.

I woke in the chill of early morning to the sound of sheep leaving the bed ground. Ewes blatted in low, fussy tones, and husky lambs replied. Hooves rattled a chorus as the sheep moved out, and the smell of dust marked their passing. I sat up in my blankets and looked around.

Darkness lay heavy on the land, but lamplight

shone at the sheepwagon's open door. Haggis climbed stiffly to the ground and stood, listening. Then he stepped out of the light and into the blackness behind the wagon. I pulled my boots on and knelt to roll my blankets.

A moment later, Haggis came back into the light, leading his Jimmy horse and followed by Tip, his dog.

"Good mornin', laddie," Haggis said. "I hae t' gang wi' ma sheep, but stay as long as ye like. There's tea on the stove."

"Much obliged," I said, "but I need to be goin', too. Take care of yourself, Haggis."

"I will," he said. "Ye do the same."

I watched the big Scot walk away into the gloom and disappear. In the east, stars grew pale and winked out. Above the mountains, coming daylight softened the darkness. Minutes later, I had closed up Haggis's wagon and saddled Rutherford. With a nod to the camp, I swung into the saddle and set the buckskin on the trail back down to Red Rock Springs.

Abel's camp was up and doing when I rode in. Sunlight filtered through the trees and caught in the rising smoke of a campfire. Out on the thick grass of the meadow, dewdrops sparkled like diamonds. Abel himself served beans and biscuits from the Dutch ovens, and men squatted on their heels around the fire as they ate.

I rode Rutherford over to the tree line and

stepped down. Loosening the saddle's cinch and slipping off the bridle, I left the buckskin to graze in his hobbles before turning back toward the fire. It was then I saw Ian coming to meet me.

"Morning, Merlin," he said. "How was everything up at Haggis's camp?"

"Haggis is doin' fine," I said. "I left just after he took the sheep out."

Ian took his hat off and ran his fingers through his hair. "Guess I'll be staying on for a while," he said. "Dad wants to me to help him move both Haggis and the new herder this week. They'll still be on range claimed by the Circle R, but we're hoping there won't be any trouble."

He frowned. "When Dad asked me to give him two weeks, I couldn't say no. But somehow I need to tell Morgan. Is there any chance you . . ."

How did I ever get involved in this durned romance, I wondered. *Playing cupid is the last thing I need.*

"Yes," I said. "I plan to ride out to the Circle R tomorrow or the next day. I need to tell Zack your dad agreed to meet with him. Besides, I want to look in on Morgan and see how she's getting along. I'll tell her about your delay."

Ian's honest blue eyes met mine. He seemed unable to speak. Then he said, "Thanks, Merlin. I mean, really, thanks."

Don't mention it, I thought. *It's all in a day's work for a soft-headed deputy marshal.*

. . .

An easy breeze stirred the aspen trees above McKenzie's ranch as I rode Rutherford out onto the upper pasture. Below, the main house and out-buildings slept in the warmth of early afternoon. Atop the ridge overlooking the house, Al Wilson watched my descent.

I drew rein at the picket fence that enclosed the front yard and waited. A moment later, Teresa McKenzie opened the screen door and stepped outside. She wore the open-necked cotton blouse and full skirt she seemed to favor, and her black hair shone in the sunlight. Shading her eyes, she looked up at me. "Hello, Merlin," she said.

I touched my hat brim. "Ma'am."

She searched my face, questions in her dark eyes. "Did he . . ."

"Yes. Ian told his dad he was leaving the county. Said he and Morgan planned to be married."

Teresa frowned, her face tense. "How . . . how did Abel . . ."

"He was surprised, at first. Then he seemed to accept Ian's decision. He asked Ian if he'd stay two weeks, help him move the mountain camps. Ian agreed."

Some of the tension left Teresa's face. She smiled. "Have you had your dinner?"

"I figured I'd wait 'til I got to town. I should be movin' on."

"I won't hear of it," she said. "There are corn

dodgers and chicken fixins on the stove. More than the children and I can possibly eat. Please, come inside."

"Well," I said, but her mention of chicken fixins had already persuaded me. I stepped down off Rutherford and tied him to the McKenzies' hitching post. "Much obliged, ma'am," I said. "Where *are* the young'uns?"

"School," Teresa said. "And don't call me ma'am. I think we know each other well enough by now for first names."

Inside the McKenzie kitchen, Teresa set a place for me at the kitchen table and set out the chicken and corn dodgers. Pouring a cup of coffee for each of us, she sat down across from me and watched in silence as I ate. I have to say that being studied by a lady as attractive as Teresa McKenzie unsettled me somewhat. It wasn't just that I feared my table manners might not be up to her standard, although that sure was part of it. Teresa was a mighty handsome woman, and being alone with her there in her house made me feel a mite fidgety somehow.

I pushed back from the table. "I surely do thank you for the dinner, ma'am . . . I mean Teresa. You're a fine cook."

She stood, but her eyes never left my face. "Bring your coffee into the parlor," she said. "I have something to tell you."

Well, what could I do? The way she said it left no

room for me to say no. I picked up my coffee and followed her.

Teresa showed me to a bentwood rocker in the parlor and sat down facing me. I wondered at the change in her. She had surprised me the day Ian made his announcement by how upset she seemed. Up until then, I'd believed her to be a person who never lost control of her emotions. Now she seemed different in still another way—controlled, but intense, and *desperate* somehow.

"I don't really know you all that well," she said, "but somehow I feel I can trust you. You've been a friend to my son, and you've obviously earned his trust. You've done your job in this sheep and cattle feud without playing favorites. You've shown courage and character. And you've proved you can keep a secret."

Teresa hesitated. She seemed to be gathering her thoughts. Then she turned her attention back to me. Leaning forward, she began to speak.

"What I'm about to tell you is known only to me. No one else—not my husband, not Ian, not Doc Reynolds—*no one* knows my secret. I always believed no one would ever *need* to know. I was wrong."

Teresa closed her eyes. The tension in her face went away. It may have been a trick of the light, but she almost seemed to grow younger as I watched. With her eyes still closed, she smiled.

"Twenty-one years ago," she said. "You should

have seen this country then. Grass as high as a horse's belly. Open range, free for the taking. No roads or railroads, only buffalo trails. And one man, Zeb Rainford, with a vision to fill the land with cattle.

"The town of Reata grew up to serve him, and it wore Rainford's brand, just like the cattle that covered the plains. Rainford built the bank and then the hotel. Saloons popped up like mushrooms after the rain. And at his trading post down on the Yellowstone, Ignacio Sanchez, my father, saw his own opportunity.

"Papa packed up his merchandise, his wife, and his daughters, and moved to Reata. He built his mercantile at the center of the town, across from the hotel. He worked hard and prospered."

Teresa paused again, remembering. Her jet black hair shone in the afternoon light, and her eyes seemed to glow. *Teresa McKenzie is a handsome woman,* I thought. *She must have been a beautiful girl.*

She took up her story again. "Homesteaders came, just a few at first. A church was established, and then a school. Dr. Reynolds opened his office. And my sisters and I grew up with the town.

"Those were exciting times. We worked in Papa's store, and we helped mother with the housework. But there was always time for play: sleigh rides and skating in winter, picnics and swimming in the summer.

"And the dances! Always, there seemed to be a dance somewhere. Dressed in our best dresses, we would crowd into Papa's surrey or a neighbor's wagon and drive to a ranch far from town. Entire families came—the old, the young, toddlers, and babies.

"Cowboys galloped in from the ranches, wild as the horses they rode. Bashful and bold at the same time, they swaggered onto the dance floor in their big hats and boots, pretending to take no notice of us girls. Ah, but we *knew* they noticed us—and we certainly noticed them!

"It was at one of those country dances that I met the man I would marry, my husband Abel. He was dashing and reckless like the rest, but there was an honesty about him that touched me. We danced, and we talked. He was sunny and open. Abel loved life, and he had a way of telling stories that made me see the people and events he described with humor and good will.

"As we danced for what must have been the fifth time that evening, he told me his best friend and 'pardner' was Zeb Rainford's son, Zack. When the dance ended, Abel introduced me to him.

"Zack was handsome as homemade sin and already something of a ladies' man at nineteen. He had a dark, brooding quality that girls found attractive. Of course, the fact that he was heir to the Rainford cattle empire made him an even bigger attraction.

"In those days, Zack and Abel competed in nearly everything. If Zack rode a wild bronco, Abel had to ride a wilder one. They raced their saddle horses. They held shooting contests, roping contests, and drinking contests.

"Sometimes, out of sheer high spirits, they fought each other in bloody, bare-knuckle brawls. Afterward, they shook hands and made up. They didn't fight often, you understand. Their battles were the sort that brothers who love each other fight, but they definitely fought to win.

"Of course, it wasn't long before they began to compete over me. I was flattered at first, and the envy of my friends. Abel and Zack kept me busy at the dances, each trying to have one more dance with me. Abel came to our house in town and took me away on a picnic. When we returned, my sisters told me Zack had come by after we'd gone, only to learn Abel had been there first.

"If Abel gave me a present, Zack gave me two. Zack has a good singing voice, while Abel can't carry a tune in a bucket. One night, Zack came to our house to serenade me. The next night, Abel hired musicians from one of the saloons to play and sing love songs outside my window.

"It was a contest only I could decide. And when Abel came to the house one night, fresh from the barber and dressed in his Sunday best, my heart made its decision. He asked me to marry him, and I accepted eagerly. I had no doubts that we belonged together. I was surprised at how certain I was.

"I knew we would have to tell Zack and that he would be disappointed, but I was so happy I couldn't think of anything but marrying Abel. He said I shouldn't worry, that he'd let Zack know. Zack was his friend, he said. Zack would understand and be happy for us. I wasn't so sure."

Teresa paused. She looked down at her hands. Silence crowded the room. After a few seconds, she raised her head and looked directly into my eyes.

"Two days later, my parents and my sisters went out for the evening to visit friends, but I didn't go. I thought Abel might come to town, so I waited at home. When I heard the knock on the door, I ran to open it. It was not Abel; it was Zack.

"I saw that he was in one of his moods and that he'd been drinking. He said he was pleased that Abel and I had found each other, but his words rang hollow. I tried to console him. I told him how much we valued his friendship, how much we admired him, but he seemed not to hear me.

"The more I tried to reassure him, the more sullen he became. I grew angry—at Zack for spoiling my happiness, and at myself for catering to him. As I talked, it almost seemed I was apologizing for loving Abel!"

I fidgeted in my chair. "Mrs. McKenzie . . . Teresa," I said. "You shouldn't be tellin' me all this. I don't . . ."

"No!" she said. "I have to tell you *all* of it . . . and you have to hear me!"

Teresa closed her eyes and slumped back in her chair, seeming suddenly older than her years. When she spoke again, there was sadness in her voice that hurt me just to hear it.

"What happened next changed everything. There, on the floor of our sitting room, Zack held me down. He hurt me. He took me by force."

Again, Teresa fell silent. Tears brimmed in her eyes.

"When it was over," she said, "he seemed to realize what he'd done. He apologized. He begged my forgiveness. I heard his words, but I couldn't answer him. I couldn't look at him. When he reached out his hand in a clumsy attempt to comfort me, I flinched and drew away. Some time later, I sat up and found that he'd gone.

"I learned I was pregnant the week before Abel and I were married. Four weeks later, I told Abel I was expecting. Eight months later, Ian was born.

"Abel was pleased as punch. I put the past behind me and made a home for my husband and my son. I made a solemn vow never to let Abel know the truth about Ian, and I have kept that vow.

"Ian has become a fine young man. Abel and I, and his sister and brother, love him and are proud of him. He's been loyal and hardworking. He has put his own needs aside to help us on the ranch and stand with Abel in this feud with Zack. But now

Ian is in love with Morgan. Naturally enough, he wants to make a life with her."

Teresa raised her eyes to mine. "No matter what we have to do, we absolutely *cannot* allow that to happen," she said. "Morgan Rainford is Ian's *half sister!*"

TWENTY-TWO
▼
SECRETS AND SORROW

The echo of Teresa's words hung in the room like the silence after a gunshot. She leaned forward in her chair and touched my hand. "Forgive me for burdening you with my secret," she said. "It's a terrible way to repay your kindness."

She sighed. "What a cruel joke fate has played on my son, and on us all," she said. "Ian has fallen in love with the one girl in the entire world he must *not* marry."

I didn't know what to say. "Are you sure? Maybe Doc Reynolds . . ."

Teresa smiled a twisted smile, but there was no humor in it. "I'm sure," she said. "Besides, Dr. Reynolds doesn't keep secrets. He sets them free.

"I'll do what I must to protect Ian," she said, "even if I have to tell him everything."

Teresa's voice broke. Seconds passed before she could speak again. Then she said, "If it comes to that, *everyone* will be hurt: Abel, Ian, Morgan,

Zack, and Melissa. And the feud will continue. It will probably grow even worse.

"I'm asking you to do whatever you can to keep Ian and Morgan from making a horrible mistake. I'm sorry to involve you in our troubles, but you're the only person I can ask."

Teresa crossed her arms, holding herself. She seemed smaller, frailer than I recalled. Only her eyes, warm and deep brown, seemed alive. They pleaded for a help I didn't know how to give. I have at times been the object of a person's hope, but never before had I been someone's *only* hope.

I didn't mean to make her cry, but that's how it turned out. "I'll do what I can," I said, and her tears began to fall.

As I set out on the road to Reata, I couldn't help but wonder why people kept telling me their secrets. I was a peace officer, not a priest. The kind of confessions I usually dealt with were more likely to lead to prison than to absolution. Now it seemed I was not only *hearing* people's secrets, I was somehow expected to be a *party* to them.

The secret Teresa McKenzie confided in me was so personal and delicate I scarcely knew what to think. Normally, a woman would tell such a thing only to her dearest, closest sister. Why had Teresa shared it with me?

Even as I asked myself the question, I knew the answer. Teresa, like many another mother, loved her children more than herself. She loved her son Ian, and she could not allow him to enter a marriage that promised only grief and misery to so many. She was desperate to find someone who might help her change his mind.

I had gone from learning about Ian and Morgan's romance to being in cahoots with the lovers. Now Teresa McKenzie was asking me to help break up that romance, and I'd told her I'd do what I could. Right then it seemed the only constant thing about my life was its changeableness.

In Reata, Leviticus Glick convened a coroner's jury at the funeral parlor. A panel of local citizens heard the testimonies of Sheriff Ross Friendly and me concerning the discovery of Loco John's body. Both Doc Reynolds and Leviticus offered opinions regarding the cause of death, agreeing that John was shot through the heart with a large-caliber weapon.

Travis Burnett and several other Circle R cowboys were questioned. They all admitted they were at the sheep camp that day. They said they had bedeviled and harassed John some—"just havin' a little cowboy fun"—but no one knew anything about his death.

"The crazy old coot came out of his wagon with a rifle," Travis said. "Went to shootin' at us."

"So you boys returned fire?" Leviticus asked. "You fired back, and you killed him."

"Not us," Travis said slyly. "We don't know anythin' about a killin'."

This testimony prompted Doc Reynolds to observe that since apparently nobody killed the unfortunate herder, he must still be alive. In that event, Doc said, it would be "imprudent and premature" for us to bury him.

In the end, the jury reached the only verdict it could: Loco John died of a gunshot wound to the heart, inflicted by person or persons unknown. Leviticus dismissed the jurors, and they all retired to the Longhorn Saloon for a nightcap.

I stood with Sheriff Friendly outside the funeral parlor and watched the Circle R cowboys mount their horses and ride off into the night.

"This has been a bad evenin' for justice," I said. "We both know those boys murdered that old man."

The sheriff shifted the tobacco quid in his cheek and spat. "*I* don't know any such a thing," he said. "Anyway, I've got all I can do solvin' crimes I can prove."

I turned away and stepped out onto the street. "Me, too, Ross," I said. "That's why I aim to keep workin' until I prove *this* one."

In my room at the hotel, I stretched out on my bed and stared up into the darkness. For all my bold words to the sheriff, I had doubts aplenty. Sometimes it seemed that for all my effort, I'd done little or nothing to bring peace to the valley. A shooting war seemed *more* likely, not less.

Zack Rainford claimed the grazing land above Vendetta Canyon as his own. He still saw Abel McKenzie as a trespasser and an enemy. The two stubborn men had agreed to meet face-to-face, but I held little hope their meeting would end the feud.

Somewhere, Griff Tallon, self-styled stock detective for the cattle interests, roamed the plains and mountains like the angel of death, hunting for cow thieves and rustlers.

Travis Burnett, Zack's range boss, seemed eager to prove his loyalty by harassing Abel's herders and sheep. Burnett was cunning and ambitious. I figured him for a man who'd do anything to achieve his ends.

The raids on the McKenzie sheep camps had led to the death of one herder and the wounding of another. Sheep had been clubbed to death. A horse and dog were shot. A herder's wagon had been burned.

At first, learning about Ian and Morgan's secret romance gave me hope. Surely, I thought, a marriage between Abel's oldest son and Zack's only daughter would bring the two families together and lead to peace. Teresa's revelation dashed that hope.

Now, I had agreed to try to *prevent* a marriage between Ian and Morgan! I had no idea how I could accomplish that, but Teresa's story fully convinced me of the need.

I was long on good intentions but short on accomplishments. I tried to tell myself just *having* good intentions was worthwhile, but then I remembered what hell is said to be paved with.

Like a dog chasing its tail, my thoughts kept running in circles, going nowhere. I don't know how long it was before I finally dropped off to sleep, but when next I opened my eyes, the eastern sky was red above the mountains.

I stood at the window of my room and looked out on the quiet street.

Down the block, lamplight shone at the Uptown Café. I splashed water on my face, stepped into my clothes, and made my way downstairs. Two minutes later, I was the Uptown's first customer of the day.

When I left the café, I headed up the street to Peabody's and saddled Rutherford. Leading him outside, I set foot in the stirrup and swung up onto him. Then, as the sun topped the eastern mountains, I turned the buckskin out on the road that led to the Circle R.

As if I needed a reminder that a range war was still a threat to the peace, Cotton Smith rode up again to meet me at the ranch gate. Recognizing me, the gunman lowered the carbine he carried and nodded. "Mornin', deputy," he said.

"Mornin'," I replied. "I'm here to see Zack. Is he at home?"

"He's out with the wagon, brandin' slicks. He know you're comin'?"

There was something about being questioned by a hired gun that rubbed me the wrong way. "I guess he will when he sees me," I said. "Stand aside."

Smith studied me through narrowed eyes. I saw his glance drop from my face to my deputy's badge. "Sure," he said. Dismounting, he opened the gate and swung it wide.

"Just doin' my job."

"Blessed are the watch dogs," I said and passed through.

Melissa Rainford walked out on her porch to greet me as I approached the house. She wore a handsome dress of green silk, with lace trimmings and a bustle. Her fine blond hair was pulled back in a tidy bun, and she carried herself with pride and dignity. "Good morning, Merlin," she said. "It's good to see you again."

"Likewise, Miz Rainford. How is Morgan doing?"

A shadow seemed to pass over her face. Tiny frown lines appeared and quickly disappeared. "Morgan's burns are healing nicely," she said. "Dr. Reynolds believes there will be little or no scarring.

"She has recently presented us with something of a dilemma, however. She says she intends to marry Ian McKenzie. She and Ian plan to leave

Meriwether County and make their home else-where.

"My husband is quite adamant. He told Morgan he will never give his permission for such a match. She replied that while she would like our permission, she does not require it.

"My husband says he will cut her off without a penny if she marries Ian. She will have no dowry and no inheritance. Morgan says she cares nothing for such things. She and her young man will live on love, apparently. They will, Morgan declares, earn their own way in the world. And, she says, they will be happy."

Melissa looked out toward the hills beyond the ranch buildings. Her voice fell and was so soft I barely heard her words. "Perhaps," she said, "they will."

She turned back to me, and there was pain behind her gray eyes. "And so goes the war," she said. "Not between our family and the McKenzies or between cattlemen and sheepmen. I'm afraid *this* war is a *civil* war."

Melissa's eyes narrowed. She said, "But then you probably know all this. Morgan says you're her friend—hers, and Ian's."

If you only knew, I thought. *Yes, I sympathize with their romance. I understand their wish to be free of the bitterness between their families. I am their friend. Because I am, and because of my promise to Teresa McKenzie, I now have to* oppose *their marriage. Life sure takes some surprising turns.*

"I know some of it," I said. "May I see Morgan?"

"Of course. Please, come in."

I stepped down and tied Rutherford to a hitching post just off the porch. As I did so, I heard hoof-beats coming up behind me. Turning, I found myself face to face with Travis Burnett!

Burnett looked startled. He reined in the chestnut gelding he rode, staring wide-eyed at me. He seemed confused. A spasm of irritation crossed his face.

"Travis," I said.

He had not expected to see me at the Circle R that morning. He'd come to the house to speak to Melissa, but each time he looked at her, his eyes darted back to me. I smiled, enjoying his confusion.

"Yes, Travis?" Melissa said. "What is it?"

The Circle R range boss was off balance and trying to regain his self-control. "Uh, yes, missus," he said. "We're brandin' slicks up on Badger Creek today. Zack asked me to fetch his tally book. Said you'd know where it's at."

"Yes," Melissa said. "Wait here." Then she turned and went inside the house.

Burnett sat his saddle. He was edgy, and the chestnut picked up on its rider's mood, as horses will. The gelding was fidgety, fighting the bit.

Burnett kept checking the animal's movement, tightening and then slackening the rein.

I didn't make it easy on him. "Can't you hold that horse still?" I asked.

Burnett made no answer but kept his eyes on the door Melissa had entered. He tried to shrug off my presence, but his curiosity was too strong. "You here to see Zack?" he asked. "He's . . ."

"I heard. He's brandin' slicks up on Badger Creek."

Burnett stared at me, waiting for an answer to his question. I declined to give him one. A moment later, Melissa came out with the tally book in her hand.

I didn't like Travis Burnett. He was cruel and he was arrogant. I was as sure as I could be that he murdered Loco John. I wasn't about to cut him any slack. "Right now," I said, "I'm here to see Morgan."

Burnett's face flushed. His eyes bulged. He slacked his rein and spurred the chestnut forward. Bending in the saddle, Burnett reached out and took the tally book from Melissa's hand. Then he jerked the horse around and rode down past the charred ruins of the barn and up the slope beyond.

I turned back to Melissa. She watched as Burnett topped the rise and disappeared over the crest of the hill. Looking at me, she smiled her cool smile. "Come," she said. "Morgan will be pleased to see you."

Melissa led me to a sunny corner room at the back of the house. "I'll put on a pot of tea," Melissa said. "I'll leave you and Morgan alone."

Across the room, Morgan reclined on an upholstered divan, her feet resting on a padded footstool. She lay back, gazing listlessly out the window. I wondered, *Is she waiting for Ian to come for her? Is she eager to begin her new life as Ian's bride?*

Well, of course she is, I said to myself. *You do ask the durnedest questions sometimes.*

"Hello, Morgan," I said.

She turned toward me, and her smile lit up the room. "Merlin!" she said. "I'm so glad to see you!"

Gauze dressings covered Morgan's arms and hands. A Windsor chair stood beside her divan, and she directed me toward it with a gesture. "Come," she said. "Sit beside me and tell me all the news! Have you seen Ian? Did he tell you . . ."

I sat down. "Whoa, Morgan," I said. "First, I want to know how *you* are."

She shrugged. "Burns on my arms still hurt sometimes, but they're getting better—beginning to itch. Doc Reynolds says that means they're healing. The worst part is not being able to get out and ride. I do miss Sheba."

"Now, please," she said, "did Ian tell you the news? We're getting married! We'll be leaving as soon as he comes for me."

Her happiness was so obvious it nearly broke my

heart. "Yes," I said. "I was there when he told his folks."

"What did they say? Did they accept our decision? Were they . . ."

I looked away. "Well," I said, "Ian's mother is . . . opposed to the idea."

Morgan's face turned serious. "Yes. I thought she might be. Poor Ian.

"I've had my own battles here," she said. "Mother seems to understand, a little. But Dad refuses even to talk about it. He says he'll disown me. He says he'll never speak to me again if I marry Ian."

"Oh," I said. "I don't think he means that. He just needs time to get used to the idea."

Morgan's jaw took on a stubborn set. "Ian and I have given *enough* time to our parents and their stupid feud," she said. "We're not waiting any longer."

"I know how you feel," I said, "but I really think you ought to put your wedding off for a while."

Morgan frowned. "You, too?" she said. "I thought you were on *our* side."

"I am. But takin' a little more time can do no harm. Your folks might change their minds."

"No. We aren't waiting any longer. Ian and I have decided."

"I hear you. But, well, Ian's dad asked him to put off the wedding for two weeks. Ian agreed."

"Ian . . . agreed? Two *weeks?*"

"That's right," I said.

"He wouldn't do that without talking to me! Where is his letter? Did he send a letter for me with you?"

I felt sick. It was hard for me to breathe. "No," I said. "I guess he was just too busy workin' with his dad to write you."

Tears brimmed in Morgan's eyes. She turned her face away, toward the window. "I'm glad you came, Merlin," she said, "but maybe you should go now. I'm feeling a bit tired."

"Sure, Morgan. I didn't mean to play you out. Get some rest."

I met Melissa on my way out. She appeared in the doorway with a teapot and cups on a tray and questions in her eyes.

"I'm sorry, Miz Rainford," I said, "but I can't stay. I have to ride up to Badger Creek and talk to your husband. Tell Morgan I hope she's feelin' better soon."

Outside again, I untied Rutherford and stepped up into the saddle. *You durned hypocrite,* I said to myself. *You hope Morgan's better, but you're the one who just caused her unhappiness.*

I turned the buckskin down across the barn lot and rode him up the hill the way Burnett had gone. I didn't feel so well myself. I felt like I'd just kicked a puppy.

TWENTY-THREE

▼

A NIGHT VISITOR

Badger Creek originated in the Flint Creek Hills just five miles north of Circle R headquarters. While I was not all that familiar with the creeks and drainages of Meriwether County, I had studied the courthouse maps and had a fair working knowledge of the region. Leaving the home ranch, I picked up a well-traveled trail that bore hoof-prints of shod horses and tracks of the outfit's wagon. A short time later, I found the branding crew hard at work.

Like most cow outfits on the northern plains, the Circle R held its spring roundup in June. Riders gathered cattle from every corner of the range, branded and marked the calves, and made a head count before turning the herd out on summer grass. I'd heard in town that Zack Rainford had wrapped up his roundup two weeks earlier. The fact that he'd taken the wagon out again told me the Circle R was now branding some of the calves they missed.

A crooked line of trees marked the course of Badger Creek as it flowed out of the hills and snaked across a broad valley. Out on the plain, riders worked the herd, roping calves and dragging them to the flankers and the hot iron men.

I drew rein atop a low hill and just sat for a while, watching the branding crew. I recognized some of the boys—Travis Burnett was one of the ropers, Harve Rawlins was an iron man—and there were others I'd seen before but didn't know by name.

Before I became a peace officer, I worked roundups as a horse wrangler back in Progress County. I always enjoyed seeing how other outfits worked livestock, especially since I no longer had to.

Maybe a half mile to the east, on Badger Creek, stood the Circle R's mess wagon and tent. The cook busied himself with his Dutch ovens and kettles, while a young yellow-haired wrangler rustled firewood from a stand of cottonwoods. Across the creek, dust drifted up from the milling hooves of the cattle, where riders held the herd apart from the branding crew.

I spotted Zack astride a high-headed bay at the herd's edge, keeping a careful eye on the proceedings. He was a man with much on his mind, I knew, and it didn't all have to do with running the Circle R.

After nearly losing his only daughter Morgan in the barn fire, Zack was now threatened with losing her in another way. Morgan had announced her intention to marry Ian McKenzie, the son of her father's enemy.

Zack had been—how had his wife, Melissa, put

it?—adamant. He had no doubt used all his powers of persuasion to change his daughter's mind, and when that failed, he had turned to threats. Morgan would be disowned. She would be disinherited. Zack would never speak to her again. Zack blustered. Morgan stubbornly held firm. And in the end, Morgan held the high cards. She was of age. She didn't need Zack's approval or his blessing. She would marry Ian as she planned.

Now, working cattle with his men, Zack sat his high-headed bay and went through the motions, but I knew where his thoughts were.

There was an irony in the deadlock with his daughter that Zack could not appreciate. He was right, after all—Morgan must *not* marry Ian. She must not, for a reason only Teresa McKenzie and I knew. If Morgan married Ian, the father of the bride would also be the father of the groom.

I turned the buckskin downhill at a walk. Zack looked up as I drew near. He must have had mixed feelings at seeing me, but if he did, he didn't let them show.

"Fanshaw," he said. He made it sound like a question.

"Mornin', Zack. I need to talk to you when you have a minute."

"No time like now," he said. "Let's ride over to the wagon."

Zack raised his hand, and an older cowpuncher left his place with the herd and rode up beside us.

Drawing rein, the man cleared the dust from his lungs and took his hat off. He was bald as a door-knob, and he wiped a sweat-stained bandana across his scalp before donning his hat again. Zack handed him the tally book. "Keep the count for me, Curly," he said. "I'll be back d'rectly."

Zack turned his thoroughbred toward the wagon on Badger Creek, and I fell in beside him. From behind us, I heard a calf bawl as a hot iron marked its hide.

The Circle R mess wagon setup was typical of most outfits on the northern range. A canvas fly stretched from the rear of the wagon to the cook tent, providing shade from the summer sun. Dutch ovens and kettles simmered in the fire pit and atop the stove. A two-gallon coffee boiler hung by a chain from a tripod above the coals.

The cook bore the marks of an old-time cow-hand, game leg and all. He watched us draw near with neither greeting nor comment, save for a slight nod to Zack. We tied our horses to a willow beside the creek and ducked under the fly. Zack helped himself to a dipper of water from the barrel on the wagon's side and drank deeply. Then he said, "All right. What's on your mind, deputy?"

"I talked to Abel," I said. "He has agreed to meet with you. Two weeks from today, at the hotel in Reata."

Zack made a wry face. "I'll meet him because I

said I would. But I wouldn't get my hopes up if I were you."

"My hopes are always up," I said. "That's just the way I am."

"Maybe you've got more reason for hope than I do. You don't have to deal with my bull-headed daughter."

I nodded. "I spoke with her today, back at your house. The conversation ended when I said she should put off her wedding plans."

"The hell you say. Morgan told me you're in *favor* of a marriage between her and the McKenzie kid."

"I was, at first. Thought it might bring your families together. I've changed my mind."

Zack sighed. "Now if somebody would just change *Morgan's* mind."

He studied my face. "But you didn't ride all the way out here just to talk about Morgan," he said. "Like I asked you before, what's on your mind?"

"Mainly, I wanted to let you know the time and place for your meeting with Abel. But there is something else. A coroner's jury ruled this week that Loco John died at the hands of person or persons unknown during a raid by your cowboys on his camp. The jurors expressed no opinion as to whether the killing was accidental, self-defense, manslaughter, or murder.

"I believe one of your men killed Loco John in cold blood. I won't rest until I know how it happened and who pulled the trigger. There's a blood trail, and I aim to follow it, no matter where it leads. I just wanted you to know that."

I had strong feelings about John's death, and I'd been plainer spoken than I intended. Zack Rainford was the big he-bull of Meriwether County, and people didn't generally talk to him the way I had.

Zack looked at me as if he was seeing me for the first time. Then the tension left his face, and he smiled.

"I wouldn't have it any other way, deputy," he said.

Zack invited me to stay and eat dinner with the branding crew, but I declined. I figured I'd be about as welcome among the cowboys as a clown at a funeral. I shook Zack's hand, swung up onto Rutherford, and lit out cross-country to pick up the road to Reata.

Back in town, I found a telegram from Ridgeway waiting for me at the hotel. The marshal had received my earlier report and wanted to know what progress I'd made in investigating Loco John's death. There was little I could tell him, but I replied that I was still looking into the matter and expected a breakthrough at any time.

Of course, Ridgeway was an old hand at dealing with his deputies. He would recognize my answer for what it was, an admission that I hadn't made a lick of progress since my last report, but we'd both play the game in spite of what we knew.

• • •

I caught up on some long neglected personal tasks. I took some clothes to the Chinese laundry. I treated myself to a shave, haircut, and bath at the barbershop, and I paid a kid two bits to shine my boots.

Come evening, I looked up Doc Reynolds over at the Longhorn and drank a few beers while he caught me up on the latest local gossip. As usual, Doc was more than willing to do so, and he was eager to hear any news, scandal, or rumor I cared to pass on.

I told him it had been a dull week and I had nothing to relate, but I couldn't help thinking I knew the granddaddy of all tales had I been inclined to tell it.

That's where Doc and I differed. Doc loved being in the know, and he was happy as a magpie with a dead mule whenever he heard a fresh item of gossip. Not me. Teresa's story was a heavy burden that stole my sleep and troubled my mind. I'd have given a thousand dollars (if ever I *had* a thousand dollars) *not* to know what I knew.

Two nights later, I ate an early supper at the hotel and stopped by Peabody's Livery to check on Rutherford. The buckskin stood in a stall, his head down and his eyes dull. He seemed not to know I was there, and he didn't move when I spoke his name.

Cal Peabody, the stable's owner, had gone for the

day. His night man, a part-time drunk and full-time loafer name of Fred Leach, said the buckskin had been off his feed since I brought him back from the Circle R.

"I gave him fresh hay, like you told me," Fred said. "Oats, too. But far as I know, he never et a bite."

"That's not like him," I said. "I hope he's not comin' down with colic."

I walked back to Rutherford's stall with Fred. "Keep an eye on him tonight," I said. "If he breaks out in a sweat or shows any other signs of colic, let me know. I'm in room number five, over at the Rainford."

Walking back to the hotel, I have to admit I was worried some. I don't know why, but the Almighty made horses so they can't throw up. If a horse eats moldy hay, too much green alfalfa or something, he's pretty much stuck with it. The animal develops a big time bellyache, can even bust a gut and die. I went to bed still thinking about Rutherford and hoping the town had a good horse doctor.

I must have dozed off, because the next thing I knew, someone was banging on the door of my room and calling my name. I threw the covers back and both my feet hit the floor at the same time. The room was dark as the inside of a cat, but my hand found the grips of my forty-four without seeing it.

I pulled the gun from the leather. "Who's there?" I asked.

"It's me, Fred, from the livery!" the voice outside my door said. "Your horse is doin' worse, deputy. He's down and can't get up!"

"I'll be right there," I said. "Wait for me!"

I fumbled in the darkness until I found the matches atop the table by my bed. Lighting a lamp, I slipped into my pants and shirt. I pulled my boots on, buckled the forty-four about my waist, and grabbed my hat. Seconds later, I opened the door to my room and stepped into the hall. Fred was already headed for the staircase, and I was one step behind.

We started up the street at a run, but within half a block, Fred became winded and stopped. "Got me . . . a side ache, deputy," he gasped. "Go . . . on ahead. I'll . . . be along."

I left Fred where he stood and ran on down to the livery barn. Stepping inside, I stared into the dimly lit space. A smoky lantern, turned low, hung from a wire just inside the door. Dark shadows filled the corners of the room. Taking the lantern from its wire, I started down the row of stalls to the one that housed Rutherford.

From somewhere behind me, a voice broke the stillness. "Hands up, deputy," it said. "I've got a gun trained on your back."

The voice was familiar, a man's voice. I'd heard it before, but I couldn't put a name to it. "Unbuckle your gun belt and let it drop," the voice said. "Use your left hand."

I figured I could either do as I was told, or throw the lantern, spin, and try to shoot it out. The first choice would put me at the mercy of a man with a gun aimed at my back. The second choice would be brave and bold, wild and woolly. And stupid.

I unbuckled my forty-four and let it fall to the stable's floor. "All right," I said. "Now what?"

"Step away from it and turn around."

I turned, still holding the lantern. The man took a step forward, a Colt's revolver pointed at my middle. I knew the man. It was Harve Rawlins, the cowboy who helped me take care of Loco John the night I fought Travis Burnett.

"Well, Harve," I said. "I never expected you'd pull a gun on me."

I turned the lantern up. Harve looked sheepish. He looked down at the revolver in his hand. "I just want to talk. But on my terms."

"All right if I see to my horse first?"

"He's all right. He got better just after you left this evenin'. I gave Fred three dollars to fetch you. Told him to say the buckskin was sick. I figured you'd come runnin' if you thought your horse was in trouble."

"You thought right. You had Fred pegged, too. There's not much he wouldn't do for three dollars."

Harve bent down and picked up my holstered forty-four. "Let's go into Cal's office and set," he said. "I wouldn't want certain folks to see us together."

I opened the door. "Sure thing," I said, "but you don't need that gun, Harve."

"Maybe I don't. And maybe I do. Set over there on the sofa."

I put the lantern on Cal's cluttered desk and took a seat. Harve sat down in Cal's chair and laid my belted forty-four and his own revolver on the desktop. "I ain't no gunhand," he said. "Most of the time, I don't even carry this old lead chucker. But I figured she might come in handy tonight."

Harve fell silent. In the lantern's dim light, his face looked troubled. He looked down at his hands and then raised his eyes to mine. "I don't know if you remember," he said, "but I helped you take care of Loco John the night Travis Burnett took the sheep shears to him."

"I remember," I said. "I appreciate your help."

"The way Travis and the boys did him that night wasn't right. I took no part in it, but I didn't try to stop it, either. I've always felt bad about that."

Again, Harve fell silent. In the stillness, I could hear the sound of his breathing. His hands opened and then balled into fists.

"I was with the boys when we struck that old man's camp on the mountain," he said. "We were like a damned pack of wild dogs! Whoopin' and hollerin', shootin' and clubbin' sheep. Seems like we all went a little loco.

"We killed John's sheepdog. Killed his horse. And, when he came out of his wagon, we killed *him*. Harmless old mutton puncher, helpless as one of his lambs."

Harve's voice broke. After a moment, he spoke again. "I keep seein' his face. Poor devil was so scared . . .

"It was Travis Burnett who killed him," he said. "Travis shot him down in cold blood, and laughed when he did it."

I held my breath. Then I asked, "Did John put up a fight? Was he armed?"

"Hell, no. He just jumped out of his wagon with his hands up, and Travis shot him in the chest. Travis found that old single-shot rifle in the wagon and laid it next to his body."

"You did the right thing, tellin' me," I said. "Will you testify against Travis in a court of law?"

Harve shook his head. "Sorry, deputy. I can't do that."

"Burnett needs to stand trial for what he did. Without your testimony, he'll never be convicted."

"I can't help that."

"You're not tellin' me everything," I said. "I have a feelin' there's more."

"You're right, deputy. I'll tell you the rest of it. Travis Burnett is a man of big ambitions. He plans to take over the Circle R someday, and he's workin' his plan. It ain't enough for him to be Zack Rainford's ramrod; he's got his sights set on ownin' the outfit.

"The way he figures to do that is to marry Zack's

311

daughter. Never mind that she despises him. Never mind that Travis is the last man in the whole damn world she'd take up with. Travis sees her as his way to the top, so she's elected.

"Travis has made Zack's feud with the McKenzies his own, both to gain Zack's favor and because, in some crazy way, he already thinks the ranch is his. He'll come against anything that seems to get between him and his ambitions, and he'll come against it hard."

Harve paused. He fixed his gaze on me, and his eyes shone in the lantern light. "That's the other reason I came here tonight," he said, "to warn you. Travis thinks *you* are in his way."

"I guess I am," I said. "I want him for Loco John's murder."

"That ain't it, deputy. Travis thinks you're courtin' Zack's daughter, Morgan. He's seen you come visiting. He's watched you share supper with the family. He's wondered about your private meetings with Zack, both at the ranch and the other day out on Badger Creek. He's heard about your savin' Morgan from the fire at the barn. In short, Travis sees you as a threat to all his plans."

I laughed. "Travis is crazy as a root cellar rat."

"Maybe so," Harve said, "but I'd watch my back if I was you. Crazy or not, Travis Burnett wants you dead."

Twenty-Four

▼

Dead Reckoning

"I've got my failin's, deputy," Harve said. "Even when I know what's right, I tend to be slow to act. I was late offerin' my help the night Travis took the sheep shears to Loco John.

"I was late believin' Travis's big talk about killin' sheepherders. Then I saw him gun down Loco John and burn his wagon. I was late tellin' you about the murder. Didn't want to rat on my boss. Trouble was, I kept seein' the killin' over and over in my mind. Kept rememberin' the look on that old man's face just before Travis shot him.

"Now, Travis has his sights set on you. The way he figures, you stand in the way of everything he wants. He aims to kill you, deputy."

I shrugged. "Bunkhouse brag, that's all. I'm no helpless sheepherder."

"You ain't bulletproof, either."

I got to my feet. Nervous, Harve reached for the six-gun that lay before him.

"You're not going to shoot me," I said. "We both know that."

I picked up my belted revolver from the desk. Harve made no move to stop me. "I'm takin' my forty-four back now," I said. "If what you say is true, I'll need it.

"You're a better man than you think you are," I told him. "That's why you're losin' sleep over John. That's why you came to warn me. And that's why you'll do what's right and testify against Travis Burnett."

Harve shook his head. "I told you I can't do that."

"Why not? Afraid of his friends?"

"Not hardly."

He slumped back in his chair. "I . . . I just don't want to call attention to myself."

I buckled my gun belt about my waist. "Are you on the dodge?"

He nodded. "Wyoming. Two years ago. Shot a man in a card game and lit a shuck for Montana. Harve Rawlins ain't my right name."

"I didn't hear that," I said. "And I won't press you. I'm obliged for the information, and for the warning. But I still believe you'll do the right thing when the chips are down. Bein' a good man is a hard habit to break."

Harve was still sitting at Cal's desk when I walked out of the livery barn and turned up the street toward the hotel.

I came back at eight the next morning to check on Rutherford. Cal Peabody was on the job at that early hour, wheeling a loaded wheelbarrow of horse manure up from the direction of the stalls. Fred Leach was nowhere to be seen.

"Just the man I wanted to see," Cal said. "That buckskin horse of yours like to have filled up his stall with horse manure last evenin'. You can help clean it up."

"Not me," I said. "You're the man who chose the horse manure business." I nodded at the wheelbarrow. "Besides, I don't know all that much about machinery.

"The buckskin had me worried," I said. "When I looked in on him last night, he looked colicky, like he was maybe plugged up."

Cal snorted. "Well, he ain't plugged up now. The dam has broke, and women and children are headin' for the hills."

He grinned. "Come on into the office. I'll pour you a cup of coffee while I figure out how to charge you for excessive road apples."

"I never saw a man so ungrateful," I said. "Here I talk my horse into providin' you with free fertilizer, and all you do is complain. How much you figure to charge me for the coffee?"

Cal led the way into his office and poured us each a cup from the pot atop his stove. He sat down behind his desk, where Harve sat the night before. I took the same place I'd occupied on the sofa. It was a strange feeling.

We sipped our coffee while Cal offered opinions about the weather, the high price of feed, and the difficulty of hiring good help. He remarked upon the shiftless qualities of Fred Leach, his night man, and offered profane speculation as to Fred's possible ancestry.

One thing about Cal—when he was on a roll, a man didn't have to worry much about holding up his end of the conversation. I offered an occasional "uh-huh" and "you bet" from time to time, but other than that, I was free to think about my next step in the Loco John murder case.

I decided to seek out and arrest Travis Burnett. True, Harve Rawlins said he wouldn't testify in court, but I could run a bluff. I could tell Burnett I had a witness to the crime—which I did, even if I couldn't use him. If I described in detail the events of the murder, Burnett might break. He might even confess, I thought, although I knew that would be a stretch.

I could haul him in and lock him up, at least for a day or two. Harve might change his mind about testifying by then. Nothing was sure, but sometimes a man has to go with what he has. It was better, I thought, than waiting for Burnett to come to me.

Cal finally ran out of chin music and made signs of returning to work. I was grateful the subject of Morgan and Ian hadn't come up. I had given Cal to understand that I was, like him, friendly to their romance. It would be hard to explain why I now opposed it. I thanked him for the coffee and made my way back to Rutherford's stall.

• • •

Whatever the source of the buckskin's previous distress, he showed no sign of it that morning. Rutherford was his old self, eager to travel and curious as a cat. I rode him out on the now-familiar road to the Circle R with an eagerness of my own. I had held second-best cards in the game too long. Now, at last, I felt my luck was turning, and I was ready to bet the limit.

I wondered where I would find Burnett. Would he be at the home ranch when I rode in? Would he be out on the range with the wagon? Would I be able to find him at all?

And what of procedure? Was it foolhardy for me to go up against Burnett alone? Should I tell Sheriff Friendly of my plans, ask him to back my play?

Everything I knew about Ross Friendly told me I couldn't trust him. Clearly, he was a friend of the Circle R. He would raise objections, urge delay. He would demand to see my evidence and question my witness. He would hinder the cause of justice, not help it.

Harve Rawlins was an eyewitness to the killing of Loco John, but he refused to testify or sign a deposition to that effect. The truth was that no matter what I knew and no matter how I knew it, I had no legal cause to arrest Travis Burnett.

My choices were few. I could back away or shoot the moon.

That's cold comfort, said a voice inside my head. *Those are the same choices Custer had.*

It was just past noon when I turned Rutherford off the main road and onto the track that led to the Circle R. Beyond the gate laid a broad sagebrush plain, bounded by low hills. Scrub cedar and pines crowned the hilltops, and wooded coulees tumbled down from above to meet the tableland. Clouds drifted over the valley, racing their shadows across the plain below.

The day was sunny and warm, with a following breeze that kept the smell of crushed sage with me. Rutherford held a steady trot along the wagon ruts, and only the sound of his hooves broke the silence. I felt ready for my showdown with Burnett and confident I could deal with anything that might arise.

And then, for no reason I could put a name to, a powerful sense of dread came over me. I saw nothing, heard nothing, and yet a feeling of danger quickened my breath and sent a chill up my spine. I narrowed my eyes, scanning the hilltops and coulees. Nothing. I twisted in my saddle, looking behind me. Again, nothing.

I looked at Rutherford's ears. Ears that are stiff sometimes mean a horse senses danger. The buckskin's ears were flopping off to the side. He was relaxed, intent on keeping his steady pace.

¡Cuidado! Back in Dry Creek, Ridgeway had

warned me. *Be careful! Notice everything! Expect the unexpected!* I shifted my weight in the saddle, lightened my foothold on the stirrups. Sweat crawled from beneath my hatband and inched down my face. My mouth was dry.

Rutherford kept his pace, dog-trotting across the big open. I looked down, past his shoulder, and saw the fresh dirt of a new badger hole. Rutherford could break a leg if he stepped in it! I jerked on the reins, checking his pace and turning him aside.

A bullet streaked past my chest, ripping the air. The sharp crack of a rifle shot broke the stillness. Startled, Rutherford bolted. I tried to reach my saddle gun but lost a stirrup and then my balance. The reins burned through my hand; I felt myself falling. Prairie sod rushed up and met me. I landed hard, rolled, and lay still.

Silence. My heart beat loud in my ears. I took inventory. No pain. *Good*, I thought, *nothing is broken*. I lay on my belly, my face in the dirt. The sound of the rifle had been loud. I guessed the shooter was fairly close, a hundred yards or less, on one of the hilltops. He would be watching me, ready to fire again.

Where was Rutherford? He wouldn't go far. I could get to my feet, make a dash for safety, but where could I go? There was no cover this side of the hills themselves. I lay still and strained my ears to listen.

Seconds turned into minutes. I tasted dirt and

slowed my breathing. My right hand inched closer to the forty-four on my hip. I waited.

Was the shooter still watching? Had he left me for dead and gone away? Or was he coming to finish the job? With my ear to the sod, I listened. Time passed.

Faintly, I felt the heavy footfall of a horse approaching. Was it Rutherford, coming back for me, or the bushwhacker? The vibrations grew stronger and then stopped. I held my breath.

My thumb slipped the thong that held my revolver in the leather and settled on the forty-four's hammer. And then I heard it, close at hand, only yards away—a man, walking through the grass! Slowly he came, his spur rowels chiming softly with each step. The footsteps stopped. I could wait no longer.

Rolling sharply away, I pulled my revolver and brought it up. The bush-whacker stood not ten yards away, his carbine in his hands. I saw his eyes go wide, and I recognized him—Travis Burnett!

Hurriedly, Travis fired the carbine. Dirt clods exploded where I'd just lain. The forty-four bucked in my hand, and I saw Burnett take the slug in his chest and go down. On his back in the grass, he levered the carbine to shoot again, but I was on him and jerked the weapon out of his hands. "Give it up, Burnett," I said. "I don't want to kill you!"

Burnett bared his teeth, his eyes hot with hatred.

"I believe you already *have*, god damn you!" he gasped.

"Hold still," I said. "Let me see where you're hit."

Burnett closed his eyes and sank back into the grass. He wore a belted Colt's revolver, and I took it from him and stuck it in my waistband. Tearing open his shirt, I saw the dark hole my forty-four had made. Bright blood bubbled from the hole, and I saw that the slug had punctured a lung.

Burnett groaned. "Hurts . . . like hell," he said.

I pulled my bandana from my throat and pressed it over the wound. "Lay still," I said.

Burnett's chestnut gelding stood maybe twenty yards away. Rutherford had wandered farther and watched warily from about twice that distance. I wondered if I should try to get Burnett back to ranch headquarters but decided against it. His skin was pale and clammy to the touch, and his breathing was ragged.

"I was coming for you," I said. "Coming to arrest you for Loco John's murder."

"You can't . . . prove . . . a goddam thing," he said.

I heard a rustle of movement. A shadow fell over me and Burnett. A voice from behind me said, "I think maybe he *can*, Travis."

I turned. Harve Rawlins looked down at me from the saddle of his horse. "Followed you, deputy," he said. "It's true, what you said. I aim to do what's right."

Harve stepped down and knelt beside Burnett and me. "There ain't but two choices. Either a man does right or he does wrong. I'm through doin' wrong."

"You . . . *told* him," Burnett said. "You spilled your guts!"

Harve looked at Burnett. "Damn right. I told him *everything*. Watched you try to dry-gulch him just now, too. Saw it all through my field glasses."

"A man . . . takes what he wants," Burnett said, "any way he can. I'd gun down that raggedy-ass sheepherder again . . . if I had the chance. Him . . . and a hundred more like him."

Burnett closed his eyes. He clenched his jaw, and his features twisted. Suddenly, he raised himself and glared at Harve. "You goddam rat!" he choked. "You *couldn't* have told him everything— you don't *know* everything!

"I've been stealin' Zack Rainford's cattle for years! High an' mighty cattle king never suspected a thing. Dumb sum'bitch blamed it on the nesters and sheepmen! Hell, I even burned his damn *barn* so he'd blame the sheepers!"

"You were gone that day," I said. "You were miles away."

"Poured . . . coal oil up in the loft. Left a lit candle in a pan. When the candle burned down . . ."

"You almost killed Morgan," I said.

Burnett coughed and then closed his eyes again. His breathing was labored, and his voice a harsh whisper. "Silly bitch . . . had no call . . . to go in that barn!"

His eyes opened suddenly. Burnett glared at me. "I . . . damn near . . . had it all," he wheezed. "You . . . meddlin' son of . . ."

His fingers clutched my arm. Struggling, he pulled himself up. A sudden spasm shook him and his body stiffened. His breath left him in a long sigh, and Travis Burnett fell back dead.

In the silence that followed, I heard Harve clear his throat. "I guess," he said, "that's what you lawmen would call a death-bed confession."

TWENTY-FIVE
▼
UNANSWERED QUESTIONS

The body of Travis Burnett lay on its back in the grass, staring at the sky with sightless eyes. I stood, feeling the tension ebb within me. Harve dismounted and walked up beside me. "Killin' a man is a damned serious thing," he said. "You take everything he is and everything he'll *ever* be."

"He *gave* it away when he tried to dry-gulch me. But you're right. Killin' a man is a damned serious thing."

I bent over the corpse and closed its eyes. "Give me a hand," I said. "We'll load him on his horse and take him to the Circle R."

Harve rode over and caught Burnett's gelding.

When he led the animal back, we lifted the body and laid it face down across the saddle. Tying the dead man's hands and feet to the cinch rings, I slid his carbine into its scabbard. Harve held the horse while I caught Rutherford and rode back to him. "Lead out," he said, and we turned our mounts out on the road that led to Rainford's.

Approaching the home ranch, we passed through the last gate and looked down on the house and outbuildings of the Circle R. At the barn lot, the ashes and burned wood from the fire had been hauled away, and carpenters were busy framing a new barn. I turned to Harve. "Ride back and take Burnett down to Zack's office," I said. "I don't want to parade his body past the women at the house."

Cotton Smith saw our approach. The gunman came riding up the hill at a lope and reined his horse to a sliding stop. He couldn't take his eyes off the corpse. "What the hell?"

"Burnett tried to dry-gulch me," I explained. "It didn't work out."

Smith stared, first at me and then at Harve. He seemed to be seeking a further explanation. I didn't offer one. "Do you know if Zack's at home?"

"Yeah. I think he's over with the carpenters."

"Tell him there's been some trouble," I said. "I'll meet him at his office."

Cotton stared at the corpse again. He looked at me, questions in his eyes. Then he turned his horse away and rode down to the barn lot.

Zack Rainford met us beneath the willow trees at the old log house he used for an office. He listened as I told him of the ambush and of Burnett's guilt in the murder of Loco John. I told him of Burnett's boast that he'd stolen Circle R cattle for years. I recounted Burnett's confession that he started the fire that burned the barn and nearly took Morgan's life. Harve Rawlins confirmed each statement and added observations of his own.

Through it all, Zack listened without comment or expression. The only time he showed any reaction was when he heard about the fire. At that point, the cattleman's eyes grew hard and his jaw muscles tensed, but he said nothing until he'd heard it all.

Then he said, "I think I always knew Travis wasn't quite on the square. I saw his ambition and thought it a good thing. I saw his hatred for nesters and sheepmen and regarded it as loyalty. I guess I didn't see his flaws because I didn't *want* to."

Half a dozen Circle R men gathered as we talked. They stood, twenty feet from the chestnut gelding that held Burnett's corpse, their faces hard as flint. Waiting in silence, their eyes traveled from the dead man to Zack.

Zack turned to the men. "Travis tried to bush-whack a lawman," he said, "and got himself a pine box for his trouble. No matter how you boys feel about Travis, or the outfit, that's the straight of it."

Zack spoke to the balding cowhand I saw at the branding. "Curly, hitch up a team and bring a wagon around. We're takin' Travis to the undertaker."

Twenty minutes later, with Curly at the reins and Zack, Harve, and me serving as outriders, that's exactly what we did.

The shooting of Travis Burnett was the talk of the county. For the second time that month, a coroner's jury convened in Reata. The county attorney questioned both me and Harve Rawlins. Even under some fairly heated questioning by Sheriff Friendly, Harve stuck to his testimony like a burr to a blanket.

Doc Reynolds and Leviticus Glick examined the body and found the cause of death to be consistent with my account—a gunshot wound to the chest, resulting in shock and respiratory failure. The jury took only minutes to rule that the killing was justifiable homicide.

Although I expected the verdict, I was relieved to hear it. Even when it's done in the line of duty and in self-defense, a killing brings mixed emotions. At first, I was just glad to be alive. Then, feelings of sadness and guilt crept in and troubled my mind.

I can't say I really felt much regret, though. When it comes to sudden death by gunshot, I tend to prefer someone else's death to my own.

• • •

As agreed, Abel McKenzie and Zack Rainford met face-to-face at the hotel the following week. According to the waiter who served them, the two men met alone for nearly four hours in a private room just off the main dining area. At first, the waiter said, they ordered a pot of coffee and two cups. An hour later, they sent out for a bottle of the hotel's best bourbon. An hour after that, they asked for a bill of fare and ordered supper.

Curious, I asked, "What did they order?"

"A rack of lamb and a sixteen-ounce T-bone," the waiter replied.

I rode out to McKenzie's that same week and found Abel in a contemplative mood. I have to admit I was curious as to how his meeting with Zack had gone, but Abel offered no information, and I didn't feel it was proper to ask. I took comfort in the fact that he didn't revile Zack as he usually did, but neither did he seem inclined to sing his praises. He talked about how well his lambs were doing on the mountain and said his herders had met with no more trouble from the Circle R cowboys.

Teresa McKenzie greeted me with her usual warmth, but she seemed tight-lipped and edgy, and her bright smile was eclipsed by what I figured were personal concerns. I knew, or thought I knew, what those concerns were.

In spite of Teresa's efforts to change Ian's mind, he was still determined to marry Morgan Rainford. Ian saw his mother's opposition to the marriage as unreasonable and spiteful and a stubborn continuance of the family's feud with the Rainfords. Her pleas and demands only hardened his resolve.

Teresa had enlisted my aid, but short of telling Ian the truth about his birth, which I would not do, I could think of nothing that might dissuade him.

I found Ian and a ranch hand fixing fence in the pasture below the sheep sheds. They were replacing rotted posts and stringing new wire, and the day was hot and sweltering. Ian saw me come riding down from the house, and he smiled.

"Long time, no see," he said. "How have you been, Merlin?"

"No complaints. Any day above ground is good."

His expression turned somber. "Yeah. I heard about the shootout. Maybe Loco John will rest easier now."

"Maybe so," I said.

Ian took off his hat and mopped his brow. He turned to the ranch hand. "Take a break, Ed. I'll be with you directly."

Ian nodded at the stretch of new fence. "Sheep and cattle war special," he said. "Two strands of barbed wire on top, to keep the cattle out. Woven wire below, to keep the sheep in."

A canvas water bag hung from a gatepost on the

shed's shady side. Ian drew the cork and drank deeply. His blue eyes searched my face for a moment, and I met his gaze. I remember thinking I'd seldom seen such sadness in the face of one so young. I saw his question coming and braced myself.

Ian re-corked the water bag and hung it back on the gatepost. "Have you seen Morgan?" he asked.

"I saw her two weeks ago, before my shootout with Burnett. Her burns were nearly healed, but her folks were keepin' her pretty close to home."

Ian frowned. "They've made it clear they don't want her to marry me. Zack says if she does, he'll disown her."

I didn't know what to say. Ian and Morgan had my sympathy, but I could no longer encourage their plans for the future. I played for time.

"Have you tried to see her?"

"I rode out to the Circle R a week ago," Ian said. "A cold-eyed guard with a Winchester turned me away."

"Cotton Smith," I said. "One of Zack's hired guns."

Ian looked into my eyes again. "I heard about the meeting you set up between my dad and Zack. Dad hasn't said much, but he doesn't seem quite as down on the Rainfords as before."

"That's good news," I said.

"Truth is, he doesn't seem as opposed to Morgan and me getting married as he was, either. It's a different story with Mother, though."

I'll bet it is, I thought.

Ian continued, almost as if he'd forgotten I was there. "When I try to talk to her about it, we always seem to end up in a shouting match. Mother just keeps saying I can't marry Morgan Rainford. She asks me to promise I won't, but I can't do that.

"I tell her I love Morgan. Mother gets so worked up she starts speaking Spanish! Then she breaks down and sobs like the end of the world has come. I hate it when she cries like that. I can't understand how she can be so *against* a fine girl like Morgan."

He turned to me. "Is there something here I'm not seeing? What's so wrong about Morgan and me wanting to spend our lives together?"

"You ask good questions," I said. "Trouble is, I don't have any answers."

Ian looked beyond the sheep shed at the unfinished fence repairs. The ranch hand called Ed lay on his back in the shade of a box elder tree. "Yeah," Ian said. "Well, I guess I'd better get back to work. You're a good friend, Merlin."

For a moment, the sadness left Ian's eyes and mischief took its place. "I don't suppose you'd care to finish fixin' that fence for me, would you?"

I smiled as I picked up Rutherford's reins. "I'm not *that* good a friend," I said.

Back in my room at the hotel, I wrote up a detailed report for my boss on the killing of Travis Burnett and the current status of the range war. I wrote that since the murder of Loco John and Burnett's confession, the raids against McKenzie's sheep camps had diminished and nearly stopped.

I wrote of the private meeting between Abel McKenzie and Zack Rainford and stated my belief that their discussions would lead to a more peaceful situation in the county.

Finally, I said there had been no further encounters with, or sightings of, the so-called stock detective, Griff Tallon. I offered my opinion that he had either left the area or had been reined in by Rainford and the other cowmen. Either way, I said, Tallon was conspicuous by his absence and no longer a major threat to public order.

I ended by suggesting my assignment was completed and said I would await his orders. Then I signed the report and mailed it.

During the years I'd worked as Ridgeway's deputy, I had learned what to include in a report and what to leave out. As I waited in Reata for Ridgeway's reply, I had to admit I'd left out quite a bit.

I had no idea what Abel and Zack talked about in their private session, nor did I know whether their talk would help bring peace in the county.

I had no way of knowing if the raids on the sheep camps were truly at an end. Cowpunchers, full of bias and cheap whiskey, could ride through a band of woolies and gun down another sheepherder at just about any time.

I was no closer than when I first rode into the county to knowing whether or not Griff Tallon was still killing men he claimed were rustlers.

Last but not least, my thoughts were occupied with concerns that had nothing to do with my work. I'd come to like both Ian and Morgan, and I had hoped their romance could beat the odds. At one point, I even thought it might bring the two families together.

Now, their hope for a life together was doomed by a secret they were not allowed to know. The threat to their becoming man and wife was the marriage itself. It would make them criminals under territorial law, and it would threaten any children born to them. Teresa McKenzie would prevent such a union even if she had to tell them the truth, and even if it broke her heart to do so.

Years before, an old cowpuncher back home in Dry Creek summed up the way I felt right then. "It's *hell* when it's like this," he said, "and it's like this *now.*"

Two days later, I was returning from my noon meal at the Roundup Café when I saw a handsome team hitched to a top surrey in front of the hotel. The horses were a matched pair of blacks, groomed and curried until they shone in the sunlight. The surrey was black, with red striping and wheels. It was a fine rig, and I remember wondering who it belonged to. I didn't wonder for long.

Coming into the hotel lobby out of the bright sunlight, it was a second or two before I recognized her. Melissa Rainford rose from the low divan and smiled. "Good afternoon, Merlin," she said. "I've been waiting for you. The desk clerk said you'd be returning shortly."

Melissa wore a stylish suit of brocaded blue silk, with a matching hat set low upon her forehead. Her fair hair was drawn back at the sides and gathered into a bun at the nape of her neck. She looked altogether elegant and cool, and her smile lingered as she looked into my eyes.

I doffed my hat. "What can I do for you, Miz Rainford?"

"Please," she said. "Call me Melissa. After all, we're old friends by now."

"Melissa, then. How can I help?"

"The surrey outside is mine. I need you to drive me somewhere."

"I'd be glad to, Miz . . . *Melissa*. But why . . ."

"Why don't I drive myself? That's a good question. Obviously, I know how. I drove here from the Circle R. The answer is my destination may not be a safe one. I need a driver who knows the way, one who can protect me."

Melissa lowered her eyes and raised them to mine again. "I want you to drive me to the McKenzie ranch. I should like to meet Teresa McKenzie."

TWENTY-SIX

▼

THE SECRETS OF WOMEN

The road fell away behind the surrey in a ribbon of dust. Melissa Rainford sat beside me, her gloved hands folded primly in her lap and her back as straight as a cadet's. She carried herself with assurance, and she struck me as a woman accustomed to having her wants met, whether by men or the Almighty.

I drove the team south toward the McKenzie ranch with questions on my mind. Why, after all the bitterness of their family feud, had Melissa chosen this time to meet with Teresa McKenzie? Melissa was a well-born daughter of eastern wealth and privilege, cool and self-controlled. Teresa was a child of the frontier, full of passion and spirit. Melissa was ice; Teresa was fire. What in the Sam Hill did the two women have in common, save marriages to proud and willful men?

Even as I asked the question, I knew the answer. Melissa and Teresa were mothers, mothers who loved their children. And their children, now independent adults, had come to love each other.

Morgan Rainford and Ian McKenzie had made their intentions clear. They would turn their backs on their families and build a life together in a place of their own. Their mothers had never met. Melissa Rainford had decided it was high time they did.

We left the highway and turned onto the road that led to McKenzie's. Melissa sat quietly beside me, occupied with her own thoughts. My occasional attempts at small talk were mostly met with a polite smile and a brief nod. In the end, I fell silent and gave my full attention to the road.

It must have been close to two in the afternoon when we rounded the last bend and rumbled across the bridge at McKenzie's. Bill Packer met us at the gate. His eyes narrowed as he looked at me, his face hard with suspicion.

"Howdy, Bill," I said. "It's me, Merlin Fanshaw. Got a lady here come to visit Miz McKenzie."

Packer's face relaxed, but not much. "Come ahead," he said. "I expect she's up at the house."

The gunman swung the gate wide and held it as I drove the team and surrey through. Melissa gave him her cool smile as we passed, a queen acknowledging a hireling.

Low and rambling, the McKenzie house seemed to slumber beneath the summer sun. Rascal, the McKenzie's old sheepdog, offered a half-hearted bark as I drew the team to a stop. Then, as I stepped down, he recognized me and apologized with a wag of his tail.

The screen door opened, and Teresa walked out. Seeing me, her face brightened. "Hello, Merlin," she said. "If you're looking for Abel and Ian, they've gone back up on the mountain." She looked past me to Melissa and the surrey. Shading her eyes against the sun, Teresa seemed uncertain. "You have someone with you," she said. "Who . . ."

I turned. Melissa descended from the surrey and walked swiftly toward us. Her eyes were on Teresa. Smiling, she said, "I do hope you'll forgive the intrusion, Mrs. McKenzie. I'm . . ."

"I know who you are," Teresa said. "I've seen you in town. Please, come in, Mrs. Rainford."

"Thank you," Melissa said, "but perhaps we could dispense with the formalities. Call me Melissa."

Teresa smiled a nervous smile. "All right. And you must call me Teresa."

Holding the screen door open, Teresa ushered us inside. As we passed through the kitchen, I caught the smell of fresh-baked cookies. Teresa was talking to Melissa. "Ginger and Keith, my two younger children, are at school," she said. "I usually bake something on Fridays as an after-school treat.

"Please," she said, "Go on into the parlor. I'll put on some tea."

I figured it was time to excuse myself. I told Teresa so. "Miz Rainford asked me to drive her here," I said. "I'll just set out here on the porch while you ladies talk."

Teresa smiled. "If you wish," she said. "As I

recall, you prefer coffee. I'll bring you a cup. And don't worry; I'll bring you some cookies, *también.*"

I found a chair on the porch and sat down. Teresa brought cookies on a plate and a cup of coffee and then disappeared back inside the house.

At first, I just ate cookies and drank coffee while I tried to ignore Rascal's sad eyes. The old sheepdog watched as I took each bite, doing his best to convince me he'd die of starvation if I didn't give him some. However, Rascal was fat as a boar hog and his act didn't convince me. Besides, someone told me once that cookies aren't good for dogs.

I was sitting near an open window, and the sounds from inside the house rang sharp and clear in the stillness. I heard Melissa cross the parlor, the heels of her shoes sounding sharp and clear as she crossed the hardwood floor. I heard the creak of the bentwood rocker as she sat down.

From the kitchen came the sounds of Teresa brewing tea and the soft clink of china cups against their saucers. I heard Teresa walk into the parlor, her footsteps softer and slower than Melissa's. Teresa would be carrying the tea service and cookies, sandals on her small feet instead of the high-heeled street shoes Melissa wore.

I heard Teresa ask, "Do you take sugar?"

"Thank you, no," Melissa replied. "Milk, if you have it."

A teaspoon tinkled against a cup. In my mind's eye, I pictured the two women sitting across from each other, Teresa nervous, and Melissa cool and prim in straight-backed dignity. The women would be sizing each other up, like boxers waiting for their match to begin.

Suddenly, I realized I could hear every word the women said. I really didn't mean to eavesdrop, but I have to admit I was curious. Before I could move away from the window, I heard Melissa open the conversation, and my curiosity got the better of my manners.

"You and I are strangers to each other," Melissa said. "Our backgrounds are very different. Under ordinary circumstances, it is unlikely we would even meet, much less share our thoughts over tea. Everything we know about each other comes from what others have told us.

"We really have only two things in common. We are women in a world dominated by men, and we are mothers who love our children. Is that not true?"

"Yes," Teresa said. "That is true."

For what seemed a long time, neither woman spoke. Then Melissa said, "This trouble between our husbands has been a burden for us both," Melissa said. "Our homes have become armed camps, surrounded by gunmen and malice. And yet somehow, your son and my daughter have found each other.

"Morgan tells me she is determined to marry your son Ian, with or without our approval. To say the least, my husband opposes their marriage. Morgan is our only child, and Zack has a different future in mind for her."

"And you?" Teresa asked.

"My daughter's happiness is my chief concern. Everything I've heard about Ian tells me he is a decent and honorable man. Morgan asks nothing more of life than to become his wife."

Teresa sounded weary. "What difference does it make? They are of age. They will do what they please."

"The difference," Melissa said, "is that if we continue to oppose them, we may lose our children. They may leave Meriwether County and build a new life somewhere else, a life we will not share. I love my daughter more than my own life. I do not intend to lose her."

Once again, the parlor fell silent. I thought I heard a sniffle from inside. I figured it must have come from Teresa. I was chewing on a cookie at the time, but stopped in order to hear better.

"These past few weeks have been eventful," Melissa went on. "The confession and death of Travis Burnett has removed a major obstacle to ending the violence. In addition, the private meeting of our husbands leads me to believe that peace between our families may yet be possible."

"If only it could be so," Teresa said sadly.

"We can *make* it so! It wouldn't be the first time women have made peace in spite of their men's stubbornness.

"Zack realizes he's gone too far in opposing their marriage. He has threatened to keep Morgan from Ian by force. He has threatened to disinherit her, disown her. Of course, he never really would.

"The trouble is, Morgan is stubborn, too. The more Zack threatens and blusters, the stronger Morgan's resolve grows."

For a moment, neither woman spoke. All I could hear was the ticking of the mantel clock in the quiet parlor. Then Melissa continued. "From what Morgan tells me, you are firm in your opposition to their marriage. Ian says you've told him he absolutely must not marry Morgan. He says you've begged him to *promise* he will not.

"That's why I've come here today. I need to understand. Why are you so against our children's marriage? Do you have something against my daughter?"

Teresa sighed deeply. I heard the scrape of a chair leg, and then the soft shuffle of her sandals on the floor. "No," she said. "Everything I've heard about Morgan—from Ian and others—tells me she is a young woman of honor and character."

"Then *why* do you oppose their marriage? Mrs. McKenzie . . . Teresa . . . Speak plainly, I beg you! I want Morgan to be happy. I want some day to know our grandchildren."

The despair in Teresa's voice hurt me just to hear it. "Our grandchildren," she said, "are who I'm *thinking of.*"

I held my breath. *Teresa was going to tell Melissa about Ian's true father!*

She began as she had begun with me. "What I'm about to tell you," she said, "is known only by me . . ."

She paused and added quietly, "And one special friend."

Sitting there by the window, I listened as Teresa told Melissa the complete story of Ian's conception and birth. She talked about growing up in Reata during its early years. She spoke of the friendship and rivalry between Zack and Abel, and of their growing competition for her affection. She told of Abel's proposal of marriage, of her acceptance and her happiness.

Her voice broke when she told of the night Zack came to see her at her parents' home. Recovering quickly, she told the rest without stopping. Zack had been drinking. Zack was sullen. He would not be consoled. He made advances. He forced himself on her. And the week before she was to marry Abel, she discovered she was pregnant with Zack's child.

"Ian was born eight months later," she said. "No one knew the truth—not Abel, not Zack, not even Doctor Reynolds, who delivered him. Only me.

"Abel and I have built a good life together. We

love our son, as we love our other children. We are a close family. I thought nothing would ever change that."

Teresa paused, and then continued. "Now my son loves Morgan and he wants to marry her. What should be a time for celebration has become a time of sadness. Ian has chosen the one woman in the world he must *not* marry. *My son and your daughter have the same father!*"

In the silence that followed, I tried to imagine the scene in the parlor. Once again, Teresa had told her story. I figured she would be in tears or nearly so, but whether her tears would be of grief or relief, I had no idea.

I figured Melissa would be stunned. She had listened to every word. Not once had she interrupted to ask a question or deny Teresa's claims. Would she accept the story as true or would she refuse to believe it?

When she spoke, Melissa's voice was calm and controlled. "Thank you for telling me, dear," she said. "I have to confess I already knew some of what you've told me. Reata is a small town. People still talk of the days when my husband and yours were friends, and how they courted you."

Melissa paused. For what seemed a long time, the only sound was the ticking of the mantel clock. Then Melissa continued. "Let me tell you a bit of *my* story. I was born into a well-to-do Chicago family and was educated by my father in the ways of the business world. Father was a banker, and he saw that I attended the finest private schools in the area.

"My friends and acquaintances were children of wealth and privilege. We attended concerts and lectures, dances and dinners, and associated almost exclusively with our own kind. As women, we were encouraged to marry well and perpetuate the species.

"The winter I met Zack, I was keeping company with a young man who worked in my father's bank. He was pleasant and polite, something of a poet, and he was determined that we should marry. I found little joy in the prospect. I was fond of him, but I did not love him as he seemed to love me. I had no wish to rush into marriage.

"He was impatient, but seemed to accept my reluctance as maidenly constraint. Then, at a charity ball one evening, we both had rather more champagne than was prudent. My young suitor became at first amorous, then demanding, and, well, things went farther than we intended.

"Our courtship cooled after that. Awkwardness developed between us, and everything changed. A week later, we agreed to go our separate ways. He resigned his job at the bank and left the city. Some of my friends said they heard he'd gone out west somewhere."

Melissa paused. "And then," she continued, "like you, I found myself unwed and expecting a child. Two weeks later, I met Zack Rainford."

"Zack came to Chicago to see my father about financing for the Circle R. Father invited him to dinner at our home and introduced us. To put it simply, Zack quite literally swept me off my feet. Before his visit ended later that week, he proposed and formally asked Father for my hand in marriage.

"Father was reluctant at first. He and Zack's father were friends, and he liked Zack, but he felt the idea of marriage between us was a bit precipitate, to say the least.

"In the end, Father's misgivings were overcome. Zack and I were married in Chicago, and I came back here with him to the Circle R. Eight months later, Morgan was born. Like yours, my baby was . . . apparently . . . somewhat *premature.*"

Melissa's voice took on a friendly, warm tone. "So you see, my dear, you aren't the only one with secrets. The truth is, your son and my daughter do *not* have the same father. I can think of no good reason Morgan and Ian should not marry if they wish."

Seated in my chair on the porch, I had been leaning closer and closer to the open window as Melissa told her story. When she came to its end, I lost my balance and fell to the floor of the porch with a crash. Aside from embarrassing me and scaring Rascal some, no harm was done.

Concerned that the sound might have startled the ladies, I rushed inside to let them know what had happened. When I got to the parlor, I saw I needn't have bothered.

Teresa and Melissa either hadn't heard my fall or didn't care. They were standing together in a close embrace, and they were both weeping. I didn't know then, and I don't know now, all that much about ladies, but I figured they were weeping tears of happiness.

EPILOGUE

So it was that what some folks call the Meriwether County War came to an end in the summer of 1887. Of course, the trouble between the county's cowmen and sheepmen never did rise to the level of outright warfare. Rather, an old feud between strong-willed men threatened the peace for a time before it was resolved by the dying confession of a killer, the love two young people held for each other, and the secret alliance of their mothers.

Earlier that year, my boss, U.S. Marshal Chance Ridgeway, had sent me out with the words, "Storm clouds are gatherin' over Meriwether County." Well, by midsummer, the clouds had parted and allowed the light of reason to shine through.

Of course, that didn't mean all the cowhands and

sheepherders in the region forgot their bias and took a liking to each other. Every now and then, some big-hatted cowpuncher would get roostered and ride his horse through a band of sheep out of sheer cussedness. Sometimes a sheepherder would encourage his flock to trespass on cattle range, even cutting a fence or two to facilitate the process.

Old enemies didn't become friends overnight, nor did they become perfect. They did, however, remain mostly law-abiding, and that was enough for me.

Early that fall, Ian and Morgan were married in an afternoon ceremony at the Community Church of Reata. According to the story in the *Reata Weekly Roundup*, the wedding was the social event of the year, and well-wishers filled the little church to the rafters.

The bride's father gave her away—reluctantly, I expect—and attendants included the groom's brother, Keith, and his sister, Ginger. A reception and barbecue were hosted by the bride's parents at the Circle R, and the newlyweds left for a brief honeymoon in Yellowstone National Park.

In October, Abel McKenzie and Zack Rainford announced the formation of the Cabin Creek Land and Livestock Company. The company merged the assets of the two men in a partnership devoted to land acquisition and the raising of sheep and cattle.

According to a statement made to the editor of the *Roundup*, the partners also look forward to expanding their families through the birth of grandchildren. They have, they said, made their wishes known to their married children.

In early November, nearly three months after Abel McKenzie moved his sheep down from the mountain, an elk hunter made a grisly discovery. Suspended by rope from an ancient pine tree, the badly decomposed body of a man hung head down above a rocky shelf, its hands tied behind its back.

Meriwether County Coroner Leviticus Glick determined the cause of death to be a bullet wound to the chest. Although the body was nearly unidentifiable because of its exposure to carrion birds and weather, both Glick and County Sheriff Ross Friendly expressed their belief the corpse was that of Griff Tallon, range detective.

Neither a suspect nor a motive for the killing was ever established.

Center Point Publishing
600 Brooks Road ● PO Box 1
Thorndike ME 04986-0001 USA

(207) 568-3717

US & Canada:
1 800 929-9108
www.centerpointlargeprint.com